She wanted him desperately

Fury and love spilled into Vanessa's blood. Every nameless fascination she'd ever felt for Alex as he'd lain in his coma assailed her. Her hands pulled free of her sleeves and met the warmth and furriness of his chest, and her breasts flattened against him.

She began returning his bruising kisses. His tongue plunged into her mouth and hers fought back. Against her frantically pulsing neck he commanded, "Say you love me, Cat."

"No!"

He relaxed his hold. "Say it, Cat."

"No..."

He released her, jamming his hands into his pockets. "Say it, Vanessa. I won't ask again."

"You haven't asked yet," she answered defiantly. "You've only *told* me—" But her heart was clamoring and she knew if ever there was a time to shut up, this was it. Her eyes glanced heavenward and she swallowed her tears. "All right, Alex *mou*, I love you."

Carly Bishop's favorite fairy tale is "The Sleeping Beauty." When she started writing novels she wanted to use that theme in a book. The result—*Prince of Dreams*.

A medical technologist, Carly has a demanding job in a hematology lab by day. No wonder she enjoys exploring a world of fantasy in her time off—and creating stories where love and light vanquish fear and darkness. This bright new author lives in Denver with her husband and daughter.

CARLY BISHOP

PRINCE OF DREAMS

Harlequin Books

TORONTO • NEW YORK • LONDON
AMSTERDAM • PARIS • SYDNEY • HAMBURG
STOCKHOLM • ATHENS • TOKYO • MILAN

To Steve because I love him,
and my Sarah because she is,
and everyone who made it possible
for me to be who I am . . .
You know who you are.
Yiassou

Published August 1990

ISBN 0-373-79004-X

Cover illustration © Joe Ovies/The Image Bank

Chapter One

Red thread, twisted well,
Neatly wound upon the reel;
Set the reel a-turning, do,
And *paramithi*, I'll tell you.

ALEX WOKE.

It wasn't a real awakening. Instinctively he knew that. If it were, his eyes would open, his body stretch, and his mood heighten. He prided himself on the ability to waken easily. This wasn't quite the same.

His spirits rose anyway. He'd been sleeping for a long time. It felt... wonderful. Even natural. Fairy tales neglected to mention how good it felt to sleep on and on and on. Nothing frightening about it.

So why the sliver of doubt festering into fear?

He heard distant sounds, but only as if through a tunnel. The satisfying purr of expensive cars pulling into the quarter-mile-long circular drive. The masculine timbre of his brothers' voices, the lilting feminine pitches of their wives... the boisterous clamor of his nephews.

He knew where he was—not in his own home, but at the family compound above Evergreen, Colorado. It didn't occur to him to wonder why he was there, sleeping in his old rooms. For now he was content to listen. It'd been a month of Sundays since he'd seen any of his family. Was it just a dream conjuring their voices for him because he'd missed them all so much?

Closer sounds he heard with exquisite clarity. A steady drip. An incessant, soft, clacking noise. Knitting needles? Quiet breathing, the soft, familiar creak of a rocking chair as it moved, back and forth, back and forth in the deep pile carpet.

Thought. More than the smattering of those images began to crowd in on his sensory-starved brain. He couldn't see because his eyes wouldn't open, and he couldn't feel much of anything because his body wouldn't move, but he could hear, and he could smell.

His mind leaped to life. He felt the sudden activity as he never had before, the processes of thinking, the mental gymnastics. Part of him rejoiced. Another part was caught in sleep-ridden confusion.

The fuzziness, the mild bewilderment irritated the hell out of him. Alex Petrakis had no earthly excuse for such frailties in himself.

He began laying waste to the confusion with a systematic mental inventory of the family compound: a spectacular marble-floored entry; his father's study to the left; a living room graced with a Bosendorfer grand piano to the right; a dining room to seat thirty-some guests, supported by a kitchen with no less than four double ovens; and Nanny Bates's quarters beyond. Upstairs, an even dozen bedroom suites, each with its own bath.

Apart from the mansion itself, the compound sported a nine-car garage, Papoo's greenhouse, a guest cottage, weight room, tennis courts and a nine-hole golf course kept in prime condition. During congressional breaks when his father had chaired the powerful Senate Foreign Relations Committee, the place had hummed with activity. It rarely did anymore. The staff had been reduced to Nanny, who had once truly been a nanny but was now the housekeeper and cook, a grounds-keeper, a chauffeur and an outside cleaning service.

Wealth certainly had its amenities. Alex was the second son of only the second generation removed from equal wealth in Greece, and his suite in the south wing of the Petrakis mansion might have easily accommodated an entire family.

Bored with the brief, self-imposed test of his mental acuity, Alex let his mind roam until it snagged again on the sounds and odors that hadn't fit and didn't belong.

Her scent gave her away. An older woman, he decided at last, sat nearby in the rocker—the rocker used by three generations of Petrakis women for nursing their babies. The rocker did not belong in these rooms, *his* rooms. Nor did the woman belong in the rocker.

She was not his mother. Helen Petrakis had died in a freak Alpine avalanche many years ago. How many now? Eight? No, ten. A decade ago.

Nor could this woman be his grandmother Eleni, who had died three years ago in the spring, or any one of his sisters-in-law. None of the Petrakis women smelled like this woman did—as if she'd been around ointments and medicines and a sterilized environment all her life.

A nurse? he wondered at last. But why?

A sudden panic swept over him. His lungs felt as if he'd been plunged into an airless vacuum, and his palms itched with sweat.

Relax, Petrakis, he urged himself. This was just one of those nonsensical, annoying dreams that come when you're only half awake.

Still, he wanted to tell *this* woman to get the hell out of his bedroom. The gall of it—what a colossal nerve! But he was so sleepy... so damn tired.

Vague images darted through his mind, impressions he had no keen desire to entertain. Of the nurse shaving him, forcing his limbs this way and that, crooning at him as if he were a stubborn child and not a man. He drew away, refusing to believe she was anything more than a figment of his imagination. She left him coldly indifferent to waking up.

Other equally uncertain memories arose as well, memories he would far rather ponder. Of Papoo telling tales Alex had never heard before. No one could spin such magic as an old-time Greek storyteller such as his grandfather was. For as long as he could remember, Alex had wanted to create such wonderful stories himself.

Now he had the bewildering sense that the old man had spent many more recent hours with him. Had Papoo also urged him to leave this sleep behind in time for... what? His *onoma*? The feast of Saint Matthew after whom Papoo had been named. Yes. It must be November then. November sixteen, six days after Alex's thirty-fifth birthday.

Many happy returns, Petrakis, he thought. Somehow it was unimportant that a birthday had come and gone without his notice...

Why, though? *Why?*

He should be out there on the three acres of lawn playing King of the Mountain with his nephews before Nanny served up brunch, catching the scent of snow to come, or... already here? But he wasn't. He must have gone on one helluva bender to think he'd slept through so many weeks.

November? Christmas and then the Epiphany celebration would come soon. His lust ought to be peaking as his wedding to Elizabeth drew close, but it wasn't. Not because he hadn't had his bride-to-be countless times. He had. It was important to him, though, that she would be his in name and in fact as well as in body.

But then an astounding thought came to him. Liz would never sit in the achingly familiar old rocker. Elizabeth's breast would never nurse a Petrakis baby, his baby.

He couldn't even summon a mental image of Elizabeth, or feel his thick sex swell with the need of her body. After two months? Impossible.

He succeeded at last in recalling the scent of her, rich and musky, more sexual than sensuous, more predatory than feminine. With it came revulsion and a surge of very real fear.

Why?

Confusion spiraled at the chain of events forming the half-blurred images in his dreams. A cloudless Mediterranean day. The jet-propelled speedboat bearing down on him as he struggled in the turbulence of its wake. Blond, Nordic Liz at the controls, laughing drunkenly. Himself swimming, his powerful shoulders heaving, his body fighting to get clear of the speedboat. Liz screaming... The awful cracking noise in his head after the bow struck him.

The pain.

The panic.

The blessed loss of consciousness...

Black anger replaced his uncertainty. He hadn't been on a bender of any sort. He was still sleeping off the effects of being struck by the *Persephone IV*.

There was no longer anything even slightly vague or hazy about his recollections. An official investigation would have had to clear Liz of any ill intent. An official investigation would have missed altogether the nuances of her chancy, defiant games.

Her presence in his life had taken the edge off his loneliness. She could flirt in five languages, more even than Alex spoke with his command of the Greek dialects, Portuguese and English. She'd memorized every one of the ten thousand lines of the *Erotokritos*, an epic poem of Crete, just to please him. Liz was brilliant with words. Liz was capable of carrying on a challenging, intelligent conversation.

Liz had the emotional complexity of a walking, talking hormone.

She hadn't endeared herself to Alex's brothers, or his father, or even Papoo with her feats in Greek literature, either. And God knew half the American Petrakis spouses were *xenoi*, non-Greeks. Before this moment Alex had only begun to understand what an exotic amusement he was for her.

He remembered now the distinctive bottle of Metaxa she'd been carrying around on the yacht. Liz wasn't a lush, but she'd killed that flask of Metaxa single-handedly. And if she was drunk, it was because she was bored—hadn't she warned him? And if she was bored, it was because he'd paid her so little attention.

He'd already had enough of jumping through her prove-your-macho hoops. Too damn much. The accident was just one more in a complex strand of her amusing but relentless challenges to his masculinity. Maybe if he'd shoved back, hard, from the start, it might have been different.

Maybe. Now, he doubted it.

Half-pleased with the clarity of his thoughts, half-angry that thoughts of Liz had spoiled his euphoric mood, Alex turned them all aside. But then the antiseptic odors of bleach and rubbing alcohol and ointments riled him all over again. What in the hell was going on?

What if he didn't wake up? What if he did? His life would never again be the same after this day. He knew, and couldn't fathom how he knew. But *what ifs* were his game, and he was clearly in this one to the bitter end. Or, perhaps, the better end.

So, what if?

His mind refused him an answer. God, but he really ought to get up...to live, to touch, to love and make love, to hold off the loneliness.

And to have babies. Before today, he'd never been so aware of such desperate longings.

He would do all those things, too. Just as soon as he got up...

DR. VANESSA KOURES sat cross-legged on the foot of Sarah Gilles's hospital bed, choosing her discards from the pathetic cribbage hand the little girl had just dealt her.

"So much for mercy, Sarah Suzanne," she groused. This sweet-faced little innocent, hooked up to a heart monitor, was ten going on forty and a regular shark at games. "Cut the cards, monster!"

Sarah picked up two-thirds of the deck and Vanessa turned over the jack of hearts.

Sarah grinned and pegged the two points coming to her. "It's your go, Nessie."

Vanessa slapped down a black queen. "Ten."

Sarah matched her with another face card. "Twenty."

"Thirty."

Sarah pounced with her ace. "Thirty-one!" And took her point. And then another and another. And then counted, "Fifteen-two, fifteen-four, a double run for—"

"You win, *koukla*! You're out. No need to rub it in."

Whatever happened to card games like old maid or fish? Children shouldn't learn cribbage from someone else's great-grandfather in a hospital solarium.... Sarah shouldn't have a congenital heart condition, either, but she did.

"Oh, Nessie, it's okay! You just got crummy cards."

"I'm not pouting, honest," Vanessa assured her. "Only wondering. What'll we do now for thrills and chills?" Sarah's parents would be coming soon, but on this cold November Sunday morning it seemed to Vanessa that Sarah needed more than usual to be entertained. Vanessa herself needed another excuse to put off completing more funding proposals. Her post-doctoral program in exercise physiology and rehab medicine had blossomed too far, too fast for the available funds.

"Some string games?"

"Okay. But I lost at cards so I get to pick, right?"

Sarah nodded, causing her little blond braids to bob up and down. She lifted the new string games book from beneath a coleus plant and handed it to Vanessa. Cat's cradle had become old hat, and Sarah could whip out a Jacob's ladder faster than Vanessa could visually follow.

"You pick, Nessie."

She paged through the book looking for something different, but her thoughts took off on a tangent. There ought to be a quicker way, a simpler way of getting research money. An 800 number. Dial-a-grant. Something. She should be grateful that funds were available at all. At least she wouldn't wind up further in debt than medical school had already left her. Still, there weren't enough hours in the day for her cardiac rehab patients, let alone hours to spend groveling after money.

Time for Sarah was especially precious. Blond and petite, with little bow lips and too-large brown eyes, the child had more gumption and spirit than her heart could handle. She wore a pediatric hospital gown with colorful hearts and rainbows and flying unicorns on it, but there was no missing the chest pocket with the telemetry box that transmitted her heart signals to the monitors. Or the wires that disappeared beneath the collarless neck of the gown.

On days like this, when the overhead monitor recorded only rare abnormal blips, it was hard to think why such a sweet bundle of life as Sarah should be confined to the hospital at all.

"How about this one? 'Two boys running away.'" Vanessa held the book so Sarah could see the miniature silhouette the string figure would portray. "Look like fun?"

"Le'me see!"

Vanessa watched Sarah's eyes darting over the picture. As if God handed out compensations, the child's mental capacities more than made up for the physical limitations of her heart condition. Ordinary puzzles were just too simple.

Her mischief overflowing, Sarah giggled. "Oh, Nessie, you'll never get this one. Will you try though? Really try?"

"Sure." Poor child had picked up on Vanessa's distractions as easily as she'd read the string instructions. "Let's give it a shot. You want to do the directions or should I?"

"I will! I will! Just let me see here...."

Vanessa smiled. Having spent so much of her life following endless medical dictates, Sarah eagerly snatched any chance to dictate back.

Vanessa spent the next fifteen minutes with her fingers tied up in string, trying to come up with a pattern even faintly resembling the complicated one in the book. She became so caught up in following Sarah's instructions that she missed the twist of conspiracy on the little girl's face.

By the time she saw the glimmer, her hands were well and truly occupied and it was too late. Warm masculine fingers whisked aside the wavy auburn weight of her hair and a pair of lips planted a melodramatic kiss on the back of her neck. There was no mistaking Nick Petrakis—fellow doctor, and most days, Vanessa's best friend.

"Pray, fair Vanessa," he pleaded, "marry me, do?"

Sarah shrieked with laughter and sank back onto her mountain of pillows. "Oh gross! Not *again*, Dr. Nick!"

For the brief instant before her eyes darted to the heart monitor, Vanessa nearly panicked. Her own heartbeat, wildly echoing Sarah's, had nothing to do with Nick's sexless, frivolous kiss. It had everything to do with what had happened to Sarah in that moment. Three jagged peaks charting the little one's excited outburst were followed by the return of normal strength and rhythm patterns.

Relief flooded through Vanessa.

The monitor might as well have been connected to her. It would have recorded the same thing—precisely. Sometimes, only sometimes, her body reproduced unerringly the symptoms of her patients. There was nothing new or unexpected about this special empathy of hers. But familiarity didn't take away from the relief she felt for Sarah now.

Vanessa let the string fall from her fingers, then smiled and shook her head as Nick whipped a chair around and straddled it. He gave her a leering wink for Sarah's benefit—his oft-repeated proposal had become a standing joke among the three of them—but Vanessa knew he knew what had just gone on.

Still smiling widely, Sarah pounded both hands down onto the sheet covering her slight figure. "*Why* does he keep on doing that, Nessie?"

"He wants something, *koukla*, dolly," Vanessa explained. "He knows if he asks me to marry him I'll say no. So then, the least I can do if I won't get married is to do whatever else he wants. See?"

Sarah narrowed her eyes. "Why don't you just ask, Dr. Nick? I bet the Little Prince would just ask."

Nick bounced the heel of his hand off his brow in a why-didn't-I-think-of-that gesture. "Do you suppose that'd work?"

"You could give it a try," she assured him with an earnest nod. The card shark was gone, replaced by the ten-year-old who believed in fairy tales.

He picked up Sarah's well-worn copy of St. Exupery's famous story, *The Little Prince* and shook his head in doubt. "I don't know... Why would a guy live on a planet so small he could just move his chair a few steps to see the sunset forty-four times in one day?"

"That's 'cause he was sad and his planet is so little! He's really very clever, you know."

Vanessa watched them fondly. Nick had given Sarah the book in the first place, and he knew perfectly well why the fictional Little Prince did those things. Nick would have been a wonderful pediatrician. Instead he was the most talented, compassionate neurosurgeon she knew.

He shoved one hand through thick, springy hair the color of sand. "What's so clever about that?"

Sarah looked positively perplexed. "'Cause it's so pretty! When you're sad you *should* watch the sunset— or something else pretty. My mom says the smartest people are the ones who take time to look at all the beautiful things, and that's why I'm so lucky. I got all the time in the world to be smart."

Lucky? Hardly. If Vanessa ran the universe, there'd be no use for hospitals at all. Nor for pediatricians or neurosurgeons or rehab specialists. Sarah had never even ridden a bike, or screamed down a snow-covered slope on a sled.

Vanessa watched the light of belated understanding dawn in Nick, and then Sarah's self-satisfied delight. Adult or child, it didn't matter. Dr. Petrakis of the large and superbly skilled hands, Nick of the bold eyebrows and sensitive brown eyes left them all smiling. Entranced. Happier and maybe that little bit healthier. And like Sarah, they all loved him.

"So, Sarah," she teased, "what'll it be today instead of marriage, d'you think? Green eggs and ham?" Sarah went into peals of laughter again over the Dr. Seuss formula, and again Vanessa's eyes darted to the satisfyingly stable heart monitor.

Nick spread wide his upturned hands. "A simple game of touch football. Is that so much to ask?"

Vanessa winked at Sarah. "See? Compared to marrying this sentimental jerk, all I have to do is play touch football." Turning to Nick, she asked, "Where? With whom?"

"Family. Up in Evergreen. Besides, Van, you know you've been dying to see my uncle's estate—"

"Phooey. I could go a whole lifetime without that honor, Nicholas."

"Oh, Nessie, go! Isn't that where your grampa's greenhouse is, Dr. Nick?"

"Yep. And if you promise not to groan next time I propose to Nessie, we'll bring you back a baby fern for your collection. What do you say?"

"Please, Nessie? I don't have any ferns!"

"Yeah, Nessie," Nick mimicked. "And you know you don't want to go back to your pencil-pushing, money-grubbing—"

True. Absolutely true. Vanessa laughed and gave up. "All right, already. Shall we try this 'two boys running away' one more time before I go?"

The expression in Sarah's eyes turned carefully neutral. She closed the book and settled back against her pillow.

"Maybe I better take a nap. Bonnie and Sean will be here soon. We're going to have lunch and ice cream in the cafeteria."

For one shadowy moment, Vanessa felt a dark wave of emotion—Sarah's battle with fear telegraphing itself to her. She exchanged a quick glance with Nick. Both of them knew Sarah called her parents by their Christian names only when she needed to put on a brave front. They lived in Creede, far away in southern Colorado, and rarely visited. Bonnie was five months pregnant again and hadn't handled the specter of a second surgery down the line for Sarah well at all.

The moment passed, and Sarah pasted on her normal brave smile. Though she tired easily, her circulation seemed as stable for the time being as her heart action. Otherwise her lips and the beds of her fingernails would've turned an icy blue.

Vanessa reached out to stroke Sarah's cheek. Nick took her hand and said gently, "You're one tough little cookie, Sarah."

This time her smile was fainter. She was asleep before Nick and Vanessa left.

Or so they thought.

"Dr. Nick?" her little voice followed them.

Both of them turned, and their eyes met for a second. Vanessa squeezed Nick's fingers for a dose of courage.

"What is it, princess?"

Sarah giggled softly. "Remember next time...just ask!"

SOMETHING WAS definitely wrong with the heating system in Nick's vintage Datsun. Burrowing down into her shocking-pink jacket, Vanessa tried prying answers out of him again. Nick had finally confessed that there was more to his invitation than just another ball game. Could there be anything casual or random about a request made by Constantine Petrakis?

"I just want to understand this thing, Nick. Constantine Petrakis, *the* Petrakis in fact, specifically requested that I join you?"

"Yeah. Today. Not tomorrow, not next month. Today."

"And you have no idea why?"

Nick smirked. "Maybe he just wants to meet the amazing Alpha Woman."

"Today." She treated Nick to a withering stare. She'd been dubbed Alpha Woman the year they'd put in as co-chief residents—the same year she'd left neurology for rehab medicine. It hadn't taken the intern gossip mills long to make a big deal out of their both being Greek. She became "Alpha," and Nick "Omega." Together they were the "beginning" and the "end" of the neurology rotation.

"Still sounds like a Saturday-morning cartoon to me, Nick. But why today?" She had a vague, disturbing feeling that something big was coming at her. Like a freight train, maybe, and she was chained to the tracks. Her hyperactive imagination, surely. *Today.* "Anyway, I'd feel a whole lot better if I knew what was going on."

But Nick's uncle—the imperious, demanding, immensely powerful Constantine Petrakis, the Hellenic answer to the Italian Godfather—was obviously not one to be questioned or refused. Vanessa had never refused Nick anything but his marriage offers, and now she knew why. He'd come by his talents honestly.

Nick rounded the final curve through a stand of pine trees. Vanessa had never seen anything half so magnificent as the snow-covered grounds or the mansion itself. There were sculpted hedges along a circular drive. There were pillars—marble pillars. And there were armed sentries who activated an electronic gate when they recognized Nick's car.

Nick drove through the gate. Vanessa turned in her seat to stare at the guardhouse. "Nick?"

He smiled at her and shrugged as he guided his Datsun to a place in the circular drive filled with Mercedeses and BMWs. "Life-style of the rich and famous, Van."

"Which explains why you work twenty hours a day—and why you're driving this rattletrap!"

He shut off the engine and bounced his fist playfully off her shoulder. "I never said it was *my* style, Van. Relax, okay? It's only a game of football, and they're all just family."

This family, however, was unlike anything Vanessa knew. An only child, she had often envied the boisterous, exuberant family-sized pandemonium that went along with a clan like this. She was instantly one of them—they would settle for nothing less—and it took her no more than ten minutes to discover there wasn't one of Nick Petrakis's cousins not bent on getting his own way. But Constantine Petrakis, the patriarch who had passed on such single-minded determination, was nowhere to be seen. His absence left her somehow unnerved.

The family had a thing for hyperbole, too—a penchant for taking a point and stretching it. According to them, the sexual prowess of the Petrakis men was legendary. Before the game even started, nine little boys under the age of ten had been bundled off to the playroom, and Vanessa had had an earful of fun-filled boasting.

The eldest son, Nick's cousin Matt, for instance, was divorced and an incomparable chef of Greek cuisine. And he could turn up the heat to scorching. Sexual heat, of course....

Second son, never-married Alex, was an international playboy and movie mogul. Vanessa remembered going with Nick to a couple of box-office smashes his cousin had produced. To hear the men talk, though Alex wasn't quarterbacking this game and no one really had any idea *where* he was, maverick Alex played hard. And when he played, women naturally forgot that there might be other players.

Third son and also unmarried, Chris was an arson specialist. The fires he lit were incendiary compared to the ones he extinguished.

And cousin Nick, of course, could doctor the nurses into a frenzied passion, or so went the family banter. Vanessa had to laugh at that one. Neurosurgery made a demanding mistress, and Nick didn't have the time of day to give one woman, much less time to seduce them all.

It was a darn good thing, Vanessa thought, that they started choosing up sides. The truth was, she would rather play football than listen to any more ribald innuendos. Constantine Petrakis had five married sons, and it was one thing for them to be such unrepentant braggarts. It was something else altogether that their wives egged them on so outrageously. Lorna wasn't about to be outdone by Julie where her husband's manhood and prowess were concerned. Or Julie by Michelle, or Michelle by Connie, or Connie by Andrea, who was pregnant and loving it.

Midway through the game the players took a break, poured Bloody Marys in spite of the forty-five-degree weather and volleyed more rapid-fire insults than Vanessa could count.

Matt snapped off a bite of the celery out of his drink and pointed what was left of the stalk at Vanessa. "So. Do you cut and paste brains like cousin Nick, here?"

"Cut and paste *brains*!" Vanessa choked. She might have expected such gallows humor, but before she could retort, Nick interrupted.

"Naw." He stuck his thumbs under his armpits and rocked cockily on his heels. They had the attention of everyone now. "Vanessa finally recognized superior cutting and decided to go make miracles elsewhere."

"Rehab medicine," she interjected idly, for her eyes were drawn to a set of windows, three stories up on the south-facing wing of the mansion. She realized this wasn't the first time, either, that her gaze had strayed to those windows.

"What'd I tell you? Miracles."

"Yeah . . ." Vanessa refocused her attention and mimicked Nick's overweening body language. "When the cutting is over the job is only half-done!" The Bloody Marys made it easy for her to fall into easy irreverence. Sometimes miracles happened in her rehab labs; more often they didn't, and never would.

A chorus of "ooh-wows" went up all around the refreshment table at Vanessa's volley. And then Andrea, flaunting her pregnancy, put in the clincher. "Yeah. You guys may plant the seeds—" she paused for dramatic effect "—but it takes a woman to deliver the miracles!"

Vanessa felt an odd bolt of jealousy toward all these smugly shameless women, and then told herself that such overkill sexuality was all in fun. But there was an edge to it, a finely-honed truth that made hash of her sensibilities. The bawdy verbal play made her skittish and uncomfortable, and she'd really rather have gone back to her money-grubbing, as Nick had so bluntly put it, than to examine all the reasons this family of men and their consummately satisfied women intimidated her.

Only, then came the final play of the game. Her team trailed by three points, and Matt, who was quarterbacking the other side, needled her again.

"Got any miracles up your sleeve, Vanessa? About now you could use one. A miracle worker is a miracle worker, on or off the field. Right, guys?"

So. She could either prove herself and her outrageously overblown miracles now or suffer the dire consequences of a besmirched reputation. Put up or shut up. Her honor at stake, she couldn't very well let that happen. She'd take the hand-off and run for the game-saving touchdown.

"Miracles are a dime a dozen, Petrakis," she taunted. Her eyes were drawn yet again to that third-story window, and in those few seconds, her primed and overactive imagination toyed with all sorts of exotic scenarios. She dismissed the sense that something was awfully wrong and tossed off a dare. "Catch me if you can!"

"Seventeen . . . thirty-twoooo . . . siiix . . . forty-sevennn . . . seventy-threee . . . niiinety-nine . . ."

"Hellfire and thunderation, Nick! Will you just throw the ball?"

"Hike!"

Vanessa fought her laughter as she ducked around the guard, ran past Nick, took the hand-off and headed down field. The football clutched to her middle, she ran for all she was worth. The laughing, threatening, thundering herd of Petrakises behind her hadn't a chance. At thirty-three, unlike her father who'd suffered a crippling heart-attack at that age, her small, lithe body still ran like the wind.

She crossed the goal line marked by the end of the patio far to her right, spiked the ball in the imaginary end zone and spun around. Her team members hoisted Vanessa to their collective shoulders and carted her off the lawn. They'd just been witness to a Koures miracle, beating Matt's team by the margin of her score.

Someone thrust a hot toddy into her fingers. Andrea gave her a hug for upholding the women's honor. It was Nick who followed her gaze to the third-story windows and noticed her puzzlement. Their eyes met, and Nick nodded. Vanessa understood the nod to mean he'd go find his uncle and put an end to her anxiety over being summoned here.

And it was anxiety, Vanessa realized, overtaking her again despite the carefree afternoon. In search of a private moment she wandered toward the far end of the patio, next to the greenhouse. Nestled in a protective glass cocoon, bougainvillea and roses, exotic lilies and hybrid orchids defied the overcast skies and the flurry of snow-flakes. The fragile, sensuous blooms beckoned to her soul in ways she was too preoccupied to probe.

At last she spotted Nick pushing his way through the crowd. He sank gratefully into the cushioned chair next to her. Rolling his shoulders—the entire family spoke more eloquently with gestures than with words—he teased, "Don't rush a Petrakis, Van. You should know it can't be done."

"Nick, I've spent the whole afternoon wondering what I'm really doing here. It's been fun, but it isn't as if I don't have better things to do." Her pile of funding pro-posals, for instance. Her programs would be out of funds in three short weeks, and her publisher wasn't advancing any green stuff for months.

"We're about to find out. Uncle Con has asked me to relay his greetings. We're expected in the study. Ready?"

"More than ready," she assured him.

She followed Nick into the mansion through an enor-mous kitchen filled with the aromas of the family feast—scents that tugged at tradition and memories so in-grained in her that she couldn't have pinpointed their beginnings. She was perversely grateful for being too rushed now to be drawn in by them.

Pulling off her ski cap, she tried to smooth her wildly wavy auburn hair. It was too late to wonder if she might pass for presentable. Too soon Nick held open the door to Constantine Petrakis's study.

A fire crackled and hissed in an enormous moss-rock fireplace. Nick cleared his throat. The short, powerfully built patriarch stood wrapped in a smoking jacket, star-ing into the mesmerizing flames. Without looking up he asked, "Would you care for a brandy before dinner, Dr. Koures? A Metaxa perhaps."

"No, I—"

"Nick, see to it," the older man ordered, despite her refusal. He turned, then, and fastened his dark eyes on her in a way that made her think of relentlessness. His quick, brittle smile did nothing to change her perception. "You may find yourself with cause for celebration."

Celebration? Vanessa exchanged startled glances with Nick before he shrugged, smiled and then turned toward the brandy decanter at the wet bar.

"What cause, Mr. Petrakis?"

"Constantine, please," he countered. "May I call you Vanessa?"

"Please."

"You are a colleague of my nephew, is that right?" It was a rhetorical question and typically chauvinistic. Especially to a man of Constantine's generation, even to many of Vanessa's own age, a truly good Greek girl didn't live independently even if she pursued a demanding career. A good Greek girl lived with her parents until marriage. Even in America, even in this day and age. Vanessa could have told him she'd given up being a good Greek girl.

"And you are working on cardiac rehabilitation, a post-doctoral extension of your exercise physiology program," he continued in a tone meant to conceal what Vanessa took for a surprisingly sharp interest. "You left the practice of medicine for unspecified reasons to pursue such a course. Is that right?"

"Yes."

"Why?"

He knew all the right terms, spouted all the right buzzwords. Either Nick had been spilling his guts to his uncle, or Petrakis had done his homework. Because he'd summoned her, he must have liked what he'd found. But she didn't need this grilling—no matter how powerful, wealthy or demanding the man. Her hazel-blue eyes narrowed in Nick's direction, silently accusing as she sipped at the brandy.

He took the hint. The time had come that a Petrakis *be* rushed. Nick had incurred his uncle's displeasure before; he wasn't afraid of it now. "Uncle Con, Vanessa is my guest. Is there a point to all this?"

Petrakis gestured broadly, took the wing chair opposite Vanessa's and smiled disarmingly. "Of course. I wish merely to determine the extent of Vanessa's talents and interests. Please. Indulge an old man. Tell me, why did you leave the practice of medicine?"

Said the spider to the fly, "Come in, please, to my parlor." Although it intrigued her, Vanessa wasn't fooled by his sudden expansive charm. How could she explain to Nick's uncle when she hadn't been able to explain it to her university mentors? Something compelled her to try with a small part of the truth.

"I think I work better with patients who are rehabilitating. When I...my father died when I was twenty-five. He'd had a debilitating heart attack many years before that, and I felt that if he'd had the kind of rehab we can do now, he might have lived a better life."

Vanessa watched him digest what she'd said, and then exchange meaningful glances with Nick. Her answer wasn't the one he'd expected. Again she wondered exactly how much Nick had told his uncle.

"You've quite a reputation for working miracles with your patients."

"I help them, yes. But the human body works its own miracles."

Leaning forward, apparently deep in thought, Constantine steepled his fingers. He appeared ready to phrase his next question when a knock came from the study door. A mite of a Scotswoman poked her gray head in the door.

"You'll be comin' to dinner shortly?"

"In a moment, Bates." He waved her on while Vanessa glanced at Nick.

The woman clacked her tongue imperiously but closed the door quietly behind her.

"Just one more thing, my dear. Is your expertise limited to the rehabilitation of heart patients only?"

"No. That's the focus of my work now, but I've handled the whole spectrum of patients."

"And your funding?"

Vanessa shot Nick another accusing glance. "I've run out ahead of schedule, as I'm sure your information has told you."

At last Petrakis sat back, smiling. "Just so. My dear girl. I propose to fund the completion of your postdoctoral research. I propose to build the cardiac rehabilitation center you have only dreamed of. I will deed you the ground, construct the building, supply state-of-the art equipment and a forty-thousand dollar a year stipend to you for a period of three years."

Petrakis hadn't missed a single item on her life's professional agenda.

Vanessa sank back into her wing chair. Her hands went clammy; her throat refused for a moment to deliver a suitable answer. She stared numbly up at the world-renowned restaurateur, the retired senator from Colorado, the man who could snap his fingers and fulfill her every notion of success. Why?

Sudden apprehension gnawed at her. Constantine's behavior upheld every tenet of Greek-American hospitality. One of his sons' generation, she was already on a first-name basis with him. And she'd seen his charismatic power in action. The entire nation had witnessed his wrapping the most contentious of congressional witnesses around his little finger in more than one Washington, D.C. scandal. But now she found in the older man's tired dark eyes the disturbing need for a miracle, and she couldn't imagine what he needed of her to justify his offer.

At last she managed to summon her voice. "All this...in exchange for what, Constantine? What could you possibly need of me?"

"My son Alex is lying unconscious upstairs, Vanessa...."

"He's what?" Silent until now, Nick erupted.

As if lightning had struck her mind, an image of the third-story window filled her.

Constantine met Nick's stunned question tonelessly. "Unconscious. For the past eight weeks."

"For the love of—" Dazed, Nick broke off his curse. "Con, what happened to him?"

Constantine held up a hand. "Please...Nicholas. Allow me to finish." He looked suddenly decades older, but addressed Vanessa with as much conviction as ever. "Alex's body will soon begin to shrivel and waste away. You ask what you can do? In return for my very generous consideration, you will take over his care before that happens. When he comes out of it, you will have delivered him back to me. Whole and strong."

Vanessa swallowed hard. Matt's taunt on the playing field slammed into her mind. *Got any miracles up your sleeves, Vanessa?*

Constantine turned to Nick then, and offered his open hands in a gesture of apology. "No one in the family knows of this but your grandfather. I..." For the first time the father's voice choked. His eyes shone with tears, but he made no move to hide the fact from his nephew or Vanessa. A Greek man was man enough not to fear a show of his real emotions. Such a man was never more vulnerable than when his children suffered.

Vanessa's throat clogged in acknowledgment of his distress, as Constantine drew breath enough to continue.

"In the beginning I hoped Alex would recover before t became necessary to say anything to the family. I was...mistaken in that, I suppose—futile, in any case. I have told you now, and you, Vanessa, ahead even of Alex's brothers, because I wished to have your answer first. If you've any inclination to refuse my offer, speak now."

Shaken beyond any response at all, Vanessa covered her quavering lips with cold-stiffened fingers. In spite of the warm, crackling fire, she shivered violently.

As stunned as she by his uncle's disclosure, Nick rammed his fingers through his hair and cleared the dismay from his own throat. "Con, my God, what happened?"

"I would rather save the details for all the family to hear. Vanessa," he implored, "may I also tell them you will consider undertaking Alex's recovery?"

Vanessa wanted to ask how such a decision, such a commitment could be made in the space of these few moments. Her gaze flew to Nick's familiar golden eyes, filled now with an unfamiliar confusion. How could she refuse? How *could* she agree?

Hearing no refusal from Vanessa, Constantine forced his emotion-strained features into a smile that spoke volumes on the subject of a father's gratitude and departed.

Chapter Two

A SHOCK-RIDDEN SILENCE followed Constantine's exit. Numbed by the enormity of the arrant miracle Constantine Petrakis required, Vanessa got up and circled her wing chair. Her neatly trimmed, unpolished nails dug deeply into its amply padded back. Flames crackled in the fireplace. She found herself mentally noting the texture and feel of the rich burgundy leather, the heat of the flames, the taste and distinctive aroma of the Metaxa— all those real things—against the chance that she'd been dreaming Constantine's magnanimous offer.

That too had been real.

His bombshell revelation explained his tension, the uncharacteristic edge to his Old-World charm. It also explained why her attention had been pulled again and again to the third-story window. A shiver of foreboding passed through her.

She turned her gaze away from the fire toward Nick, who was slugging down a double shot of brandy. Inanely it occurred to her that he was still on call. That he never, ever drank while on call. "Nick?"

Nick swore succinctly. "Do you see now why I bury myself with work at the hospital and drive a junkyard reject? The press wrote me off years ago for a total bore. When you become this filthy rich and famous you'll pay any price to keep your crises off the evening news, even if it means keeping your family in the dark!"

"You knew nothing about this, then." All Vanessa's cultural baggage told her how very betrayed Nick felt. Family was everything. Honor and tradition and loyalty and responsibility were bound up in it. Vanessa remembered her Aunt Ennea telling her of a prominent Greek family in Chicago that had recently pushed their only daughter into a marriage she didn't want because she was pregnant and the honor, the *philotimo*, of the entire family was at stake.

It made perfect sense for Constantine Petrakis to shield his son's condition from the world, but from family?

"He's very upset, Nick. Don't take it personally—"

"Don't take it personally? How in blazes do you suggest I take it? *I'm* the neurologist! Don't you suppose it might have made a grain of good common sense to call me?"

"You're *family*," Vanessa argued gently. "If anyone else were to ask you if a doctor should treat a member of his own family..." Vanessa trailed off. Nick needed no lectures on medical ethics. Nor would he have undertaken his cousin's treatment, but he could have *been* there, lending his educated support. "Let it go, Nick. Not telling the family was a judgment call—maybe hasty or wrong—but whatever your uncle has done, he obviously cares very much what happens to his son, to Alex."

"Yeah. Alex." The mention of his cousin's name checked Nick's anger at having been kept so long in the dark. He placed his empty brandy snifter into the wet-bar sink and then dragged a hand through his hair. "He could be in deep trouble, Van."

Vanessa drew a deep, shaky breath. Her mind focused now beyond the panes of that third-story window to the man lying beyond them. "I don't know what I can do, Nick, or what your uncle expects...."

Nick approached Vanessa, and with his arm around her shoulders, guided her toward the door. "I don't either, Van. I don't either."

THEY ARRIVED at the elegant dinner table as all of Nick's cousins, their wives and sons jockeyed for places. This was a celebration meal in honor of Papoo—the old man's Saint's Day feast, his *onoma*—and the boisterous mood of his grandchildren didn't slack off just because they now occupied the formal dining room.

Papoo clung fervently to the old-country tradition of honoring one's patron saint instead of birthdays. It was out of respect for him that the family gathered at this time each year. But Papoo's mood didn't match the happy pandemonium, didn't admit to a celebration or cause for a party.

Papoo knew. The family had yet to learn of Alex's coma.

Nick and Vanessa exchanged glances as he touched his grandfather's shoulder. "Papoo, this is my friend and colleague, Dr. Vanessa Koures. Will you welcome her to your *onoma*?"

The old man's rheumy topaz eyes seemed for an instant to fill with tears. Elderly at eighty-five, mustachioed and deceptively frail looking, there was something in his bearing and in the weathered look of him that told Vanessa he'd lived through a great deal in his long life. The old man took her hand and nodded. "Please," he said. "Sit here beside me."

It had been a very long time since Vanessa had sat at a table so full of the sights and scents and flavors of her heritage. Distracted by knowledge of Alex Petrakis's condition in the face of his family's unknowing exuberance, Vanessa could no more enjoy the feast than the old man next to her, or Nick, or his uncle could. She began to wonder when Constantine would put an end to his long silence. And somewhere between the *arni paragemisto*, Papoo's favorite stuffed lamb, and dessert, the family began to grow quiet.

"What is it, Papoo?" Matt finally asked. "Nanny's cooked you a fine feast here!"

Nanny Bates, whom Vanessa knew had truly been a nanny to Nick's generation of Petrakises, began moving around the table collecting empty plates. Her Scots lilt brooked no flippancy. "Y'll not be needlin' y'r grandfather, Matthew." She glanced defiantly at Constantine, but held her tongue with noticeable effort.

Nanny would have to know as well, Vanessa realized, and knowing such a secret made Constantine's continuing silence on the subject of Alex's coma unbearable.

Nanny marched off into the kitchen, having said all she dared to prod the man whose family she had served for so many years. Twenty-three pairs of eyes flew to Constantine. He put down his napkin and gave the kitchen door a half angered, half long-suffering glance.

Vanessa clasped her hands in her lap. Constantine's moment of truth had come. Hers would follow, if he had his way.

Again Matt spoke for all of them. "Pop? What's going on?"

Constantine drew a long breath and sat back. "Your grandfather isn't much in the mood to celebrate tonight because Alex cannot be with us."

"The hell with Alex, Papoo!" Chris, the third son, exclaimed. "He was off somewhere with Liz last year too, but—"

Vanessa flinched at the brash interruption. Papoo choked. And Matt, sensing unpleasant news, interrupted his younger brother by passing him the wine decanter. "Here, Chris. If you're going to stick your foot in your mouth, you may need this to wash it down."

Nick wadded his napkin up and threw it down beside his plate. "Con, this has gone—"

Nanny Bates entered carrying platters filled with cheese and fruit for dessert. Constantine allowed her time to serve the old man before he suggested she take the children to the kitchen for ice cream. Once the rambunctious little boys were gone he took a deep breath. "Alex was severely injured in September. He's lying upstairs in a coma. Naturally Bates is aware of the fact, as is your grandfather. I asked Nick to bring Vanessa here today because she is a physician and a specialist in rehabilitation."

The whole room became silent and very still. Chris swallowed hard. "Oh my God, I'm sorry, Papoo...."

The old man waved off Chris's apology, and Vanessa could feel the helplessness roiling up in him. More, she felt every one of the family glancing at her. Without knowing what had happened, or why Alex might need her or whether she could help, they were prepared to believe in her infamous miracles.

Again, Matt spoke for them all. "What happened, Pop? And why hasn't the press got a hold of this?"

"You know, perhaps, that Alex and Liz were yachting over Labor Day in the Mediterranean. I understand from Liz that they'd taken the speed boat out, that Alex was swimming, and that she somehow lost control of the boat. Alex was knocked unconscious when the *Persephone IV* struck his head and back."

Mechanically, absently, the cheese and fruit were passed from hand to hand. No one picked up a fork or knife. The laughing, boisterous crowd had been reduced to a horrified audience. Vanessa felt her own stomach turn over.

Constantine reached for his wine goblet, drained it and continued. "They were apparently close enough that Liz's screams reached the yacht. Andrikopoulos stabilized Alex's body on a stretcher so they could haul him out of the water...." Constantine hesitated and glanced at Vanessa. For her benefit he explained. "The ship's captain is a retired physician as well.... When Alex was brought aboard the yacht, Andrikopoulos contacted me for instructions."

Sick at heart, Vanessa reached out to squeeze Papoo's hand, but the old man was cutting his fruit into tiny pieces now. Perhaps, Vanessa thought, to keep his mind off the awful events. A few others followed suit, just to be doing something, anything.

For the first time Vanessa truly understood what it meant to be so wealthy and powerful. Alex had been flown to a US military base in a helicopter owned by equally moneyed relations in Greece—and from there to the Walter Reed Army hospital in the States. The Petrakises, she learned, were more than adept at closing ranks against *any* public notice, and Constantine's still-influential government connections made the secret transfers possible.

Chris finally interrupted, his eyes dark and turbulent. "How did Liz manage to lose control of the speedboat?"

"According to Andrikopoulos she'd been drinking," Constantine replied. "I understood that she and Alex had not been on the best of terms."

"So. Is she rotting in some medieval dungeon?" Chris demanded.

Nick glanced at Vanessa. "Liz Pederson is Alex's fiancée," he murmured. "Not a popular choice even before this...."

Vanessa watched Constantine framing his answer. If he thought, as Chris did, that Liz should be locked away, it was equally clear he had other considerations. "Liz has spent the past several weeks at her family's villa in Italy. Bringing charges against her might be the most gratifying option in the short term, but—" Constantine shrugged "—it would accomplish nothing. She is wealthy enough in her own right to tie the matter up in the courts for years. And it gains Alex nothing."

"So she's off the hook, is that what you're telling us?" Chris railed.

Papoo spoke out for the first time. "She'll meet her Maker with this guilt on her hands."

"Ah, Papoo, that's a bunch of claptrap—"

"Enough!" Constantine interrupted. "Liz conceded to bow out of Alex's life—permanently—in exchange for such a reprieve. Now we must do whatever is necessary to bring him out of this. I have asked Vanessa to take over his . . . recovery."

There seemed no question but that they would all do as their father asked—whatever was necessary to see Alex through this disaster. But the looks that passed among Alex's brothers and their wives told Vanessa they were split on the issue of his fiancée.

"Do you think that was a good idea, Pop?" Matt asked. "I mean, if Alex loves Liz, maybe she would help pull him out...."

"Liz is the last woman on earth Alex needs now," Constantine snapped. But then he admitted to having asked her to come for precisely the reason Matt suggested. "She refused."

Angry murmurs ran around the table. Vanessa wondered if Liz would have returned had someone other than Alex's imposing father asked her. But by the time Nanny Bates cleared the dessert plates, Liz was written off for a bad penny and the matter settled. All Alex's brothers would visit his rooms after Vanessa had seen him and given them her answer. Though their high spirits didn't return, the family at least felt encouraged. Alex would be in the hands of someone able and talented.

Vanessa's spirits plummeted deeper. She hadn't even *seen* Alex Petrakis yet. And now, confronted with Constantine's expectations and the entire family's hopes . . .

Heaven help her.

PAPOO AGREED to help his grandchildren teach their little ones a folk dance while Vanessa and Nick returned with Constantine to his study. Once settled, the older man proceeded with a more detailed explanation. "Alex suffered a concussion. The CAT scan showed evidence of hemorrhage and swelling, but the intracranial pressure was never critical enough to warrant surgical intervention. His spinal cord was bruised. His neck and back appear to be mangled, but apparently they were not. The specialists believe his coma is a subconscious, psychological defense against the trauma and that he is not physically paralyzed."

Vanessa flipped through a mental catalog of medical outcomes of psychogenic coma. Less than half of head-injury patients survived a coma as long as Alex apparently had.

Weariness invaded Constantine's eyes and his voice. "I am told hospitalization is no longer required. I am given to believe the prognosis for regaining consciousness is poor. Papoo is in favor of anything, *anything* that will bring Alex back. That is why I have turned to you, Vanessa. There are no other medical options."

"Constantine," Vanessa interrupted softly, "you've consulted with the finest specialists. What more can I possibly offer you? Alex must surely be getting the care he needs at this point—"

Constantine cut her off with an impatient gesture. "Of course, of course. But his care is inadequate to his needs. The private nurse will give you a complete history."

"Presuming I accept your offer," she stalled. "I'm not—I appreciate your faith in me, but if Alex has had a private-duty nurse well-versed in range-of-motion exercises and electrical stimulation, my taking over would be a ridiculous waste of your money and my time. Right now he needs ordinary nursing care and a program geared to keeping his joints flexible. There's very little else I can do."

The look that came over Nick's face shook Vanessa far more than she had already been. It was a look that combined speculation with sudden insight. "Wait, Van. That's not exactly true—"

"A ridiculous waste?" Constantine interrupted. "Nothing I ask is a waste of your precious time, Dr. Koures. Or have I been misled by Nick? Can your reputation be so overblown—"

"My reputation is not the question," Vanessa snapped. "My professional opinion is that your son could benefit most from the rehab I would prescribe if and when he is out of his coma."

Constantine stood abruptly. "What if that doesn't happen by next week? Or the next? Or next month, Dr. Koures? Are you telling me I should stand by and watch him *waste*, instead of investing my money and your time?"

"Van, can you make that kind of judgment call before you've even seen Alex?"

She could scarcely believe the swift change in Nick's attitude, but she could understand it. She'd probably be grasping at straws herself, if Alex were someone she'd known and loved all her life. She just wasn't willing to be that straw, to make promises she couldn't deliver on. Alex Petrakis might never come out of his coma.

"Under any other conditions I would never second-guess you," Nick continued. He cast a scathing glance at his uncle, as if to say he'd fight this battle, but that it would have gone far better if he'd had a chance to prepare her. "But as a neurologist—"

"You're not second-guessing me, Nick! I haven't said or done anything to second-guess. You're playing devil's advocate again, and dammit, right now it's not particularly helpful!"

Nick held up his hands. "Yeah! Maybe I am. But his chances are *far* better with you than with a nurse or a therapist."

"That's crazy! I have no idea how to do for him all the things nurses do. Alex needs care I have no experience giving!"

Cagey, manipulative politician that he was, Petrakis retired from the fray to let his nephew do his arguing.

Vanessa wasn't fooled, or inclined to cave in. Her research was at a critical point; there were dozens of patients, not to mention Sarah, who needed her far more than Alex Petrakis did right now. But she could almost see the wheels spinning in Nick's head, building to the one argument she couldn't overcome.

He knew her far too well.

He knew her uncanny empathy and he'd seen the results, the emotional stress that had forced her out of practicing medicine. He knew she would have no choice but to feel Alex's terrible isolation, make it her own and, out of necessity, find a way to beat it.

"He needs something else far more, Vanessa. I may not approve of the strong-arm tactics, or even the bribe you're being offered—" Nick paused pointedly "—but I can't help wondering if he's not right." Nick jerked his head toward his uncle, but his eyes never left hers. "I think maybe Alex does need you. Nothing happens in the real world until it happens in the mind. You know that!"

Memories churned through Vanessa's body. The first time it had happened, she'd been only ten. Her father had suffered a permanently disabling heart attack, and she'd been hospitalized too, with heart arrhythmias no one understood. She knew now what none of the doctors had been able to grasp at the time. Her healthy heart had manifested her father's symptoms.

She'd been foolish enough to think that she could bridle her empathy by the time she went to medical school. Foolish enough to think it couldn't happen with strangers. Foolish enough to take the chance because the thing she wanted most in her life was to heal her father. But Georgiou Koures died in her fourth year of medical school. Part of Vanessa had died too.

Even now she knew, just somehow *knew*, that it was Alex Petrakis's unacknowledged desperation that had drawn her attention to that third-story window again and again. But desperation was not what she wanted to live with.

"Vanessa?" Nick probed.

"I've only known symptoms, Nicholas," she whispered. "Never the answers, the remedies..." Her eyes, filled with the shadow of panic, added, *You've no right to ask this of me.*

"Empathy is empathy, Van. He'll know it. He'll recognize it. We can't afford to overlook the chance that he'll respond to it!"

It struck her then that it was hopeless to resist. Her breath came out on a sigh. "I'll see him, Nick. No promises, but I'll see him."

"Fine. We'll go have a look at his chart and you can—"

"Alone, Nick. Take his chart if you want to, but leave me alone with him."

"I'm not sure that's a good idea, Van. You'll have plenty of time—"

"You're asking me to do this thing," she said, flaring. But surprise at her own intensity made Vanessa avert her eyes from Nick's. She swallowed hard. "I'm asking both of you to let me make this decision my way. Take me to him, take the chart and get out, Nick. I mean it."

VANESSA APPROACHED Alex Petrakis's rooms with none of the foreboding she'd felt all afternoon. Instead she felt detached now, as if the decision had already been made for her and there was nothing left to do but accept it.

Perhaps it was settled in a professional sense. She probably *could* help Alex to some degree. But she knew too well the way families tended to hear what they wanted to hear from a doctor. One misplaced reassurance led to expectations that could never be met. She wouldn't fuel Constantine Petrakis's fires with false hope and yellow-brick-road promises.

A lot of other patients depended on her, God's own truth. But the things she could do, the people she could help with a rehab center such as Constantine promised made it sheer folly to refuse. That left one question—was there even the smallest chance that Alex could break free of his coma?

On her way up the elaborate staircase, she glanced at the family portraits lining the wall. And stood transfixed before the one she knew instinctively was Alex Petrakis.

His informal pose, shoulder leaning against a gorgeous maple tree, made all the other more formal portraits seem overdone. The pastel color of his shirt ought to have seemed feminine. It didn't. The collar looked so crisp she could almost smell the starch. The tweed jacket was surely hand tailored to accommodate shoulders like his.

Masterful thighs filled blue jeans that you didn't find hanging in a discount department store, and he wore a class ring set with a dark, flashing garnet—she'd bet his hand-tooled boots on the quality of that gem. Either might have paid off her remaining med school debt.

He leaned against the maple. And smiled.

Another woman might think his smile come-hither. Vanessa saw loneliness in the shape his lips had taken, sadness in the humor. But the sun glinting off his hair made it impossible to say just what shade of blond it was and his eyes, hazel with impossible streaks of gold radiating outward, said *impossible* wasn't a word Alex Petrakis had any acquaintance with. Humor was his weapon and loneliness be damned....

She stared at the almost unbearably masculine portrait. For one aching moment, Vanessa felt crazily possessive of him.

Her reaction shocked her. She was used to the impact her patients had on her, even physical, visceral impressions lodging themselves in her body like Sarah's heart skipping had this morning. She'd long since accepted them. She was a doctor, first and always, even if all she could deal with now were patients who were recovering.

She wasn't accustomed to a purely feminine, almost sexual response in herself. She denied it with everything in her and reached for whatever emotional distance she could summon. She drew within herself for a moment and gathered her defenses, every shred of professional discipline in her. She was neither a child nor inexperienced with her gift of empathy. So help her, this one time she would toy with the fire and not get burned.

She turned away from the portrait at last and followed Nick and Constantine to Alex's rooms. Chin lifted purposefully, she left the two men sitting on a sofa next to an antique occasional table in the hallway. The private-duty nurse glanced up, stuffed her knitting into a bag on the floor and got out of the rocker by her patient's bed. Vanessa held a finger to her lips to forestall the automatic report of his condition from the woman. She avoided looking at Alex at all. Taking the chart the nurse handed her, Vanessa flipped it open.

The documentation of Alex's condition appeared to be textbook in its detail. EEG readings and interpretations, CAT scan reports, the results of test after examination after test. Hourly temps and blood pressure. Anthropometric measurements—like skin-fold thickness, arm and muscle circumference—b.i.d.—twice daily.

Every set of results fell within the norm for a man of Alex's age and build. In fact, his muscle measurements after eight weeks in a coma were still at 110 percent of the standard.

All normal, except for the Glasgow Coma Scale. A score of eight indicated an intermediate disturbance of consciousness. Hopeful, but still a coma.

Vanessa didn't have to go through the reflex checks or range-of-motion movements to trust the reports. There was nothing wrong with Alex Petrakis except that his subconscious mechanisms had taken control and there seemed to be no escape. Vanessa could already feel the frustration building in her.

Was it Alex's frustration, or her own? She didn't know, couldn't tell where the feeling was coming from. And worse, she couldn't remember a time since medical school that she hadn't been able to tell the difference. Why? Why couldn't she make that distinction now?

Ridiculous, Nessa. The doubting voice in her head sounded very much like her mother's. Of course the feeling was her own. She had strong, valid reasons for her own frustration. The challenge of dealing with a coma was enough.

There were so many things she knew about the human body and mind. Take the olfactory system. Chapter and verse, she could explain the nerve location, function and chemistry involved in the sense of smell.

Or hearing. Or reflexes or pain or itches. For each she knew the cause, the result and the disease possibilities.

She couldn't explain why Alex didn't open his eyes, even to pain—score one. Or explain why he could jerk away from physical pain and yet not move when asked—score five. She couldn't have said why he formed sounds no one could understand but not words—score two. Total of eight. Coma.

But you didn't have to be able to explain electricity to use it. And the ancients couldn't have explained why gingerroot broke fevers. It just did. Vanessa couldn't comprehend her uncanny empathy, either, but she knew that what Nick had claimed was true. Given her uncommon gift, Alex's chances were better with her—if she could last long enough.

Still without looking at Alex, she escorted the nurse out to the hallway. Nick grasped her limp wrist as she handed him the thick, clipboard sheaf.

"Are you sure?"

She drew a ragged breath. Not at all. "I'm sure. He's asleep, Nick. I just need a little time alone, okay?"

She could see that her assessment of Alex's sleeping state disturbed Nick more than her insistence on being alone with him.

"Vanessa—"

She recognized his tone. "Don't start lecturing—"

"Then don't make more of this than there is," he countered anxiously. "Alex is profoundly unconscious. Technically he's always asleep."

"No," she contradicted, "he's not."

As one, Constantine and the nurse looked at her as if she'd just claimed Alex could fly. Vanessa shook her head and shrugged. Scientific evidence of brain activity proved it wasn't strictly true that a patient in coma was always asleep, and as a doctor, Nick knew it. But there was no way even Nick could understand her certainty, much less Constantine and the nurse.

"He is asleep now. Please, Nick. Go away."

She waited until Nick and his uncle disappeared downstairs, then closed the door behind her and leaned back, her hands in a death grip on the elaborate brass doorknob behind her. She couldn't bear to look at him yet, although he seemed to be in a deep, dreamless sleep.

It made no difference that at the moment she could sense none of the deep-seated despair Alex must soon begin to feel. She knew his priorities, knew his psyche, knew *him* in ways only a Greek woman might begin to understand. It was their mutual ethnic heritage that gave her such intimate knowledge.

A man, any man's self-image had as much to do with his sexuality as a woman's self-image had to do with the shape of her body. It wasn't particularly a Greek thing at all. It was human. But a Greek man born into a patriarchal world, into a family governed by a man's wishes, developed an overpowering sense of himself in control.

With the accident Alex had lost control. At some level far below consciousness, he'd regained power in the only way he could. Sleep.

Vanessa closed her eyes and stood motionless, leaning against the smooth, hard texture of the mahogany door. No matter how she opened herself to Alex now, she just seemed to touch a void.

The frustration had been her own. Surely it had.

She wondered now why she had thought a psychogenic coma unlikely. She knew, somehow *knew* now that it was true. Alex's subconscious was in total control. At some primitive level he just couldn't believe that once out of his coma he would ever again be the man he had been before.

Her task, rehabilitating him, keeping his muscles toned and strong, his body nourished and free of pressure sores, his joints flexible, his oral tissues moist, was the easy part. She could stimulate his muscles electrically. She could simulate the instructions of his nervous system. She could even manage the IVs and the nursing care with a few hours' instruction.

Could she coax him out of his cocoon? She had to touch him to see if he wanted to make it back. Then she'd know if he had the spirit to fight his way toward consciousness. He'd been asleep so long already, she couldn't help suspecting or fearing the worst. A man like Alex wouldn't take kindly to losing control, and he might not give a damn about making it back. She had to touch him.

It hurt to look at him, perfect in every way but for the intravenous feeding tube threaded into a vein below his collar bone. His pectorals cast crescent-shaped shadows onto his muscled midriff.

It offended her that any human being could be condemned to such a living hell. She hadn't been able to heal her father. She felt still more offended that a man such as this should be imprisoned. Perhaps she couldn't heal Alex, either.

The lines radiating outward from his eyes seemed etched in ink. Eyebrows still bleached blond from days, weeks in the Mediterranean sun, met in feather wisps over a proud nose. His tough, unrelenting whiskers, the honeyed shade of his hair, showed a heavy day's growth. Vanessa thought his cheeks too lean and gaunt compared to his portrait.

She watched his Adam's apple for long moments, waiting in vain for a swallowing reflex. Vanessa swallowed for him, then touched her fingertips to the pulse point at his throat.

She angled her wrist to time the heartbeats while the sounds of his breathing filled the room, threatening to overwhelm her. Twice she lost count. Suddenly she knew that he would overwhelm her in ways she didn't want to examine, and she felt more trapped than ever. Anger flared in her. How could Nick ask her to do this?

Still, Alex slept.

Unwilling to disturb him, Vanessa looked around the room. The dim light of heavy brass wall sconces cast eerie shadows. The teal carpet pile, surely an inch thick, felt unreal beneath her feet. Priceless antique paintings hung carelessly and yet somehow artfully with late twentieth-century holographic photographs on massive beige walls. One of the holograms, mounted above an antique desk, caught and riveted her attention.

A man. A naked man, relaxing in a beach lounge chair under a full, radiant moon. Drawn to the holography, the texture, the image, the unusual posture of the man's head, Vanessa felt her heart begin a slow, inevitable crescendo. A shallow breath caught in her throat. Unwilling, she moved toward the image. She had never seen a hologram more sophisticated than those on credit cards. This . . . this was art.

Loneliness wavered in every line of the man's body. He was uncompleted, unfinished, alone and aching, as if forever might come and go while he struggled on, alone. His body cried out for company, for another, for completion.

The air rushed from her lungs. She stepped back and to the side in one direction and then another, compelled to discover the hologram's secret. At last she saw the woman. A bare-breasted woman, intimately straddling the man.

Light penetrated light. Tone upon color, violet dissolved into blue into pink into flesh. Vanessa had never seen anything as sensual. As sensitive. In another moment the brutal reality of Alex's coma would consume her again, and Vanessa knew it. She allowed herself this brief instant of sheer fantasy and became that woman.

The man's fingers curved at the woman's breast. Vanessa felt the heat rising in her body.

His lips touched her throat. Vanessa's breath locked in her own.

The muscles in his body strained toward the woman as she strained toward him. Vanessa went hot and moist herself.

Her reactions were too powerful to be real. Unable to look at *The ManWoman* any longer, she backed away, her fingers balled tightly into fists. She'd been drawn out of her role as physician, as healer, by a vision. By something as simple and yet complex as a hologram.

Her stomach tightened painfully at the anger rising in her. She'd been jerked around like that before—turned on and left to cool her heels because sex wasn't an option for a good Greek girl, for the fiancée of a Greek man who would do anything short of consummation to marry a virgin. She didn't recognize her emotion for jealousy, for a need so elemental that her response to the hologram was only natural. No, Vanessa felt cheated, and she'd sworn off sex a long time ago. She wouldn't be cheated again. Not by a man, and not by a vision that left her aching.

Deliberately unclenching her fingers, Vanessa forced herself back to what was real—a hospital bed wildly at odds with the rich, male texture of the room. That and the man lying in it. Why had she cared whether or not she disturbed him? Her posture as stiff as her resolve, she returned to his bedside and demanded his answer.

"Spineless wonder or lionheart, Petrakis? I must know."

HER SCENT TUMBLED and danced around him. The scent of a woman mingled with the icy, outdoors aroma of late autumn and winter on its heels. Of fallen leaves and pine needles and snow. Of a warming fire and brandy. She lived and moved and had come from the world outside his sleep, carrying about her its essences. Alex realized that in some never-never-land dimension, he loved her for surrounding him in the sensations he had long missed.

Standing over him now, she waited. Just stood there, waiting. She wanted something of him. His hearing delivered the most subtle sounds to his brain, and he heard the slide of her throat. Then he knew that's what she wanted of him. He focused on his lips and his throat and his tongue...tried to remember the sequence of motions involved in swallowing...willed with everything in him to give her what she wanted, to show her he could.

A simple swallow. He couldn't produce it. But he was a man, Greek and powerful and resourceful. His mind wouldn't admit he *couldn't* swallow, and so churned passionately for an answer.... He lit on the reason, and wondered why it had even taken a moment's thought. He was sick to death of jumping through feminine hoops, playing Elizabeth's games. He was done with it forever. He wasn't about to accommodate this woman, this intruder.

Get out! he yelled at her. His tongue and lips wouldn't do that, either, but oddly she did move away....

Alex sensed her overpowering reaction to *The ManWoman* hologram. Feeling her emotional response was like hearing the beating of a butterfly's wings. Impossible.

But asleep like this it became surrealistically possible to see her from every angle, to feel her emotion, to hear her blood rushing toward secret feminine places. And to touch her without really touching her. He knew that *The ManWoman* had beguiled her essence.

Her curiosity, her womanly response pleased him in strangely new and intimate ways.

She evoked in him a tremor like the vibrations of one cello string causing another to resonate with the same exact tone and intensity. In spite of his resolve, his irritation with her for intruding with her ridiculous, silent insistence that he swallow, he'd never known such a moment, so barren of touch and still so poignantly fulfilled.

Alex sensed her confusion, the threat of what was real, and that too struck an answering chord in him.

But then he felt her rage in his heart, knew it had something to do with him, with being trapped. He resented that one. God as his only witness, he resented the hell out of that one. He wasn't trapped, only sleeping. Sleeping. Who wouldn't, after all he'd been through?

The vision was gone. In its place he felt as much as heard her move away from *The Man Woman* and toward him. The air shifted, currents of motion stirred as she drew nearer again.

Doubt clouded his mind.

She touched him. He could feel her fingers at his throat against his own prickly whiskers. He chose not to respond, all the while assuring himself he had the choice to make. Her touch was different than the nurse's unwelcome clinical ministrations. Delicate. Soft. Like a butterfly's wings.

In the far reaches of his memory Alex came upon his wonder-anger the day he'd first discovered his caterpillar collection emerging as butterflies. The day he'd understood they could shed their wrappings and fly away while he could not.

His heightened awareness of her mocked his still body and he couldn't fathom why waking up seemed somehow beyond him right now . . . why he didn't tell her he wasn't trapped, only sleeping. . . . Alex hadn't the satisfaction of feeling his jaw lock against the confusion. He felt cheated.

"Spineless wonder or lionheart, Petrakis? I must know."

Spineless wonder! What if this weren't all just a bad dream? No. Impossible. He'd swallow when it suited him. He'd wake up when he damn well pleased, and not for this woman. Not for a woman who came to him aroused, who got all hot and bothered with *The Man-Woman* and then had the nerve to come demanding such an answer when all he wanted was a little more sleep.

He dubbed her "Caterpillar." She was the one trapped in her own tight little body, her sexuality wrapped up like an Egyptian mummy. Caterpillar. None of this was real anyway. It couldn't be real. Why in the hell didn't she just clear out and leave him alone?

Go to hell, Caterpillar. Go straight to hell.

Vanessa picked up immediately on the physical effects of his anger. Mottled skin, increased pulse rate, a tension in his body that wasn't there before. Lionhearted, fighting reactions... She had her answer. He had the ego strength to battle the protective coma his body had forced on him.

Unexpected tears sprang to her eyes; one fell in the hollow below his powerful shoulder. She wiped at the traitorous tear and ignored the heat of his skin.

Anger she could work with, his and her own. It tore her heart for reasons she didn't want to recognize or admit, but it would work. "That's good, *andras*, man. Very good."

Anger was a beginning for him, and a course of action took shape in her mind. It began with taking that overwhelming holograph from its place above the desk and hiding it in a deep, dark drawer.

She drew a long bracing breath and left his bedside for the door. The nurse, Mrs. Hancock she learned, waited expressionlessly in the hallway. Vanessa wondered at the patience of this woman, and then realized what enormous stores of patience she herself would need.

"I'll talk to Mr. Petrakis now, and his nephew."

"I'm never to leave this area of the house, Doctor, but there's a telephone on the desk. You just dial seven to get Mr. Petrakis's study."

"Oh. Okay. Please, come in and sit down." Vanessa turned away to summon Nick and Alex's father. When they arrived only seconds later, she relieved their minds right away with a nod. But she had no idea how either of them would accept what she had to say.

She took the chair at the desk, adopting it as her own, as a symbol of her control. She intended to bait Alex, to invade his space in every way she could. To tromp all over his territory, claiming it for her own. She hoped to feed fire with fire and keep the pitch of his anger high.

Constantine dragged a chair to the desk from what appeared to be a reading corner. Nick sat on the edge of the desk, Mrs. Hancock in the rocker beside the hospital bed.

"Do all of these things belong to Alex?" Vanessa asked at last, gesturing to include the antique desk, the artwork, the furniture. "Is this his room?"

The elder Petrakis nodded. His eyes lost their focus as he remembered other, happier times. "*Yie mou*, my son Alex has a house in town, but his grandfather and I collected his belongings and brought them here." His voice cracked then, with strain and emotion. "These were his rooms twenty years ago. We wanted him here. *Ta peo politima eparhonta tou.*" Surrounded with his most precious possessions.

"I thought so." Vanessa swallowed on a knot of emotion in her throat. Constantine Petrakis, for all his connections, for all his power to keep even the press at bay, was still just a father.

"Why does it matter?"

It mattered a lot to the plan taking shape in her mind, but there were other important things to explain. "I think Alex is in an awful quandary. His body suffered an enormous trauma. A coma is a natural, protective response."

"Are you saying he won't come out of it?" Constantine demanded harshly.

Are you all crazy? Alex railed silently.

"Uncle—" Nick interrupted, but Vanessa silenced him with a gesture.

"I'm saying that there are some very powerful forces in his brain working to protect him. If I didn't think he'd try, I'd be out the door, offering you my sympathies."

Offer them anyway, Caterpillar, and get out....

Cracking white knuckles, pointedly refusing even to glance toward his mute and frozen son, Constantine stared at his hands. He had no way of knowing that Alex heard the misery in his voice. "Go on, then."

"I think you were right to ask me," she offered gently. "More right than you know. The mental part, keeping him in touch with what's real and what's only in his mind may be the key to unlocking his coma."

"Explain, Van," Nick encouraged her.

She turned toward him, growing optimistic now at the possibilities. "Think about it, Nick. Alex is angry. Really angry. He wants out of this, but at the same time he won't admit that it's all out of his immediate control."

Bullshit!

"He may even want to die. But if I can channel the anger . . . do you see what I'm saying, Nick?"

Nick grinned at her animation. "When you say something, it's heard, Van. Never seen."

"Nick, I'm serious!"

He'd expected her to share the joke. "Yeah. It is serious. But you're going to need a sense of humor," Nick warned. "What are you getting at?"

Vanessa smiled, and half wondered if she'd done so to prove her good humor was unflawed. "I'm going to move into this room with Alex."

Over my dead body!

Vanessa froze. Just froze, listening for an echo, trying to reconstruct the sound, the voice. "Over my dead body." She wanted to laugh, or to cry. Tears flooded her eyes. The intensity of her reaction threw her, scaring her even more because she didn't really know what had provoked it.

Take it easy, Caterpillar. It was a joke.

A joke? Just a joke. Her mind playing wicked tricks, since it was impossible she'd heard those words. Did Alex Petrakis have it in him to make this a laughing matter? But then...she'd seen his portrait and recognized the humor in his eyes....

Vanessa daubed at her tears with the back of her hand and swallowed hard. She assured herself it wasn't possible to hear Alex's thoughts. Her own overactive imagination, surely... But *over my dead body* wasn't an expression she'd have used in a million years....

Concerned, Constantine took her hand. "Vanessa, there are a dozen rooms on this floor. You can have your choice—"

"Thank you. I'm...I'm sure there are lovely rooms I could be very comfortable in. But I don't want Alex to get comfortable. I don't want to be comfortable. This is no easy thing, and I want him to know that. Neither of us can afford it. I'll stay here. I'll sleep here, eat here, do his therapy . . . here."

Constantine nodded his approval.

Still, Vanessa felt he had to understand the odds against them. "Alex will fight me, you know."

"For God's sake, why, when you're trying to help him?"

"He won't want my help." Vanessa shrugged. "It's . . . understandable, really. He's used to being in control. The only control he's got left is to deny that he's in any trouble at all. I'm sure Alex must think he's only sleeping off the physical trauma. Do you see what I'm saying?"

A tear slid down the older man's cheek, but the beginnings of a smile tugged at his elegant mustache. "I *hear* what you're saying, Vanessa. And I understand. We have a deal, then? *Yie mou*, my son whole and strong, in exchange for your rehabilitation center?"

Tears welled in her own eyes as she agreed. "We have a deal."

The old man smiled broadly. "His grandfather will be so relieved."

Alex wished they'd all just go away and leave him alone to sleep in peace. A coma? Ridiculous. Papoo had nothing to be relieved about. *Take Caterpillar and get the hell out, Pop. She's right about only one thing. I don't need her help.*

Chapter Three

VANESSA WOULD RATHER have walked through hell than try explaining Alex Petrakis to Sarah Gilles. It had been Vanessa's mission to see Sarah through rehab until her body recovered from the last surgery and grew strong enough to tolerate the second. Now someone else would have to bring Sarah along to that point, and the child deserved to know why. Always compensating for her body's limitations, Sarah was simply too astute for watered-down excuses.

Vanessa had no qualms about entrusting the child with the truth. But the truth, even to Vanessa's own ears, sounded like something out of a Greek myth. Mere mortal Vanessa Koures versus all the gods on Mount Olympus.

After her Tuesday-morning therapy session, Vanessa brushed away the tears forming on Sarah's lashes and hugged her hard. "I'll be back before you know it, sweetheart. And you'll be graduating to the exercise cycle by then. Won't that be something?"

Sarah's little bow-shaped lips trembled. She nodded mutely. There was nothing she could have said that would make Vanessa feel better about it anyway.

"You're going to where Dr. Nick's grampa lives?"

"Yes. Up in Evergreen."

Sarah nodded.

"I didn't get to ask him, but Dr. Nick said it would be okay to bring you this baby fern. Do you know what it's called?"

Sarah nodded as her fingers trailed delicately along the small piece of cedar stick. "It's a staghorn. See, this is a little plantlet Dr. Nick's grampa took from the mama plant. It has to have a stick to grow next to." She hesitated for a moment, and then her brown eyes met Vanessa's. "Can you make Dr. Nick's cousin wake up, Nessie?"

Please God. "I hope so, *koukla*. That's why I'm going there. But I'll call you once a week, okay? More, if I can."

She felt the youngster's fears as if they were her own. And although there might be other doctors and therapists, others who cared almost as much that Sarah make it, Vanessa couldn't help the knot in her stomach or her own heart playing hopscotch with Sarah's. *Goodbye*, she thought, must surely be the hardest word in any language.

Vanessa made sure the little girl had met "Dr. Mark" Bledsoe, her replacement, then took one last look at Sarah's still-pale face and almost changed her mind about going.

"Don't look so sad, Nessie! You mustn't be sad," Sarah cried.

"Why mustn't I? I am sad, you know. I don't want to leave you."

"But the man can't wake up. I can!" Sarah shook her head and turned to "Dr. Mark" as Vanessa backed away, struggling against tears. "Grown-ups. It's very tiresome for children to always be explaining things."

Or so it said in *The Little Prince*.

When Vanessa left Sarah, it was to keep her appointment and make the necessary explanations to her director. Charles Ferhedy was more than willing to take over when it appeared that Vanessa's bread was being buttered quite nicely. If she'd fallen into an anonymous, untapped source of research money, so much the better.

Endless details consumed Vanessa's afternoon. Catching up on directives for the therapy on half a dozen patients. Ordering a computer search of the latest literature on coma. Rummaging through her desk for an article she'd promised the rehab director. Finally, a note to Mark Bledsoe. "Remember Sarah's plants and string games. Think you're up to a Cat's cradle, Dr. Hotstuff?"

And you, Alex Petrakis? How about a nice Jacob's ladder?

And you, Vanessa Koures? she chided herself. Sarcasm, her papa had always said, was more suited to the Chicago mobsters and gangland hoods than to a sweet little Greek girl. "*Koukla mou*, what has happened to make you so unhappy?" he'd ask. Oh, Papa, she thought. You just wouldn't believe this one.

Constantine Petrakis had given her all of two days to rearrange her life. She was tense and nervous and snappish. There was no one to blame, and no one to vent her frustration on. Even Nick was lying low.

It seemed unlikely that anyone would be needing the closet space she called her office, but some compulsive part of her insisted she leave an uncluttered desk. Muttering under her breath as she gathered up boxes of research material to haul to the Petrakis mansion, she cursed Nick for a consummate coward.

Maybe she'd have time to continue her research update. Maybe Alex would be interested in hearing it.

At home in her condo near the University Hospital, there was the laundry, the newspaper to cancel, her plants to parcel out. She was suitably vague with her neighbors about "a short sabbatical" out of state. And finally, after four suitcases and nine boxes were packed and ready, Vanessa went to her postage-stamp-sized kitchen and faced the last detail—calling home. She poured herself a Diet Coke, splashed ice cubes into the glass and dialed Chicago's 312 exchange before she could change her mind and put off calling her mother at all. He's Greek, Mom, she thought to say. And he's beautiful, but he won't wake up....

"Hello?"

"Hi, Mom. It's Vanessa."

"No one else calls me Mom, Vanessa."

"Are you crabby tonight?"

"Even if I am, it's not your place, *koukla mou*," Althea Koures chided. "But then, when have you ever known your woman's place? Why should I be surprised? It's late. I've just gotten in from a concert in the city. Why are you calling? Are you all right? Is something wrong?"

Vanessa's fingers tightened on the receiver. Ever since Papa died, his favorite endearment for her, *koukla*, my little doll, made a lump rise in her throat. It did now, too, despite the fact that she herself used it with Sarah. And in spite of her mother's short lecture. "No, Mom. Nothing's wrong. I'm okay."

"Then what?"

"I'm...I'm going to be away from my condo for a while. I just wanted to let you know so you wouldn't worry if you couldn't get hold of me."

"Away? A trip?" Another mother might have found the prospect exciting. Althea Koures conveyed a thorough disapproval in three short words.

Vanessa could hear the tinkling sounds of a spoon in her mother's teacup, and that too brought her memories of Papa. His lone concession to the kitchen had been to brew Althea's tea.

"No. Not a trip." Should she tell her mother all about Alex Petrakis? Or should she just call her absence a special project away from home? No. She couldn't find it in herself to call Alex a "project." "I've met a man, Mom. Well, not really *met*," she rushed on. How stupid did that sound, as if she'd met The Man? "He was hurt in a boating accident several weeks ago and he's in a coma. I've been ... that is, his father asked me to oversee his rehab."

"Why, for heaven's sake, would you do that, Nessa?"

"Because it's what I do, Mama."

"Don't be fresh. I'm still trying to understand why this is what you do, but this! This is crazy. You say he's in a coma?"

"He's Greek, Mom." As if that explained anything. Why, why had she said that?

"And married with four kids?" Althea probed blatantly, interested now.

"Single, good-looking and rich. But so is Nick, Mom. I'm not looking."

"Well, you should be. Nick would marry you in—"

"Between morning rounds in the Neurology ward and his morning Danish. I'm doing this because the father has promised me my own rehab center if I pull it off. That's all." Or because the specter of Alex Petrakis buried alive tears me up like Papa living the life of a broken toy....

More tinkling. More tea. Mom could swallow.

"And who is he that he can make such promises, *koukla*?"

"Constantine Petrakis."

"The senator?" Althea gasped. "Nick's, what is it, uncle?"

Vanessa twined the coil of the telephone cord around her fingers. Anxiety riddled her just speaking the man's name. She daren't disappoint him. More, she couldn't fail Alex. "Ex-senator, yes. His son, Nick's cousin, is my patient. I'll be staying in their home, but I won't be able to take any calls there. Mr. Petrakis wants his son's condition kept under wraps, so please, don't say anything to Aunty Ennea or Aunty Chloe. Or anyone at church—especially at church, okay?"

Charged with a secret Vanessa knew without a doubt her mother would keep just to have something over her sisters, Althea brightened. "Of course, *koukla*. But how will I get in touch with you?"

"I'll call you every couple of weeks, but if you need me, call Nick at the hospital."

"I will. Nessa?"

"Yes, Mama?"

"You could do worse than a Petrakis. *Any* Petrakis."

Vanessa smiled hopelessly, but she took care not to let a trace of humor spill into her answer. "Yeah, Mama. I could do worse than any Petrakis."

She'd settle for bringing one Petrakis back from his unending sleep. And for a rehab center of her own.

BETWEEN WEDNESDAY morning rounds and his Danish, Nick followed Vanessa back to Evergreen, his vintage blue Datsun as loaded with her possessions as her own little rattletrap VW. He passed her on Bear Creek Road and led the way through town and the winding roads past the world-renowned Hiwan Hills golf course, and above it, the Petrakis mansion. The additional security forces Constantine had warned the family about were already in place, but the guards waved Nick and Vanessa through without delay.

She set the brake in the front circular drive and then slammed her door because that was the only way to make it close. Wordlessly, intimidated by wealth and armed sentries and her own rash promises, she followed Nick inside. Nanny Bates hustled them to the dining room where she produced two glasses of freshly squeezed orange juice.

They sat together at one end of the twenty-five-foot dining room table—itself a statement of Petrakis wealth. This morning the inch-thick beveled-glass tabletop was uncovered except for their two linen place mats. It rested, gleaming without so much as a mote of dust, on the formidable trunk of a redwood tree. With just the two of them here, it was much easier to get a perspective. The antique sideboard and all thirty high-backed chairs barely filled the room. Sunlight poured through enormous lead-paned windows.

Except for Nanny Bates, the mansion seemed deserted. Its quiet unnerved Vanessa. Two days before, the compound had been near to bursting at the seams with extended family. Then, she'd felt Alex's isolation. Now, her senses tuned toward him, she felt none of it.

"Van, are you sure about this?" Nick asked. "Do you know what you're letting yourself in for?"

"Second thoughts, Nick? It's a little late for that, don't you think. I mean—"

"I pressured you," he interrupted. "Hell. I bullied you into accepting. Frankly, right now, I'm thinking it was a mistake. That it *is* a mistake."

Vanessa stirred cream from an unusual black-walnut creamer into her coffee. "You couldn't bully me out of sharing that chief residency, Petrakis, and you didn't bully me into this. Let's be straight, huh? And if this is a mistake, it's mine."

"I want Alex back among the living, Van. But I don't want you hurt in the process. Hell, Con offered you a staff, some nurses, and he can afford to—"

She reached out to cover his hand with her own. "I know he can afford it, Nick. That isn't the point." They'd argued the point all the way home Sunday night.

"Will you get out if..."

Her eyes fell. "What *if*?" she whispered.

"If...hell, I don't know. If he doesn't respond. If he slips even further back. If, in spite of everything I know you can do, you start getting headaches or gut aches or just tired. You will get tired, you know. Van, he'll have to be turned every two hours. Can you do that? He has to be watched day and night to avoid pressure sores and infections and God only knows what all else. *You* should have some help. When I asked you to consider it, I hadn't even thought—"

Nick ended his entreaty abruptly with Nanny Bates's appearance. She served perfect eggs Benedict to each of them, poured more orange juice and clucked quietly. "I know most everything going on about the place, Nicholas. Your uncle, bless his soul, hasn't the least idea what it takes to carry out his grandiose wishes. And that woman...that nurse—" Distaste made Nanny wrinkle her nose. Obviously she wasn't a real fan of Mrs. Hancock's. "Couldn't cope if I didn't spell her some. I'll do whatever I can to help your Vanessa help Alex. Nothing against you, you know, but Alex is . . .'' Tears welled in Nanny Bates's eyes and her chin quivered uncontrollably. "Alex always was my favorite."

Vanessa smothered a smile, fully sympathizing with the tiny, aging dynamo and her obvious enchantment with Alex.

Nick caught her fluttering, liver-spotted hand. "I didn't know. You've had a crush on him all these years, haven't you?"

"Pshaa," Nanny scolded, jerking her hand out of Nick's. "You're all too pretty for your own good. Now you eat those eggs and help Dr. Missy get her things upstairs."

Nanny whipped Nick's napkin into his lap, as she'd doubtless whipped a bib around his neck many years before, and disappeared through the swinging door to the kitchen without uttering another word.

"'Dr. Missy'? The old darling!" Vanessa smiled. "Does anybody ever take exception to her names for them?"

Nick cut into his eggs Benedict with a flourish. "All of us. Used to call me Master Nicholas Beanpole. Do you?"

"Heavens, no. She's precious. I'm not sure she'll be that much help—"

"She will, Van," Nick said, grinning evilly. "Don't underestimate the power of a woman in love."

Nanny's answer came with the extraordinary din of pots and pans crashing into a stainless steel sink.

ALEX WAS IN high good humor. The nurse knew nothing of it, and that only increased his pleasure. He listened to the sometimes subtle creaking of the old Petrakis rocker grow obnoxious as she rocked furiously. Back and forth, back and forth, back forth, back forth, more agitated by the minute.

Nick and the female he'd dredged up were unloading their cars in the circular drive, preparing to move her into his rooms. Alex paid no attention to the fact that he couldn't laugh. He recognized a donnybrook coming when he saw it. So to speak, he thought, smiling in his head again.

Hancock looked on in what Alex imagined to be tight-lipped silence while Nick moved in a ton of boxes and suitcases, Caterpillar orchestrating the whole thing.

The more noise she made, the more Alex retreated into his amusement. The more she flattered the nurse, the huffier the middle-aged woman became. Alex could tell by the pattern of her breathing. When an hour or so later things were arranged according to Caterpillar's specifications and Nick had departed, the free-for-all Alex expected began.

"He's worse," Hancock snapped.

I'm not worse, you old bag of wind, Alex thought, *but please, by all means, don't mind me. Continue.*

"How is he worse?" Caterpillar asked.

Alex had to give her credit for the even tone of her voice. Home Team 0, Visitors 1.

"His reflexes were dulled this morning, for one."

It comforted Alex to know he had the control to fool the eagle-eyed old witch.

"Progress isn't necessarily measured by days, Mrs. Hancock," Caterpillar answered. "Small setbacks are to be expected."

That comforted him none at all. *Setback indeed!* But he remembered in the next instant that it was his anger she was after. Having already decided she couldn't have that, Alex laughed inside. *Touché, Caterpillar.* Home Team 0, Visitors 2.

"For another thing, I can usually detect a faint smile after I've done with his morning shave. There was none of that this morning," Hancock accused.

"A smile?" Caterpillar asked, surprise in her voice.

Who, me? Home Team 1, Visitors 2.

"Alex actually smiles?"

"Yes, until this morning."

"And you think I'm to blame for that, Mrs. Hancock?"

Sharp cookie, huh, Ms H? Catches on quick. The score is even, sports fans, 2-2.

"As a matter of fact, Doctor, I do. I think if this is your method, it's madness. I've worked for weeks to get to this point with Mr. Petrakis and you've managed to—"

"I'm sorry you're upset. But I'm not sorry it's changed the way Mr. Petrakis is responding," Caterpillar interrupted. "If he continued on that way he might never come out of it, Mrs. Hancock. You'll have to trust my judgment on this."

Good shot, Caterpillar. But suddenly Alex wasn't interested in keeping score. When the nurse muttered something about having no choice in the matter, he thought, it'd probably be best if she gave up defending him as a lost cause. The real battles were yet to come, and Alex was, had always been, his own man. He had no need of a champion for his cause. He had no need of an opponent, either, but the battles might ease the loneliness for a while.

He heard Caterpillar explaining to Hancock her precious theories. That trampling all over his privacy was bound to make him angry, and that as an emotional prod, anger couldn't be matched.

What a joke. In all the Greek language there was no word for *privacy*. No, Greeks were a highly insular and family-oriented people, and, historically, when they weren't fighting the Turks, families—even whole regions—were suspicious of each other. Privacy was a concept they just had no use for.

Alex had no use for it, either. Caterpillar might—any woman might. But he would be willing to bet an Oscar nomination on his next picture that she'd been an only child. He'd grown up with seven brothers, and still it seemed to him that he'd spent his whole life fending off loneliness. *Privacy* was just another word for *alone*.

Funny. Not funny ha-ha, but funny *ah-ha*. He'd known it all his life without being aware of it in quite this way. He'd even been willing to put up with Liz because when he was with her he wasn't strictly alone.

Alex tuned out. The fireworks he'd hoped for were dismal. He shouldn't have been surprised. Caterpillar wanted *his* anger; she'd made that much perfectly clear hours ago. How many hours Alex wasn't sure. Time had taken on a kind of unreal quality that seemed to have nothing to do with him. It simply didn't matter.

She could stoke the fires all she wanted, move in, scatter her female things from one corner of his space to another, even sleep in the bed his father and Papoo had moved in earlier. But his anger was an intensely personal thing, part of his emotional store, something he collected and hoarded jealously until it spilled out of its own accord onto paper, into his scripts. Drawers full of them.

Mentally he shrugged. Let Caterpillar try to wrestle his anger from him. The battles might even prove entertaining.

IT WAS DUSK by the time Mrs. Hancock left, and dark when Vanessa finally finished her unpacking and turned on a lamp at Alex's desk.

Nick had seen to it that her VW was tucked away in the nine-car garage. Out of sight, out of mind. Going away was no longer an option, and she'd have no need of her little car. She had chosen to come here, chosen to pit herself against the unending sleep of Alex Petrakis.

She stared out into the dark of night, at the snow falling placidly to earth. The glimmering lamplight of the wall sconces were reflected over and over again in the multipaned windows.

"You're missing the first evening snowfall, Alex," she taunted softly. "Are you a man to appreciate that?"

Silence.

"No? Yes?"

Alex was as still and silent as the falling snow.

"When I was a little girl, I'd sit for hours cutting snowflakes out of tissue paper. You know that white stuff they use to fold your clothes in the department stores? My mom used to bring home scrap pieces of it from her job."

Other childhood remembrances came—a silver saucer sled, weeds poking through the first covering of snow. She spoke about them aloud, too, but Alex remained silent. She really didn't expect anything different. Did she?

"Memories are hard enough to share when you're on speaking terms, Alex," she said. She wanted to goad him. Why did she want to share childhood remembrances, happy, simpler times? She turned toward his bed and glared at him. "Life isn't that simple anymore, Petrakis. Nor is happiness. I think you hear me. I think you know everything that goes on around here, just like Nanny

Bates does. You're holding out on me, Alex, but you don't know how stubborn I am.''

Or how tired.

Weariness overtook her in ways she hadn't begun to expect. In the hours of instruction on the nursing care Alex required, Vanessa had gained a healthy respect for the hostile Mrs. Hancock. For nurses in general.

But the worst of her weariness had nothing to do with Alex's strenuous physical care. She knew the exact moment trouble had erupted. She'd turned Alex on his side, and had discovered the remains of massive bruises on his neck and shoulders. Noting them in his chart was routine. Seeing them made her want to retch. A lesser man— a less muscled man—would have come away with a broken spine if he'd survived at all.

His body's wisdom humbled Vanessa. Until those traumatized areas healed completely, he *should* be in a protective coma.

She picked up a ten-carat gold-filled Cross pen, belonging, she supposed, to Alex, and tried to ignore the silence. Writing notes to herself for long, still moments, she transferred the relevant details to Alex's chart. Finis. At last.

Although the hours had flown by, the physical toll they had taken on her aching body was nothing short of depressing. She slumped in the chair at the desk, her knees drawn up to her chest, and locked her hands around her legs. Until this moment she'd prided herself on her prime physical condition.

The enormity of the commitment she'd made hit her hard. "Do you know what this is like for me?" she asked, knowing Alex couldn't care less.

The day had been trying for him, too, Alex thought, and he wouldn't give her the satisfaction of even thinking she'd gotten to him. So what if she'd spent half her childhood cutting up snowflakes, or paper dolls or paper airplanes? Yuppie angst he could do without.

So why did he suddenly care about missing the first snowfall?

"I feel like some storybook heroine, locked away from the world without the hope of a happily ever after."

Nothing.

"I could use some conversation here, Alex. I'm not used to the silent treatment."

Soon, maybe, she'd get used to carrying on one-sided conversations.

She opened a relatively new and unorthodox text on head injuries and flipped noisily through the pages to avoid the overbearing quiet. The print swam in front of her. Diagrams wavered and blurred. She rubbed her eyes with the heels of her hands and forced herself to focus on page one, word one.

He heard her sigh, and recognized her weariness. *Go to bed, Caterpillar. I'm tired.*

Vanessa slapped the thick text shut and headed for the shower.

He heard the water running and sensed the billowing steam . . . felt a gentle, unguarded tug inside and thought that if she had such sterling damned instincts she'd know how he envied her . . . and dozed.

Vanessa lathered her hair, gathered shampoo suds into her hands and stroked her skin with them, then rinsed and let the water sluice over her. *Alex's shower.* But the needle spray coming out of the pulsating shower head drove that intimate, nervous observation from her mind. After a while she turned off the water, toweled dry and pulled her wet-darkened hair into a braid. Finally she slipped on her worn, oversized Denver Bronco T-shirt.

And fell asleep to the sounds of Alex's breathing.

He stirred, long enough to know an unsettling sense of pleasure at the presence of this woman in his bedroom.

HER CLOCK RADIO came on three times. Alex supposed that as a doctor, Caterpillar must once have been accustomed to walking quickly, ready for whatever emergency confronted a lowly intern.

The adrenaline must pour into her system with each alarm. Couldn't she distinguish between the wakefulness needed to cope with an emergency as opposed to that necessary to shift his position and tend his needs?

He knew she suffered.

The last time the radio came on he heard her tell the blessed thing to take a break, that she'd wake to the light of dawn, as always. Instead, she woke to a gentle but insistent knock on the door and bright sunlight pouring into the room.

Papoo. His grandfather. Alex recognized the knock, but Caterpillar must have been expecting Nanny Bates with a breakfast tray. Alex heard her groan, crawl out from between what he imagined must be fragrant, sleep-warmed sheets and open the door, yet in the T-shirt that barely reached her thighs. He knew that because he'd felt the soft cotton fabric against his skin as she'd levered his body with her own to shift his position. And he'd guessed a T-shirt could no more than brush her bare thighs.

Alex pictured Papoo at the door, confronted with the sleepy feminine visage.

"Eldest Mr. Petrakis. Welcome! Here, let me take that from you."

The scent of cinnamon oatmeal and something citrus—grapefruit maybe—reached Alex as well. Listening to Caterpillar handling what should have been an awkward situation, Alex grew amused himself. Perhaps Papoo had met his match. It didn't occur to Alex that if that were true, he'd met his own match as well.

"Vanessa," the old man returned. "You *are* every bit as beautiful as my Eleni was. Here. *Yie mou*, my son Constantine asked that I bring your breakfast tray. At my advanced age I, Matthew Zachaios Petrakis, am reduced to your humble manservant."

Alex knew, and he was certain Papoo knew as well, that Nanny and his father were in a conspiracy to keep the old man active, and delivering food trays was as good an excuse as any.

Still, Alex thought, Papoo's rapier wit was in fine form this morning. The appreciation he verbalized for Caterpillar was discouraging, though. Because Alex wanted so intensely to dislike her, he'd assigned Caterpillar a miserable combination of physical traits. Buck teeth. Thin, scraggly dishwater brown hair. A Durante nose, her body the shape of a chrysalis and the personality of a Disney villainess. Cruella DeVille, perhaps.

"Perhaps, come in and sit with me, Mr. Petrakis," she encouraged. "I meant to compliment your beautiful English. My grandfather never bothered to learn."

Alex didn't care for the tone of her voice, either. *Patronizing little witch.*

"Vanessa," the old man pronounced with relish. "Greek. Butterfly." Grandfather paused. "Yes. It fits. And you must call me 'Papoo.' Of everyone in this household, only Bates dare not. Old hag," he muttered.

"Papoo it is then. Thank you."

Thank you, Alex mimicked inside, twisting her gentle thanks into an ingratiating, simpering epithet. *Why don't you go put on some clothes, Caterpillar?*

"If you'll excuse me for a minute, I'll go get dressed."

"Not on my account, I hope," Papoo chuckled bawdily.

"No. On your grandson's."

This time the old man laughed aloud. "We're going to get along very well, you and I, little Vanessa. Very well indeed."

You're welcome to her, Papoo. Very welcome, indeed, Alex thought bitterly.

But then Papoo's voice became subdued. "How is he?"

"Ask him yourself, Papoo," Caterpillar answered.

A drawer opened and closed. She moved toward the bathroom. The door closed. He was alone with Papoo, who made his deliberate way toward the bed. The old man's cool, gnarled fingers reached for Alex's hand and held tightly. For dear life.

There was an awkwardness between them Alex had never known. *Papoo, what is it?*

Long moments passed. A tear splashed onto his thumb. A tear. *Papoo, what?*

When at last the old man spoke, his voice quavered. "I haven't been so charmed since your grandmother Eleni was a girl, Alexander *mou*. This one is a beauty. Hair that is long and dark with a color to remind you of red maple leaves at the end of a long, hot summer. Skin the color of an orchid petal, enough to make an old man weep. And heart . . . such heart."

How can you tell that so soon, Papoo?

"She knows, Alex *mou*. Did you hear her tell me to ask you myself how you are this morning?" his grandfather scoffed. "Of course you heard."

I heard, Papoo. But you have known me all my life. You are entitled to me, as I am to you. That one isn't.

"She must be very, very good. She is your cousin Nicholas's equal. This is not an easy thing for me to accept, but I am old and my ideas are decrepit as this old body of mine."

Your ideas aren't decrepit, old one—

"And your father would not have promised her heaven and earth if he didn't believe in her." The old, exquisitely familiar voice of his grandfather cracked. "She'll be good for you, Alexander. Take care that you do not drive her away. A man should not do such a thing."

I'm sorry if I've disappointed you, Papoo. When I wake up, it will be because of you.... Not because of this woman.

He heard her enter the room. Felt the electricity and heard the crackling as she brushed her hair. He imagined the dark, fiery color of red maple leaves, and cursed Papoo's descriptions.

"So, Papoo. This is wonderful. Is Alex applying any pressure to your hand?"

"Of course. But it is no more than he has done for several days. Is it important?"

"I didn't see any mention of it in Mrs. Hancock's notes—"

"Bah! That woman. Talked to my grandson as if he were the moron instead of her! Muttered something about an old man's imagination when I spoke to Alex. I stole a peek over her shoulder at her precious Glasgow Scale, but I never quite understood it."

Vanessa sat down to the meal Papoo had brought her. "It's not all that complicated—just a way of evaluating his condition—"

And just what condition is my condition in, Cat?

Papoo waved off any detailed explanation. "I want to know only how it is a man can be unconscious and still smile. Alex smiles, you know."

"I haven't seen it but—"

"And he squeezes my fingers. His father tells me you are able to understand Alex in ways the others have failed to see. That you are known far and wide for the miracles you make."

Vanessa scraped at the oatmeal with her spoon, pushing the creamy stuff around in the small bowl. "No miracles, Papoo, truly."

Amen. Pack it in, Caterpillar.

"But since I was a little girl I've had this sort of empathy. If we're lucky I'll be able to reach Alex, and if we're very lucky, he'll respond."

Alex sighed. Cat wasn't going anywhere soon.

Papoo straightened hopefully. "You hear him then?"

"No, I don't. But sometimes I seem to sense what he's feeling—"

Yeah? When?

But Alex's grandfather's face lit up from inside. He clutched at her hand, and cradled it tightly between his. "You hear him!"

Alex's heart beat louder in his ears, and faster. The possibility was staggering. It was also crazy. Just crazy...

"Papoo, that isn't possible," she chided gently. Casting about for a change of subject, she gently withdrew her hand from his.

"So, anyway. How is Alex this morning?"

Papoo snuffled unashamedly into his handkerchief like the dramatic old man he was.

"Stubborn, as always," he said. "Before he wakes up he wants to know you'll be his forever."

She laughed. Alex wasn't amused, but he couldn't help enjoying the sound of pleasure in her voice.

"Anything, Papoo. I'll promise him anything."

For heaven and earth, isn't that what you were promised, Caterpillar? A rehab center of your own. How very, very noble. But the hint of sincerity in her voice, the notion of such compassion shook Alex deeply, more, even, than the possibility that she could hear his thoughts.

"Ah, therein lies the rub," the old man jibed. "Will you deliver, my dear?"

But then, because Alex hoarded other emotions than anger, pulled them apart and put them back together, piece by agonizing piece, he heard in her voice a pensive quality, filled with the specter of immense personal loss.

"If that's what it took, Papoo, how could I do anything else?"

How, indeed? was the flip answer that his jaded, leery, thrumming heart offered up. But somewhere deep inside him, Alex was touched.

Papoo gathered her hands into his again, silently thanking her for the depths of her commitment and then left. But his question, "Will you deliver?" raised all sorts of issues Vanessa had never thought to confront. It implied that Alex would recover—Papoo believed where Vanessa could only hope. It implied that she'd already made the promise herself. She stood looking down at Alex, wondering where to start with him, knowing the journey of a thousand miles must first just begin.

"Stupid to worry about it, anyway," she told herself. Things were only ever that simple in fairy tales, and she'd be the last woman on earth a man like Alex Petrakis would hold out for. "Just make a start. Somewhere. Anywhere."

She padded barefoot to the bathroom to brush her teeth. To the bathroom where her own toiletries now mingled casually with Alex's. There was nothing casual about it. To her, having her toothbrush hanging with his was the very core of intimacy, to say nothing of her tampon box next to his condoms. And why condoms? Had Constantine merely tossed them in with all Alex's things, or had Papoo? The old familiar Greek machismo, no doubt.

She'd meant to wreak havoc with Alex by presuming on his territory. So far, she'd only set herself up for a shock every time she saw their personal belongings jumbled together like that. She grabbed up the offending toothbrush and scrubbed at her teeth.

As a doctor, she *ought* to be impervious to such mundane details. Ought to be immune to the suggestion of intimacy. Ought to be clinically detached. But she'd wager the rehab center she didn't even have yet that no physician had ever been in a situation quite like this one.

She had planned to give Alex a shave, a bath, and then a session of physical therapy, but she changed her mind. Alex would pay.

"When you can answer me, Alex," she told him, "you'll get a shave. And not before."

But it was Vanessa who paid, and paid a steep price in the days that followed, and Alex knew it. She did everything herself, turning away Nanny's offers of help time and again. Why couldn't she understand, Alex wondered. Why wasn't it as obvious to her as it was to him? He'd wake up when he chose. He didn't need her to dance attendance on him every two hours, day and night.

In Caterpillar's mind, Alex thought, he was an invalid, and that made him angry. Gut-level, hell-bent-for-leather mad. But he couldn't afford to show it, or else she'd conclude she was right. The power and force of his personality—even his manhood—lay in foiling her.

And foil her he would.

Hancock had told her that he sometimes smiled after a shave. Caterpillar had resolved right then and there not to shave him if he enjoyed it so much, and she didn't mind telling him so. She was after his anger, after all. It bothered him, all right. A lot. He'd been shaving since he was sixteen years old—sometimes twice a day. But every time she offered to correct her little oversight if he'd just respond with some muscle action or another, he let his muscles go slack. Or, if she wanted him to relax a muscle, he wouldn't.

But then she let him know his resistance was okay with her. Either way, she was getting what she wanted. If she asked him to flex, and he relaxed instead, fine. Because then she'd ask him to relax, and he'd flex as she'd wanted.

He'd been outwitted. In spite of himself, he was charmed. Captivated. When was the last time *anyone* had taken the time to outwit him?

Then he started really thinking. He had to respect the energy she poured into her days with him, even if he didn't really *need* any of it. And when he listened, really listened instead of trying to twist her words, he was deeply pleased with the way she gave Papoo such daughterly respect. And with the small kindnesses she did the old man, by hearing his many stories.

Face it, Petrakis, he thought. You're tempted to like the woman.

On his eleventh night with her, twelve straight days without a shave, Alex heard her come back in after a half-hour's absence. She'd finished the supper Papoo had brought up, and had returned the tray even though she knew Nanny would scold her for doing so. Alex supposed she needed to get out of the room once in a while.

There was no cheery little greeting when she returned, though. Instead he heard her rattling around in the cabinet below the bathroom sink, and then shaking some pills out of a bottle. Water running. The clink as she replaced a glass on the sink...

She came back into the room and sank heavily into the rocker by his bed. ''I give up, Alex. Papoo thinks you need a shave, Nanny thinks you need a shave. And I don't care anymore.''

That's when he knew just how much he'd worn her down. He didn't care much for the guilt parading around in his head.

''I'll get to it in a little while. Right now I don't feel...I just don't feel really terrific.''

He knew why, suddenly. Cramps. How the hell old was she, anyway? *You should get married, Caterpillar. Have kids. Don't these things go away after you've had enough sex or babies?*

''But then, you wouldn't know about cramps, would you?''

He knew, he just hadn't ever really cared one way or the other before now. But he pictured her in the rocker, curled up with her arms around her legs and her head resting on her knees. Just sitting there in the rocker all the women in his family had used, and suddenly, he did care. *Tell me, Cat. Tell me how you hurt.*

''There's...it's nothing. When I was a girl though...''

She hesitated, remembering, and Alex found himself holding his breath. He didn't believe it was nothing to her.

"I had such pain when I first started my periods," she remembered aloud. "I missed days of school for three years, but my mother would only tuck me into bed with a hot water bottle. Finally my father made her take me to the doctor. I think I was about fifteen, then, and the doctor wanted to put me on birth control. He said the Pill would . . . make things easier. Mama nearly went into hysterics at the thought of it. Birth control! She took me away and we never went to that doctor again. . . . I never saw my Papa more angry at her, but she was years past paying attention to his wishes."

Her shared intimacies stunned him, eroding his veneer of indifference. They had a way of dispelling his loneliness, too. Cat had this way about her, a way of unwittingly offering him such intimate knowledge of herself that he knew she believed he'd forget it once he woke up.

Surprise, Cat.

Surprise, Petrakis.

There had never been a time when he'd felt more a man, because a woman was never more a female than when her body did the things Cat's was doing, and he knew about it. . . .

Or more protective, with a need in himself to ease a woman's hot, flushing aches. This woman's aches.

Tell me, Cat. What happened then?

He wanted her to hear him like Papoo did. He could almost feel her queasy, moody discomfort. *Tell me.* But the question she answered wasn't the one he'd asked.

"Things are only as bad as you think they are, *andras*. Or as good. You had a *life*, Alex, remember? It's time for you to come back."

AFTER A WHILE the mild painkillers took effect, and Vanessa knew there wasn't any point in putting off Alex's shave any longer. Papoo was upset by seeing Alex look so unkempt, and Nanny was snappish as well.

Perhaps another tactic... She got wearily out of the rocker and went to gather together her own shaving gear. While she would have chosen an electric razor for any other patient, Mrs. Hancock had said Alex didn't own a double-edge razor. She'd suggested in her written notes that "Dr. Koures keep as much as possible to the patient's preferences."

That wasn't part of her plan, and hadn't been from the beginning. But if not shaving him wasn't the answer, either, maybe coming at him with a real razor—her razor—would convince him she meant business.

She ran a metal basin full of hot water, tossed in a washcloth and marched out to do battle.

"Time for a shave, Alex. I know Mrs. Hancock told me to use your electric, but if you don't mind, I'm going to use my own double-edge," she announced. "After a shave and a sponge bath you'll feel like a new man."

Trite, Caterpillar. But if you cut me, just remember. Paybacks are hell. The mellowing of her mood pleased him, maybe because he knew she must be feeling better. He decided to play along for the moment. Besides, he relished the thought of a barber-style shave. It didn't occur to him to wonder if she were the least bit competent with a razor. Instead, the fact that it was *her* razor made him realize how far she was willing to go in trying to keep him off balance. *Sorry, Cat. Close, but no cigar.*

Now, though, she faced one more aggravation. In order to get into position at Alex's head, she had to move the bed out from the wall. "Simple enough," she muttered, but then she hadn't counted on the wheels of the bed being anchored deeply in the plush carpet. She swore succinctly when her repeated efforts to dislodge it failed. By the time she'd managed to edge the bed sideways, the water in the basin had gone cold.

Though Alex wanted a shave desperately, he was glad he was in no position to come to her rescue. This was definitely too much fun.

"Laugh, Petrakis. Paybacks are hell."

She flicked a few drops of cold water onto his chest and took a great deal of professional and personal satisfaction in the healthy response of his skin.

She stomped off to refill the basin with hot water, giving Alex time to wonder at her echo of his threat. *Paybacks are hell.*

Vanessa soaped the washcloth and wrapped it around her fingers to wash his face first. Short, gentle strokes, where her father would have taken broad, all-encompassing swipes. How many times, and how many years ago had she sat on her child's stool in the family bathroom and watched her father perform this entirely male ritual? Maybe a hundred, and surely twenty-five years ago.

"Here goes nothing," she murmured.

She shook the can of shaving cream, put a large dollop in her hand, and began transferring the creamy substance to Alex's jaw. The sensation of stiff whiskers coated with the slick foam plunged her stomach into chaos. She jerked her hand away from the intensely male feel of him.

Dammit! she railed silently as the idiocy of her reaction hit home. She put a swift end to it with a deep, determined breath and a verbal recitation of the muscle and bone underlying his heated flesh.

"Here it is, *andras*. Your anatomy lesson for this evening. This is the neck musculature. Platysma—a broad sheet, extending from the clavicle obliquely upwards and medially sideways. Here to...here." She thought for a moment how very stupid this must all sound, but it was having the desired effect of distracting her.

"This is the sternocleidomastoid along the laryngeal prominence..." Her fingers guided the razor's edge along the length of his neck. "The buccinators, here, the thin quadrilateral muscles occupying the interval between the mandible and maxilla here..."

Alex's silent laughter began with a quivering of the muscles in his torso. Vanessa's fingers halted, suspended above his face. Her eyes darted to his torso. His shoulders shook, and a deep, rumbling laugh founds its way out.

Vanessa clapped a foam-covered hand to her lips. Waves of shock and surprise and delight raced through her. An answering giggle tickled her throat. The giggle threatened to erupt into full-fledged laughter, and then did. She turned her head over to wipe a tear from her lashes with her wrist, and began laughing all over again at the wry appreciation on Alex's naked lips amid mounds of shaving cream.

After days and days of his resistance, this felt like a major triumph for her. For Alex.

For them both.

Chapter Four

PAPOO WAS READY to dance—to lead a *Syrto* in the nearest *taverna*. Nanny scolded him for his exuberance, though she was only slightly less elated over Alex's laughter. But when the old man snatched off her apron to use as a prop, she banished him from her kitchen with an elaborate imitation of her own Scots burr to counter "His Greekness"—Nanny's own version of "His Highness."

"Out! Out, y'old goat! Or I'll prromise y'a brrnnt celebrration supper for y'r trouble!" Nanny catered to his every Greek whim, though, and cooked for his sake food more ethnic than Matt served at The Apollo.

Vanessa laughed. "You're an old fraud, Nanny."

The old woman handed Vanessa a wicked-looking knife and pointed to the onions waiting to be chopped. "Maybe. He loves a good fight, and there's nary a Scotswoman alive not up to the likes of him."

Vanessa began hacking away at the onions. "You've known him a long time, haven't you?"

Nanny's hands slowed a bit in their salad-making motions. Her momentary stillness gave Vanessa a strong, almost visceral feeling of the old woman's intense loyalty to Papoo.

"A very long time, indeed. We've learned to tolerate each other over the years."

"Are you humoring him, Nanny? Do you really believe any of this is possible?"

Nanny gave the question a moment's serious thought. "If you'd been about askin' me that thirty years ago, I'd have said you were just plain daft to be catering to Alex like you are, talkin' to him, and such. Now? The older you get the less likely y'are to call anythin' impossible. How did it happen, this laughter of his?"

A deep flush stained Vanessa's cheeks—she could feel the heat of it all the way to her scalp. "I...he was laughing at me."

"Why, forever more?"

Vanessa put down the knife and clasped her hands, and the story came out in a flood. "It's ridiculous, really, Nanny. I have...for days on end I've touched him, rubbed him, bathed him. Last night I decided to shave him—Papoo seemed so upset that I hadn't. Oh God, Nanny, when I touched his beard with that slick shaving cream it was like I'd never touched a man before and I...well, he knew it. I've suspected all along that he's aware of what goes on around him, and I've waved a crimson flag in front of him. 'Do this, do that, c'mon Alex, you're such a *man*. I started naming the muscles beneath my fingers to distract myself and that's—"

"When he laughed. Oh, Vanessa! You precious, precious, child! They're all too much, aren't they...all the Petrakis men. A woman would do well to don a pair of track shoes and run for her life."

Tears welled in Vanessa's eyes. "Oh, Nanny! I don't need this. Things are complicated enough without it!"

Nanny came around the kitchen island and patted Vanessa's shoulder.

"You started something you must finish, lass. Don't you see? You've egged him on mercilessly to be a man— what else has a better chance of working with him? But then, Dr. Missy, you've got to be woman enough to handle it!''

"Is this what I've worked so hard for all my life, to come to this? That being a doctor isn't good enough. I have to be *woman enough* for him?''

Nanny shook her head. "I have lived among this family for twenty-seven years. Alex's mother, Helen, used to tell me that it was easier to handle her husband, eight sons and even her father-in-law than it would have been to raise a daughter to live with men like them in this day and age." Nanny paused, and covered Vanessa's icy fingers with her own warm hands. "They're overbearing tyrants, she would say, but they're *men*. Real men, and she was very happy."

"I would appreciate a 'real' meal on the table," Constantine interrupted from the door. Living, breathing specimen of the overweening Greek man Helen Petrakis had loved so well, and whose nurseries she had filled with sons like him. "I'm expecting an important call, and I'd as soon be done when it comes."

He was gone as quickly as he'd come, and Nanny continued as though she'd never been interrupted. "You don't have to give Alex *all* your heart, Dr. Missy. Just the part that is wise enough to play his game long enough to make him live again. And if you will, let him pay the consequences after."

Only, I'll be the one to pay his piper, Vanessa thought. But that, she couldn't say. Not even to Nanny, who loved the Petrakis family as though they were her own.

Constantine was the more formidable pragmatist. When his initial pleasure over Alex's laughter wore off, he was left somehow angry. Laughter alone should have been enough to end his son's coma. Why hadn't it, he wanted to know. Dammit, why?

But Papoo needed the reprieve of believing the laughter *had* made a difference, and for his sake, Vanessa countered Constantine's cheerless expression with a smile of her own at the celebration dinner.

Papoo was in such high spirits that afterward he helped Nanny clear the table and then wandered off in the direction of his beloved greenhouse. Vanessa had discovered days ago that Papoo spent all his emotional moments there, good or bad.

Constantine's eyes were glued to the door his aging father had just gone through and swirled the last of the retsina in his Baccarat goblet. "He expects too much."

Vanessa rested her chin on her folded hands and smiled a little sadly, a little hopelessly. "Are you speaking for yourself, or for him?"

He ignored her challenge. "He's an old man who thinks he hears Alex. He reads into every situation whatever he wants to believe."

Defiance rose up in her, and she'd had a lot of experience with defiance. "Yes, he's old. And he's terribly afraid. Sometimes it's the old ones who are better able to accept things they can't understand. How can you be so sure that he doesn't hear Alex?"

"Do you, Dr. Koures?" he snapped, clearly taking her pointed remark for an impertinence.

"Isn't that why I'm here? Isn't that why you've offered to move heaven and earth for me? Because I can hear him in ways no one else can? Because even if I don't hear Alex's words, I hear what's in his heart?"

Constantine drained the wine in his glass, then poured himself more. "And just what is in his heart? If Alex had the compassion God gave a goose, he'd know that that old man will not live long enough to see his village in Greece again if Alex doesn't get out of that bed!"

Vanessa paled. She hadn't known Papoo wanted to return to Greece, nor that he'd postponed such a journey on Alex's account. But before she could respond, the telephone rang in Constantine's study.

Alex's father shrugged elaborately. "I must go take this call, but I'd like to discuss this further. Could you join me in my study in thirty minutes?"

An overwhelming need to assert herself consumed her. "If Alex is sleeping, I'll come back down for a while. If not, it will have to wait."

"See to him, by all means, but then come down." It was understood that unless she did, he'd carry their discussion to Alex's bedside.

She met his hooded gaze, nodded and left the table.

She knew before she opened the door to Alex's suite that he was asleep within his sleep. Still she tiptoed across the carpet and stood looking at him for long, silent moments.

God help her, but she'd needed that laughter.

She needed so much more. For Alex to open his eyes. For Alex to tell her to get the hell out of his rooms. What she'd need after that, she didn't dare even think about.

She wanted to touch the shadow of a beard that had grown in since the night before. Instead she checked his IV. Pulled away the gauze to satisfy herself that it was clean and uninfected. Straightened his sheets. And eased his hand back onto the bed. There was nothing more she could do for him tonight, and still she lingered.

Please wake up, Alex *mou*. Please.

Her dreams, waking and sleeping, had been filled with ways to break through to him. With the unwanted feminine, womanly doubts Nanny had spoken of. With Papoo, and his trusting nature.

And with the hologram she'd hidden away in Alex's desk drawer. It haunted her, consumed her thoughts, ruled her dreams. She reminded herself over and over again that it was just a weird combination of high-tech, beam-splitting images. It was so much more.

Her memory worked in vague ways providing her with image and light and keening emotion.

She'd worked with Alex's body for two weeks now. She was intimately aware of the shape of him, and of his profile from any and every angle, and of the powerful contours. And the arrangement of muscle over bone. He was only human, a man with a man's body.

He was so much more.

Papoo knocked gently on the door, and let himself in. "My son wishes to see you in his study. I'll stay with Alex if you like."

"I'd like that just fine, Papoo," she whispered.

ALEX WOKE to the sounds of Vanessa leaving. He sensed Papoo's presence though, and his joy.

Papoo. What can it be that has pleased you so?

"Little Vanessa told us of your laughter. It is a portent, an omen, I think."

An omen of what, Papoo?

For long moments the old man was silent. Alex understood his silences well. For all his life such interludes had been meant as gentle rebukes. Did Papoo think him deliberately obtuse? Of course he knew Papoo thought it was "little Vanessa" who would accomplish this miracle of his waking. Alex was in no need of miracles. His sleep was wearing thin, but he needed no woman to help him out of this great dark hole.

When Papoo finally spoke again it was in the tradition of a Greek storyteller.

"Red thread, twisted well,
Neatly wound upon the reel;
Set the reel a-turning, do,
And *paramithi* I'll tell you."

Alex had heard this version of "once upon a time" many, many times.

He felt the old man lean heavily against the bed and take his hand. "There was once an old couple," Papoo began, "who were without any children. They were good people, and God-fearing, and so they prayed every day for a child—even if it were a little butterfly. And so at last God sent them their little butterfly as reward for their prayers, and the couple adopted her."

Alex recognized the story and squeezed his grandfather's gnarled old fingers. "The Bayberry Child" was an old Greek tale found in many collections of folk tales. Only in the real story, the couple had prayed for a child, even if it were a magpie.

In Papoo's version, the little butterfly took her adopted parents' clothes to the castle gardens to wash. There she would cast a spell on the gardener, take off her wings, and in the little butterfly's place would be a beautiful girl doing the wash.

Alex let Papoo's voice in the ancient Greek dialect flow over him. There was a point to this telling, he knew, but he was content for the moment to let the story unfold.

"The mother and father were very worried about the little butterfly. She was so tiny, and the load she carried so heavy..."

In the end, the little butterfly became the bride of the prince. For though she had used up the water and ruined the king's flowers and trees, she was good and beautiful, and the prince, who happened upon her one day and would not return her little butterfly's wings, fell in love with her.

"The old people went crazy with joy when their little butterfly-girl told them what had happened, and that they were going with her to live at the palace.

"And they lived well ever after, but we are even better."

But we are even better. This was the way happily-ever-after Greek stories ended. How many times, Alex wondered, had he fallen asleep in his grandfather's lap as child, hearing the stories in his sleep, only to wake up to "but we are even better."

Disney should have animated that story, Papoo. Better by far than Cinderella . . .

"You should make that picture," Papoo contradicted. He paused a moment. "Your father grows impatient, waiting on happily-ever-after-and-we-are-even-better. He begins to despair of your ever waking up."

The things Alex could tell Papoo about despair were staggering, but none of them had to do with his sleeping or waking. So his father didn't believe he'd wake up. No surprise. Constantine Petrakis had rarely had the patience even to hear out his father's stories. Where would he get such patience now?

The child in your story was a magpie, Papoo, not a butterfly named Vanessa.

"Will you be so stubborn as to miss the point, Alexander? I know that you have christened Vanessa 'Caterpillar' in your heart. But surely you know this. One must endure the chrysalis until the butterfly emerges."

Surely you know, Papoo, that I have no pressing need of either. But then he felt as if he'd been caught lying.

"I know nothing of the sort! I have seen how little your brothers' company filled the loneliness in you. Their needs were never what yours have been.'' Beyond the gentleness of a silent rebuke now, Papoo's voice shook with an emotion Alex recognized as profound anger. ''Don't speak to me of your needs if you will not be honest!''

Ah, Papoo—

The old man interrupted Alex as if he had not heard. ''Like the childless couple in the tale, I've prayed every day for someone to help you come back, even if it was only a magpie. I will not quibble with God, Alex. He sent a butterfly, and I am content. In this I am, I fear, no better than your father, who has so little faith, at times.''

Alex fell back into the deepening shadows of his unconscious, and it was like falling over a cliff into unending darkness. To endure Papoo's rare anger was bad enough. Papoo without this enduring faith was... unthinkable.

VANESSA LEFT ALEX to Papoo and negotiated her way down the broad, winding stairs and into Constantine's study through a blur of tears. Clearly upset himself, Constantine rose out of his chair and indicated that she should take the chair opposite him.

She could feel his tension, taut like a bowstring. She knew suddenly that this had little to do with her, or with Alex.

''What is it? What has happened?''

He shrugged a shoulder as if to say it didn't matter that she know. Then he cleared his throat. ''I owe you an apology. You were quite right in that I have promised to move heaven and earth for you because I thought you alone could do for my son—for Alex—what no one else has been able to do. You will forgive me if I am unwilling to accept so feeble a victory as my son's laughter.''

"So feeble a victory?" Vanessa went rigid with resentment. "Isn't that a contradiction in terms?"

"I don't care for argumentative women," he warned.

"And I don't care for tyrants."

"So." He lifted his hand to her in a grudging salute. "We understand each other well." His eyes, though, were filled with fire. "But this laughter. Mark my words. It will prove a setback for him."

"That's crazy! He's beginning to know—"

"—just how powerless he is!"

"No. You're projecting your own feelings onto Alex. It's you who are powerless in this, and you who can't deal with it."

He seemed taken aback by this, hit with a truth he was unwilling to acknowledge. Tossing his head imperiously, he glanced toward the cordless phone at his side and flared at her. "I have no need of being reminded how powerless I am when it involves the lives of my sons." He hesitated for a moment, then sighed deeply.

"I had a second call before you came down. My son John's wife, Andrea, is fourteen hours into premature labor—the infant is not due until Christmas."

Vanessa remembered Andrea well, and her husband John, the mining engineer.

"They live fifty miles up a remote canyon," Constantine continued, "and I offered to have her transported by helicopter into Denver, but John refuses. She has miscarried three times, and still they will have only a midwife present at the birth." With a look he defied her to contradict him. "I am no stranger to powerlessness. I will not apologize for wishing I were."

He was silent for long moments, and the only sound in the room came from the crackling fire. Constantine stared into the flames and Vanessa felt the rage of his impotence ebbing from him. What was left seemed only the shell of the man he was, and in spite of her own resentment, she ached for him.

"I've found myself hoping for a granddaughter. All my children's children until now have been sons."

Surprised and moved to hear him say so, Vanessa reached across the space that separated them to touch his hand.

He nodded and sighed deeply in acknowledgment of what they both knew. Male babies were more desired than females in many Greek families.

"Daughters have always been a burden to a Greek family. Precious, as every child is, but still, a burden. In the old days, it was the issue of a dowry. Now the problem is much more subtle. Most of us place high value on educational advancement. Yet for over half of us it's still unthinkable for a daughter to leave home before marriage. How do we reconcile these things? How do we make our girls conform, to bring only respect to the family *philotimo*, the family honor? It is very...heartless. Difficult, because we are not a people without heart."

A lump of some very primitive resentment rose in Vanessa's throat. "My father always wanted a son. He got me."

"And that was not enough for him?"

The discussion had become difficult for her. "No. I think he was proud of me, anyway, but I was not a son."

"Were you raised with no sense of your value as a woman?"

Vanessa bristled. "Do you count my worth in feminine wiles?"

His hands outspread, Constantine scolded gently, "Of course not. A man is a man, no matter what else he becomes. And so it should be for a woman. I meant no slight.... What of your mother?''

She understood that Constantine was not trying to be cruel, but to grasp a notion foreign to him.

''Nothing I've done with my life since I was old enough to make my own decisions has pleased my mother. Every time I talk to her she manages to remind me that I have never known my place. She's not heartless, either. She just expects...conformity.''

''You're still trying?'' To please her, he meant.

Vanessa's chin rose defiantly, as if he were challenging her instead of asking a simple question. To him it might be simple. To her it wasn't. ''No. A good Greek girl would.''

His eyes, so dark and unlike the golden-streaked hazel of Alex's, filled with a sudden understanding. ''I had only sons with Alex's mother, Vanessa, but I would have been proud to call you my daughter.''

Such things were easy to say, her expression told him.

''Perhaps you're right. *Gyneka mou*, Helen, my wife, wanted only sons. I thought I wanted a daughter, but I would have left her in her mother's hands. Perhaps I would've expected only this conformity you speak of.''

He paused for an uncertain moment, and Vanessa felt the strain in him, and the sorrow. Uncertainty must be so difficult for a man such as Constantine Petrakis.

He opened his mouth to say something more, but then the phone rang again, interrupting his thoughts.

He answered the call, listened and then smiled. Tears came into his eyes as he replaced the receiver, too emotional to comment for a moment.

''I have a healthy, five-pound, five-ounce granddaughter,'' he said at last. ''Perhaps I will live long enough to tell her that a real woman is so much more than a compliant girl. And that when my son woke from his long ordeal, it was because of a Greek woman who refused to know her place.''

THE MEMORY of Alex's laughter sustained Vanessa for days. It had now been weeks that she'd worked with Alex, all the while denying to herself any possibility of hearing him.

She called the university to ask for a literature search of the scientific evidence of psychic communication. When Nick delivered stacks of photocopies, she found justification for her refusal to believe.

Nick didn't think much of her request. He treated her to all sorts of curious looks and probing, oblique questions. Was she really buying into this? he wanted to know. She explained Papoo's belief that he heard Alex, but her casual explanations didn't satisfy Nick. He took one look at her eyes and the ever darkening shadows beneath them and begged her to allow Constantine to bring in additional help. She couldn't.

More than once Vanessa dreamed of Papoo, standing beside a sleeping Alex, demanding over and over again on Alex's behalf, "Will you deliver?"

She had told Papoo she'd promise Alex anything if that's what it took to get him back, and she had meant it. She'd not been able to help her father. If there was such a thing as justice in life, bringing Alex back would redeem that failure, restore her.

It solved nothing to remember that Alex had had a life of his own before the accident. A life and a fiancée. Vanessa knew Constantine's still-active Denver office fielded regular phone calls from the press, avid to report the whereabouts of his son. Once awake, Alex would doubtless want to take up where he'd left off—with the woman and the life he knew—in spite of his father's dictates where Liz Pederson was concerned.

She didn't believe Alex wanted any part of her promise of forever. Perhaps she'd needed such a reminder. Although she'd called Sarah Gilles every few days, and spoken to various colleagues, sometimes it seemed to Vanessa as though her other life at University Hospital were a fanciful creation of her mind—that she'd been here, with Alex, forever.

In the late afternoon of a day when Alex had seemed particularly stubborn and unmanageable, she went down the back stairs to the kitchen. Nanny would be napping, and Vanessa could brew her own cup of tea and phone Sarah—as much to remind her of her other responsibilities as to chat with her little patient.

"*Koukla!* How are you doing today?" she asked when the nurse passed the receiver to Sarah.

"Nessie, hi! Guess what? Dr. Mark says I can start on the bicycle tomorrow.... Really rad, huh?"

Vanessa smiled into the phone at the chipper little voice—and all the right lingo. Sarah might know better how to play an old man's game of cribbage than fish, but the "in" jargon hadn't escaped her. "Totally awesome, sweetheart. I guess you must be bored silly with string games by now, huh?"

"Well, nobody's as fun to do it with as you. Dr. Nick tries, and his fingers are real good, but Nessie—" Sarah's voice dropped into a conspiring whisper "—you better come back soon. He's real sad not having you around to propose to all the time. I can tell."

"He's just spoiled rotten, *koukla*. Remember all those things I do for him so I won't have to accept?"

Sarah giggled. "I *couldn't* forget! Is Dr. Nick's cousin all better now? Did he wake up yet?"

How to explain that one, Vanessa wondered. Awake, and yet not. Responding, and yet not. "No, sweetheart, he isn't. Soon, though, I hope. I really miss you."

"Yeah . . ." Sarah's voice trailed off. "I miss you, too, Nessie—but don't worry. Dr. Mark is pretty good."

Pretty good. Vanessa swallowed hard on her frustration. Neither she nor Mark Bledsoe were good enough . . . no one was. They talked for several more minutes before Vanessa promised to call Sarah again in a few days and hung up.

Her tea was already cold, and her heart colder still. No one was good enough to ransom back Alex Petrakis, either.

ALEX FELT the passing of the days, as well. Before, time had seemed to have very little to do with him. It wouldn't now, either, except that while Caterpillar occupied his room, he began measuring time by her activities—and all her activities were occupied with him.

Things were closing in on him. He heard Nick telling her she looked like a starving street urchin, that the shadows under her eyes were looking like bruises. Alex began to feel like a sadistic jerk for prolonging her back-breaking work.

His brother John and Andrea drove in from their canyon home with their infant daughter so that he would know of the birth of his first niece. All his brothers visited as they had the night Cat had first come, and Alex measured time by what was going on in their lives, but it was the ineffably sweet baby scents that got to him. The fierce longing for babies of his own flared in Alex, and yet here he was, stuck in some absurd never-never land day after day.

Ever since he'd laughed at Cat's reaction to shaving him, and she'd laughed with him, he'd been intrigued. He'd begun to cooperate with her because he thought in return she might try harder to hear him as Papoo did. A couple of times, from what she said, he could almost believe she *had* heard him.

He cared for her in ways he found alarming. In spite of that realization, maybe because of it, Alex began to hope "little Vanessa" would just disappear into the woodwork. If her mere presence was going to feed Papoo with false hopes of a sudden Lazarus-exiting-the-tomb act, Alex wanted her gone. He'd wake up sooner or later, and if he didn't, he didn't want Cat around to see that, either. He was dangerously close to losing his self-respect.

This morning Vanessa came to shave him humming a melancholy sort of tune. It did nothing but aggravate his first truly awful mood. Papoo wouldn't approve. On her first day here, Papoo had told him to take care not to drive her off.

Alex resolved to force the issue, to make her leave.

"You're scowling, Alex," Caterpillar observed.

And you're on your way out, whether you know it or not.

"You've got to help me out here," she continued. "I can't very well shave a scowling man."

So don't.

"C'mon, Alex. Relax."

There was no way he could help responding to the soothing stroke of her fingers against his taut chin.

"That's better."

Don't be patronizing, Caterpillar.

"I'm not patronizing, Alex, and stop calling me— Dammit!"

Stunned surprise rocked through him. He heard the razor clank against the metal basin and splash into the water. Caterpillar was as startled as he was to hear herself answer him like that.

Alex froze. She'd heard him. He'd hoped for this moment for weeks. Now it scared the hell out of him because he'd wanted it so badly, and he'd wanted to wake up, and if he could have one, maybe he could have the other.

Cat? he taunted to get a grip on himself. *Aren't you going to finish?*

"Shut up, Alex. I'm tired of you." She spun away from him, circled around the end of his bed and planted herself before the windows. "This is ridiculous. Papoo hears you. *I don't.*" A fluke, she thought desperately. Just a fluke chance. One in a hundred million.

He heard the note of exhaustion in her voice. In spite of Nanny's helping hand, Cat's tolerance and good humor had reached the breaking point. He found himself wanting to wipe her tears away, and then discovered that he didn't want to be the cause of them in the first place.

It won't get any better, Cat. Get out while the getting's good.

"I'm not leaving, Alex," she told the windows.

You will, Cat.

"I won't leave you, do you hear me? I won't!" She drew a deep, steadying breath, pushed off from the window and retrieved the razor from the basin. She would finish shaving him if it was the last thing she ever did. "I know you're frustrated, and I'm sorry for yelling at you, Alex. But I'm frustrated, too."

Not half as frustrated as you're going to be if you stay.

He heard the water sloshing in the basin and knew that she would empty it and begin with fresh hot water.

She refilled the basin. Alex waited, forcing himself to think, to plan his attack. He didn't want her here, filling Papoo with false hope, plaguing even *himself* with her relentless hope. He would wake up in his own time, or not at all. He had to make her understand.

It was Cat who came out swinging. "Alex, about Papoo."

Yes, Cat. About Papoo...

"He's an old man, Alex." She wrung out her washcloth, soaped it and began rubbing his shoulder and arm. "He may not live until you decide to wake up, you know. How will you live with that?"

What's between Papoo and me is our business, Caterpillar.

She massaged the washcloth on his fingers. "It's more than what's between you two. I'm in the middle of it now. He expects too much. He hurts so badly."

Ah, God, that feels good, he thought. He had to concentrate to get past the sensations caused by her strong, caring hands.

Don't you suppose it hurts me, too, Cat?

Hurts you? she thought. In her wonder, Vanessa forgot that she believed it wasn't possible for her to hear his thoughts. "How *andras*? Tell me how it hurts. How can it hurt if you won't even admit to your coma—or that you're responsible for this unhappiness!"

Alex fought the sensation of being shoved into a corner. Her calling him *andras* was a low blow, and she knew it. An attack on his manhood. *A man is responsible for his own happiness, Caterpillar.*

"It bothers you, though, doesn't it? Well, you're a selfish bastard to do this to him, Alex." Matter-of-factly, she began scrubbing his chest, but at some level she re-

alized she'd just, somehow, made a breakthrough in getting him to backhandedly admit to his coma.

Shame on you, Caterpillar, Alex struck back. *Your
Papa would turn over in his grave to hear you talk like
that.*

Vanessa felt herself pale. How did he know her father
was dead? How had she heard him? Had she heard, or
was she just feeling guilty because she'd caused her own
father pain just like she was accusing Alex of causing
Papoo? But she knew that in some inexplicable, undoc-
umented and absurdly unscientific way, she was hearing
Alex.

Caterpillar. He called her Caterpillar. Everything else
she could chalk up to her own hyperimagination, or to
her own feelings of guilt. Never "Caterpillar."

"I resent that, Alex."

Resent it all you want, Cat. Just leave.

"Why do you call me that?" she railed.

What? he demanded innocently. Anger suffused him.
He'd as much as admitted to a coma. Now let her make
a concession, he thought.

She couldn't fail to notice his shoulders twitching.
"'Caterpillar,' Alex. I hate it."

Oh, so you're admitting you hear me.

"Suppose for one insane moment that I am!"

*Suppose you get scared thinking this is just too bi-
zarre and hightail it out of here?*

"Suppose you stop using that name, *andras*?"

*Why? It's the truth, "little Vanessa." You don't feel
anything. One little sexual titter from The Man Woman
portrait and you slam the thing into a deep, dark drawer.*

"Stop it, Alex!"

*Stop what? You don't hear me. But just in case you do,
sweetheart, think about yourself spouting anatomical*

names and functions to avoid feeling anything sexual for me.

"There's nothing like that in me—"

Bullshit! You hide in this so-called empathy of yours, feeling what everybody else feels and allowing none of what Vanessa feels.... Well, without your own feelings, your own sexuality, you are one up-tight, bound-up little caterpillar. You're the spineless wonder, lady. What makes you any different from me right now?

Her fingers brought the sopping washcloth to her trembling lips. She'd finally pushed him too far, dug up and exposed his awful, unbearably perceptive anger. She understood now how much he resented her presuming to save him. How little he expected of her, believing her to be so tightly controlled that there was virtually no difference between his coma and her emotional bindings.

She wouldn't cry. Not for Alex Petrakis. Not now, not ever.

She swiped the soap from his torso and swore. "I don't fit the good little Greek girl mold any more, *andras*. I have nothing to lose and everything to gain by hounding you until you come out of your self-centered shell. At least I'm not hurting anybody else. Just lie there and rot for a while, Alex. I don't give a damn."

Vanessa carried the basin away and dumped it into the shower. She forced herself to think steadying thoughts, reassurances that whatever cultural expectations she hadn't met, she'd given Papa her best efforts. She'd tried, really tried—even if that meant going against the grain, going to med school and living on her own. Papa had gone to his grave proud of her.

Alex, for all his brutal honesty, was hurting the people who loved him—his brothers, who made constant efforts to visit him, his father, Papoo. And it was none of his damn business, she told herself, how she reacted sexually to his *ManWoman* or to him. It was totally unethical and unprofessional to respond to him, or to any patient that way. And he *is* just a patient, she reassured herself. She was more than justified in shutting down those feelings.

All the same the basin clattered into the shower and the cloth fell to the floor and Vanessa curled up on the cool ceramic tile floor while bitter, brutal tears fell.

Alex lay miserably in his bed, wondering what had possessed him to hit on her like that. She'd done nothing half as mean. In fact, she'd given and given until she dropped into bed every night. But the reality was, he didn't want her around.

He didn't know if he was truly in a coma or not. He didn't want to think about it, either. All he knew was that he wasn't coming out of it. He had no control over his sleep and maybe he never would. She was wasting her time growing frustrated with what looked to her like a failure. And maybe he'd had no right throwing "Caterpillar" and all its nasty meanings at her. But she had no right, either, dammit! None at all to think it was in her power to wake him. One way or another she'd learn.

He would play into her frustration by seeming to backslide on all the things she used to judge his progress, and maybe she'd see she had to give it up and go away. She'd get nothing more from him.

His resolve lasted most of the day. She came close enough to change the hyperalimentation bag running into his IV, and to shift his position, and no closer for hours. Instead she sat in the old rocker and read.

Hours later, having turned Papoo and his lunch and dinner offerings away, she slammed shut her book and took a deep breath.

"I'm not going to skip your therapy, Alex."

His resolve began to slip.

"Get as nasty as you want, bud. It won't help. I don't care. I've decided that my rehab center is more important than your ego or mine. You can laugh all you want—"

The laughs are over, Caterpillar. Maybe it's time you realized that. He was beginning to learn the meaning of hopelessness and fear, and he'd fight his way back to consciousness now or have no respect left for himself. But if he failed, Cat was the last person on earth he wanted around to witness it.

"I'm not here for fun and games—"

Then why? For God's sake, why?

"I'm here because ... because ..."

Because my father is your meal ticket for the next three years, huh, Caterpillar?

"Fine, Alex. If that's what you want to believe, fine."

Because you'll take the credit for bringing me out of this when I decide to wake up, and get your damned rehab center. Right, Cat? Isn't that right? Even as he thought it, he knew it wasn't precisely true....

"You want the credit, Alex? Fine. *Use* that awesome Greek body, then—"

Awesome? Gee thanks, Caterpillar.

"Use that infamous macho Greek power. Come on, Alex. Put up or shut up." She hurled the book to the floor and stripped away the sheet covering his body. Grabbing his foot, she flexed one knee, braced her weight against the plantar surface of his foot and dared him to extend his leg. "Go ahead, *andras*," she taunted. "Show me."

His resolve crumbled to nothing. All the rage at himself and his coma that he'd been carefully hiding from himself exploded in him. Damn her. Damn Elizabeth. Damn everyone for believing he wouldn't sleep this off himself!

Something warned Vanessa that he was about to unleash all the pent-up fury. A wary elation buoyed and braced her as nothing else would have. "Do it, Alex. Do it!"

He threw every bit of his remarkable, dormant strength into straightening his leg against her counterweight. She flew backward, stumbled and landed in a heap near his desk.

Vanessa should have been out cold. Instead she laughed until she cried, and the happy tears spilled over. There was a part of her that was warm and human and frenzied, needy and starving . . . a part that was woman enough to make the offer she'd waited so long to make.

"Wake up, Alexander *mou*, and I'll be yours forever."

Chapter Five

THE PASSION of that moment, the intensity of Caterpillar's naked offer brought Alex down, hard and fast. He knew her promise to be utterly honest even though it had come from the heady exhilaration of his success. The power was his, she'd granted him that. All he had to do was to wake up to make it come true.

He'd been given a lot of things in this life. A proud, ancient heritage, loving parents and family, a silver spoon in his mouth from birth in the wealthiest nation on earth. But he'd learned early on that wealth was no synonym for power, personal power, and no one had ever given him such power as Cat had just granted him.

Alex Petrakis was about power. He courted and valued it more than anything in himself. He wrote with power, but if his scripts missed the mark, he trashed them with an unforgiving ruthlessness.

He produced his films with an exacting, demanding quality that had earned him the reputation of a fourteen-carat son of a bitch in Hollywood, where competition for such singular honors was stiff. He hadn't produced a film in five years; it amused him to let the gossip rags and California potentates think he had only two successes in him. Or that he had lucked into properties worth throwing his money at. But he hadn't put together a single project that the critics hadn't called powerful, first and foremost.

He didn't want that kind of power over Caterpillar.

He discovered a swiftly burgeoning respect for her he would never have suspected—for her strength and grit and for her flying in the face of *impossible*. Control of her was the last thing he wanted.

And so, when she promised she'd be his forever if he'd just wake up, he smiled. Humor had always been his best defense. For the first time, it seemed, she seriously misunderstood him. She thought his smile meant something far different—that he had accepted her promise in the spirit of fun.

He couldn't accept that selflessness, that *gift* from her. Not in any spirit. He had nothing half so valuable to give her in return.

She was a quick study, as he'd known all along. It took her just a few moments to realize that something had gone indefinably wrong. She sat down in the old rocker and started its gentle motion.

"Lighten up, Petrakis. It was just a joke."

Another echo, like a boomerang, returning from their past. Hadn't he told her the same thing when she reacted so strongly to his "over my dead body" threat?

You scare the hell out of me, Cat.

"Why, Alex?"

Because it doesn't feel like a joke. It feels like God's own truth and I don't understand why.

She'd expected Alex to smile—even to laugh. Why this time had he grown so serious? Because he was afraid that she meant it? That she would try to bind him to her with some warped sense of honor? Scared silly herself, of hearing him now, of responding to him like this, Vanessa backpedaled. "Well, it was a joke, Papoo's joke. Remember?"

He remembered, all right. And he remembered her response, "How could I do anything else, Papoo?" But he sensed her running scared now, as he was. They were both treading on thin emotional ice, talking a future, a relationship, a forever. For one rash and glorious moment Alex wanted to explore the possibilities without feeling fear like a cold lump in his gut.

Cat?

"Skip it, Alex. It's time you rolled over onto your side so I can get some lotion on your back. Why don't you save me some trouble and do it yourself? I know you can if you want to, so you might as well just do it."

He ignored her insistent sidetracking because maybe he did have something to give her. His passion, his intensity. Qualities that made weaker women turn tail and run. Qualities that had only amused Liz because she was so disdainful of anything that smacked of meaning.

What if it weren't a joke, Cat? What would happen between us then?

Busying her hands, Vanessa turned her watchband round and round her wrist. "It wouldn't work, Alex."

Why?

"There's Elizabeth, for one thing."

Who's so devoted that she's been at my bedside day and night!

"Stop it, please! It's not funny."

No, it's not, is it? I'm serious, Cat.

"I must be going slowly insane," she cried. "It is simply not possible that we're having this discussion!"

Tell me why, Cat.

"*Because*, Alex! Just because."

Because I'm not what you want?

"No. You're everything I was ever raised to expect or dream of, Alex. But I'm not what you want or expect, and I can't change any of that."

He had never been more aware of her as a woman than he was right now. Her feminine scent, simple and uncluttered; the whisper of sound as she combed and twisted her hair with her fingers; the extraordinary sense that *she* belonged in the Petrakis rocker. And the still more extraordinary vision of her petite body swollen with his child, her woman's cramps eased for a while. His lips felt dust dry. A sweet heaviness pooled in his groin.

You're a sweet liar, Caterpillar. You promised me forever.

Vanessa rose, dipped a sponge in cool water and moistened his lips. "It wouldn't work, Alex."

You know dry lips aren't my only problem, don't you, Cat?

Her eyes were drawn to the tented sheet just above the outline of his muscled thighs. "Don't, Alex." Her whisper had within it a cry of torment. "I can't...help you."

It's your fault, Cat...

"Erections happen, Alex. Even in your sleep," she snapped. "You're a normal, healthy male and it just happens!"

This is no wet dream, Cat. This is you and me, and as real as life gets. I can smell it on you, harato mou. *You're a normal, healthy woman.*

"Tell me what's normal and healthy about a thirty-three-year-old virgin, Alex!" God in heaven, *why* had she said that? If only she hadn't hidden away *The Man-Woman*, if only he hadn't pushed her, hadn't crowded her into a feminine panic with the unerring sexual instinct of a mountain stag to a doe in heat...

But she had, and he had, and the slowly simmering sexuality between them flared.

Cat?

She bit her lip and ignored him, then came round the foot of the bed and put one knee against the water mattress form. Pulling on the draw sheet, she moved Alex close to the side of the bed, then rolled him to his side. She placed one heavy leg in front of the other, and began with the cool, soothing lotion at his shoulders.

She worked ever downward on his back, as was her pattern. Unbidden, whole passages of research papers she'd read on sexual rehabilitation in impaired patients played through her mind. On an intellectual level she understood how vital it was to Alex's very identity that his sexual, purely biological drives be acknowledged, even accepted. A man robbed of his most elemental nature was a man without hope.

For the first time, among all the times she'd touched or bathed him, her clinical detachment deserted her, heart, soul and intellect. Alex sensed her new confusion, her hesitation to reach in front and loosen the draw string to lower his pajama bottoms. Both her fists clenched into tight balls before she reached blindly.

Naturally, her fingers brushed him.

Naturally, he stiffened with unexpected pleasure.

Naturally, she trembled.

He wanted her touch again, to know her caress was deliberate, to feel her fingers close around him. Any caress would be a towering risk for her; so intimate a caress, a blind leap of faith. He wanted her actions to give meaning to her promise. But more, far more, he wanted her, desperately.

Please... Cat, please.

She did his bidding against any contrary demands of the rational part of her mind. For an instant her fingers touched him and he thought he'd forgotten how to breathe. For an instant he felt her fingers close around him. Untutored, unembellished, just closing around him, and he knew if he didn't breathe now he never would again.

For an instant. Shorter than the span of his ragged breath, long enough to be known for what it was. Dangerous.

"Damn you, Alex Petrakis!"

Ah, God. Need, hot, swelling need, overwhelmed him. And nothing she could say or deny could turn back the generosity of her touch. *You're a woman, Cat. And I'm still a man.*

"You expect too much, *andras*." Undeniable, impossible, womanly longing lodged deep in her feminine recess. Mocking the professional being she'd thought she wanted to be, adorning the primitive female that was the core of her. So help her, she wanted to touch him again.

You should expect more, Cat.

She sniffed and withdrew. And though she continued to massage the lotion into all the pressure points and muscles of his back, his hips and thighs, his calves and heels, she would say no more. Alex was left to his own interminable silence.

After a while his discomfort eased. He regretted the passing of his masculine response to Caterpillar. It was the first tangible evidence he had that his life, his male identity was still intact. He wondered now why it hadn't occurred to him, why he hadn't worried about it before.

But then he remembered he *had* thought of it—on the day Caterpillar first came.

Elizabeth. With Cat here, he hadn't thought of Elizabeth in days. Weeks even. How many now? Three? Four? How many altogether, since the accident?

Fourteen. Christmas was almost upon them. Fourteen weeks of his life. Six of them the most extraordinary he'd ever known, because of this woman God had sent him, in answer to Papoo's prayers.

It was Papoo's knock at the door that broke the spell. Hurriedly Cat drew his hospital bottoms up and covered him over once again with the sheet.

"Papoo! Come in, please."

Was it relief he heard in her voice? Or embarrassment? Please, not that. *Don't, Cat. Don't hide from what you did for me.*

Hush, andras, please! she begged silently. *This is your grandfather!*

Yes, Papoo, who would cry for joy himself if he knew.

Papoo's rheumy topaz eyes missed nothing. "Am I interrupting something here, children of my heart?"

Yes.

"No, Papoo. Of course not. Please, come in."

He brought with him an offering from the greenhouse—a delicate catelya orchid plant in full bloom. Covering the awkward moment, he handed it to her. "Put it in the window for now, little Vanessa, and enjoy."

"Thank you. Thank you very much. It's beautiful!"

Papoo waved aside her praise. "It is about to die. I'm hoping it will choose to live for you and bloom again, as my grandson has."

Ah, Papoo. You old devil.

Alex might just as well have admitted straight out that he had indeed bloomed at her hands. Embarrassment coursed through her. She spun away from the collaboration of knowing men and fussed over the orchid.

"May I sit in the old rocker, little Vanessa?"

"Of course, Papoo," she said to the window.

"It is a testament to my age and manhood that I feel so unthreatened in this woman's chair," he spouted grandly, settling down into the rocker.

"Braggart," she teased, unthreatened herself, at least, by Papoo's ancient masculinity.

"*Braggadocchio*," Papoo gestured magnificently, rolling the name off his tongue. "The personification of boasting, *Fairie Queen*, Edmund Spenser."

Vanessa laughed aloud. "Were I only half as well-read as you, Papoo!"

"You will be, should you live so long. But never mind," he waved again. "Merely the wishful thinking of an old man. Come. Pull up a chair and sit with me and Alex awhile."

Vanessa felt the remains of her embarrassment drain away under Papoo's gentle, bawdy humor. Rolling the desk chair near, she curled up in it to bask in the old man's presence.

He rocked forward and touched her knee. "My grandson tells me your uncanny way with feelings comes of 'mirroring physiology.'" Triumphantly, for heaven knew what, he rocked backward again.

For one crazy moment, Vanessa supposed he meant Alex, until she remembered Nick was also his grandson. "Nick?"

"Of course!" He slapped his forehead with the butt of his hand. "You thought I meant Alex *mou*, but no. Alex, no. Nicholas, I meant, of course. Tell me what it means, please."

"Well, it comes from a school of thought that has to do with neurolinguistics. It means that if you are able to match or follow another person's body precisely—breathing, posture, facial expression, eye position—

everything exactly so, you will know what is going on in
his head, too.''

*Is that what you do, Cat? If I show you desire again,
will you follow me?*

Andras, *please. Please don't.* She risked a glance toward Alex, then had to concentrate even more on answering his grandfather. "I don't think about doing it,
but maybe I do. I believe there's a lot to it. Kind of like
emotional charades.''

"Who knows how this communication works? But it
does, doesn't it?'' the old man asked.

Vanessa paled. "I am not able to communicate with
Alex like you do, Papoo. I know what he must be going
through and I can sometimes think what he would say if
he could. But I do not hear him.''

Alex felt a sudden stab at her denial. *She's a sweet,
chronic liar, Papoo.*

Alex, don't, she pleaded silently, but Papoo's eyes were
on her as his mind turned to Alex, and those eyes
wouldn't grant her a second's relief.

*I begged her to touch me, Papoo. As a woman touches
a man. But it's like asking a woman to love a man less
than alive.*

"Alex, don't,'' Vanessa cried.

Papoo rose to his feet and clutched at the lowered bed
rail.

*It hurts, Papoo. It hurts.... I can't touch her. I can't
pleasure her. I can't share with her.... Papoo, what does
a man do? What would you do?*

The silence was awful. Papoo had no answer, but the
tear struggling down his rugged, time-worn face mirrored the one falling on his beloved grandson's cheek,
and the ones brimming on Vanessa's lashes.

THE MASSIVE, BEIGE WALLS seemed to close in on her. She'd never been fond of the neutral color. Bright things, colorful rooms were her preference. She discovered now that she loathed neutral—neutral anything. Colors, walls, clothes, feelings.

Weeks...days on end she had spent locked away in this room, battling Alex's nonchalance, then, gradually, prisoner to his desperation and her own determination.

Suppose it was all for nothing? She had tried everything. Invading his life, only to find a comfort she'd told his father she didn't want either of them to know. Needling him to anger, only to discover his brutal honesty and redeeming humor. Making him laugh, to find that laughing with him, at herself or him, had become one of life's poignant pleasures.

And now, without quite knowing how or why, she'd made him want her, only to discover the same need in herself, so very long denied.

In the coldly rational, professional part of her mind, she knew that Alex didn't want *her* so much as to have his very masculine physiological cravings fulfilled. In the research material she'd brought along was a rough draft of an article written by a colleague in rehab medicine on the subject of dealing with the latent sexuality of impaired patients. She would probably cite it as a reference in the follow-up publication to her dissertation.

Maybe in the back of her mind, she'd expected to be confronted with the issue with Alex. She hadn't expected her own role in triggering it. She hadn't expected to confront her own need.

She should have known, ought to have seen it coming.

She ached with it. She grew hot and then unbearably cold, breaking out in sweat while she shivered in the pitch-black night, alone in the bed across the room from Alex.

And she ached for him. Papoo's tears alone would have undone her. Alex's broke her heart. She had to grit her teeth to keep from crying aloud.

Wanting only to get out, she had to remind herself that the stakes were her rehab center and Alex's life, not his sexual fulfillment. Or hers.

The alarm trilled its warning. Time to move Alex. Wearily she rolled aside her covers, lit the hurricane lamp she used in the middle of the night and padded to Alex's side.

He smiled, but his lips twisted painfully.

Her teeth caught at her lower lip. "What is it, Alex?"

What could he say? That for the first time in his life he was more in touch with another's pain than with his own? That he knew, without understanding how, that her loneliness surpassed his own? That he sensed the awful ache in her small, exquisite breasts and her empty womb and her heart? That he had never, ever been more scared in his life?

With a need so savage he could hardly stand it, he wanted to touch her, hold her, make love to her, and in doing so, drive away from her the demon loneliness. He understood himself well. Sex was far more to him than the easing of overpowering biological urges. Sex was the only way two separate people ever truly overcame the loneliness of living in separate skins.

He thought then of *Demon Alone*, the last screenplay he'd written just before he'd taken up with Liz. When he thought of the story line, the irony hit him so hard that for a moment he couldn't breathe.

The hero and heroine were Richard and Catherine. Richard the Lionhearted and...Cat. Admittedly that was stretching it—but hadn't she asked, "Spineless wonder or *lionheart*, Petrakis?" Hadn't he called her Cat?

In the script Alex had used the device of an avalanche to plunge Richard and Catherine into a living hell. In this never-never-land reality, Alex was as close to a living hell as a man could come, and Cat was living it with him.

The enigma all but blew Alex away. Life imitating art scared the hell out of him. Now, because of his coma, because of what he'd learned of loneliness, his own and Caterpillar's, he wanted to produce the film.

Now, he couldn't. He couldn't get out of bed, either, or walk through Papoo's greenhouse or make love to this extraordinary woman.

And now, in spite of the feelings he had been able to communicate perfectly to her, and the ones she'd shared with him, he could tell her none of these thoughts. He wanted her to read *Demon Alone*. Sharing the script with her seemed as close as he'd get to revealing himself to her. It seemed to him nothing less than vital.

The script was locked into the wall safe in his house on ten Spy Glass Lane. He'd tell her to go get it. She needed very badly to get out of the Petrakis compound, anyway. But first, tonight, he had to know. He had to hear from her who had driven her into her sexual cocoon, and how. Who had condemned her to her solitary life, and why.

HE SIGHED WITH RELIEF when Cat worked to position him on his back. As she readjusted his pillow and the trocanter rolls to keep his heavy legs from turning outward, he drew a deep breath and swallowed—one of those talents he'd always taken for granted, but only relearned with her endearing nagging.

Sit with me, Cat. Sit in the rocker and talk to me.

"Go back to sleep, Alex," she murmured. "I'm tired. I don't want to talk."

Tell me about the man, Cat. I have to know.

"What man, Alex?"

Don't play dumb with me, Cat. You know who I mean. The man who hurt you.

Was it so obvious? "It doesn't matter. *He* doesn't matter."

Sit, Cat. Please.

"I have a name, Alex! Vanessa. Use it."

Okay. Vanessa. Does this mean you're not going to tell me what I want to know?

"No, Alex, I'm not. It doesn't matter."

Will you sit awhile, and give me your hand?

Wearily, she sank into the rocker. "I'll sit with you, for a while."

His fingers held hers, felt as warm to her as only Colorado sunshine can on brisk winter days. To counter the comfort that spread lazily through her body, threatening to pull her into a whirlpool of emotions she didn't want to face in the dark of the night, Vanessa composed in her mind the report she would give Constantine in the morning.

Like every other morning, he would want the vital statistics, her estimation of Alex's progress on the Glasgow scale, her recounting of Alex's strength and reflex reactions, her promise of a breakthrough—soon. Though Constantine pumped her for all the scientific factors she could produce, he'd begun to place a great deal more stock in Papoo's more emotional versions.

Even now, Alex didn't open his eyes—not to pain, or to conversation. That put him at a score of one out of a possible four. Vanessa felt that in spite of the fact that he didn't actually speak except confusedly in his dreams, he deserved an evaluation of five in the verbal response category. A five meant that he was oriented. There was nothing confused or inappropriate about his communication with her, or with Papoo. His best motor response also got the highest rating of six, now. He could respond to her urgings when he wanted to.

He'd achieved a sum of twelve on the scale for which a fifteen was the highest. Constantine would be pleased—and still more pleased when she told him that in her opinion, Alex's denial stage was over.

She knew it to be over, but confessing to Constantine that Alex had admitted to his coma seemed a thoroughly daunting, unprofessional prospect. How could he have recognized his coma if he wasn't talking aloud? On the other hand, scoring Alex at a five in verbal response amounted to the same thing. Constantine was unlikely to miss the implication that she now believed she heard Alex every bit as well as Papoo claimed to hear him.

She worried that Constantine would feel slighted, left out of Alex's special circle. If Alex had been her son, she'd have been devastated by that kind of revelation.

She worried that while Constantine had been grasping at straws to believe she could make a difference in the first place, his patience would run out. But then, so had his options.

She worried most of all that she would fail Alex.

As if attuned to her thoughts, Alex squeezed her fingers tightly. *Is this going to end, Cat?*

Hopelessness welled up in her throat and closed off her ability to answer him. Yes, she wanted to say. Of course, Alex *mou*. Just a little more time. But in another few days it would be Christmas, and she hadn't imagined bringing him back would take so long.

Her silence worried him. *Cat?*

She returned the squeeze of his fingers, a little desperately. "It will end, Alex. It has to."

When?

"Soon, *andras*, soon." Surely to God, soon.

The pressure of his fingers slackened a bit. He moved a little, readjusting his shoulders. *Cat? Would you do me a favor?*

Anything. Anything at all. "What is it, Alex?"

Promise.

"Anything."

Sleep with me, Cat.

A cry strangled in her throat. Her free hand flew to her lips. "Oh, Alex!"

Sleep with me, harato mou, *my joy. There's room for you, room for your head on my shoulder.*

"No, Alex, there's not. Your IV line—"

I have two shoulders, Cat. Please. Please.

Her throat threatened to swell with the pain of his plea, and the need that rose in her. Specters of unfulfilled need from her past filled her now, and the reality of her need at this moment.

You promised, Cat.

"Yes. I promised. But what will happen next, Alex *mou*?"

Next, I'll hold you, Cat. Tomorrow may not be any better, or the day after that.

Or the day after that. She rose from the Petrakis rocker and went to him. She lowered the rail and removed the trocanter that supported his naked thigh and pulled back the sheet. Why hadn't she thought to put his hospital pajama bottoms back on?

Because he hated them. Because in spite of her plan to deny him his every whim, she conceded to his comfort at every turn. To sleep with him would be no different, just another concession to her woman's feelings in opposition to her trained intellect.

But now she'd sleep with him. She'd feel the texture of his body hair against herself. She'd know the warmth and latent strength against herself. Her eyes fell closed and she swallowed and she prayed for the strength to offer him the comfort of her body without yearning for more. She turned off the lamp and climbed into the bed next to him. Next to the man she had come, in spite of everything, to care for far beyond her professional commitment.

She turned into him and put her head on his shoulder. Drawing the sheet back over them both, she placed her leg at his thigh, to replace the support of the trocanter roll. There was nothing left for her to do but rest her arm across the broad, warm, muscled wall of his chest.

What surprised him most was that her small figure fit so closely. He laughed bitterly at himself to know he'd come to think of her stomach as rounded and full of his child.

Her hair spilled over his shoulder. He ached with the familiarity, as if he'd always known the soft, full texture of it. Her small, exquisite breasts, covered with the soft cotton T-shirt, pressed against his side. His forearm came to rest in the hollow above the sweet, feminine swell of her hip.

More than any physician he'd ever known, Vanessa healed. Her touch wrought wonders, her tender ministrations gave life where there was precious little sign of it. And her heart was as committed to the oath she'd taken as was her mind.

Alex sighed deeply. Caught between wishing she'd refused him and wishing she could relax, between the torture of having her in his bed while he was unable to do anything about it and the overwhelming intimacy of just lying with her, his heart tripped and skittered and raced with longing.

But he eventually slept as he hadn't in weeks.

And after a very long while, Vanessa slept the sleep of angels.

TEN SPY GLASS LANE. Even the name beguiled Vanessa. Deep snowdrifts left untouched by snowblowers or shovels gave the house an almost ethereal quality—tucked away amidst blue spruce and holly bushes in a pristine, sunlit land of enchantment.

It was a terrible lie. A mirage in the barren, heat-crusted desert. She felt like a character caught in a fairy tale gone inexplicably wrong.

She'd slept with Alex, really slept the night through. Her reward was the beginning of angry red, burning-to-the-touch pressure sores at Alex's hips. Because she'd slept the night through, abandoning her responsibilities.

She'd slept with him, and that was a lie too.

She stepped out of her VW, slammed its stubborn door and made her way through weeks-old drifts to the varnished oak door of Alex's house. Held tightly in her hand was the key Papoo had spirited away from Constantine's office. Held tightly in her heart was the condemning knowledge that she'd fallen for Alex Petrakis, that she'd let her fragile feelings overcome her sensibilities. And that she was about to wander through his home on her own. Proof that he had existed in this and not only the netherworld of his coma.

To touch and smell his things. His furnishings. His clothes. His bed.

To hear what he heard on lazy Saturday mornings. The hum of his refrigerator. The warbling of winter chickadees, or the occasional gusts of wind against his windows.

To see into the mirror at which he shaved his own heavy, honey-shaded beard.

To know him for the man he was outside her nightmare.

He'd sent her here to bring back something from his wall safe. What? she'd wanted to know. You'll know when you see it, he'd said. Go, he'd said, with an urgency she recognized but didn't understand. Nanny Bates and Papoo would watch over him while she went.

He knew she was scared of what had happened between them, of the pressure sores on his skin and the responsibilities she'd forsaken by sleeping with him. That she was so scared she might not come back. That Nanny and Papoo might have to watch him until his father could summon another nurse—someone who'd have more sense than to need a half-alive man.

Still, he'd urged her to go, because he trusted her to return. Alex trusted her.

You don't have it in you to abandon me to Hancock again, harato mou.

She unlocked the deadbolt and pushed open the heavy oak door. *I don't have it in me to stay, either,* she'd thought, bungling her nursing care of him because he kept pushing her to be more woman than healer. Alex had just smiled.

Inside the intricately tiled foyer she stood stock-still, absorbing the contrasts of light and shadows: dark, heavy, masculine woodwork, and sunbeams pouring in through a skylight that dominated the open beam ceiling.

To her left was a study with bay windows, a dark, Persian carpet over deeply stained bare wood floors, floor-to-ceiling bookshelves and an empty space where Alex's desk and chair had been. A black touch-tone phone, state-of-the-art photographic equipment and an IBM computer sat in dusty disuse on the floor, the high-tech cables trailing like umbilical cords over the antique carpet.

Straight ahead through a short hall lay the master bedroom suite, and to her right, a living room with bay windows to match those of the study and more bare wood floors, here left uncovered. Vanessa found the furniture more functional than not, and yet still beautiful in a dark, brooding kind of way. No neutral colors, but none of the bright, insistent shades she'd have chosen, either. Blues, forest greens, and rich, lush browns defined his personal space.

The collection of laser-engraved portraits taking up most of one wall transfixed her for long moments. None were anything like *The Man Woman* holograph. Instead of announcing a powerful *together* as *The Man Woman* did, each one of these confronted her in one way or another with a vision of separateness. Ice fields in brutal white and silver and gray and fathomless blacks. Seascapes with endless variations of green. Sunsets at sea— blue and mauve and purple. Bloodred sunrises. Mountains behind more granite peaks, snow covered and touched with mystery.

But for Vanessa the most gripping were visions of people. A shrunken old man. The famous *End of the Trail*, the Indian slumped on his horse with a spear nearly dragging the ground. A child's dirty tear-streaked face. Vanessa found her eyes drawn unwillingly to the fat, colorless tear on the child's soft, too-lean cheek.

"Pretty revealing, isn't it?"

Nick. She should have been startled, but she wasn't. The thought crossed her mind to wonder why, but she was too intrigued with his question to even say hi. Turning reluctantly she responded at last. "How...revealing?"

Shrugging, Nick ambled toward her. "Alex is obsessed. Always has been."

"Obsessed with what?" There was something vaguely defiant in her tone of voice, and an alarm sounded in her head. She wanted to drop the whole ugly situation into Nick's capable Petrakis hands and run, but she didn't know if she had the strength.

A frown creased Nick's brow. He put a protective arm around her shoulders. "It's obvious, Van. Just look at them. Alex is obsessed with the true *alone*. It's a power trip. Most of these were done before he ever got into cinema or holographs."

Power? No. How could it be? "These are portraits of gut-wrenching isolation, Nick, not—"

"Yeah, they are that," he interrupted. "But you're missing the point. Do you know what it takes to come up with these portraits? The time, the processes?"

"No. I've never seen anything like them, but what does that have to do with—"

"It's an incredible investment of time and technology, Van. The engraving alone takes lasers, computer-assisted graphics and some complicated, fancy-ass techniques Alex has taken out a patent on. Not to mention photographing the originals. He's given every image here a life of its own. Why would a man go to the trouble of giving substance and meaning to the isolation if he weren't passionate about it?"

"I don't know..."

"Believe me when I tell you this, Van. Alex looks at these as evidence of his power, his achievement, almost as though he's defeated the isolation. But he's done it over and over again, in dozens of hostile environments, which tells me he's never really quite believed that he's won." Nick hesitated. "Of course, no one wins that battle. We're born alone, live and suffer and achieve alone. We even die alone. Alex keeps trying to prove he can beat the system."

"We all do that, Nick. We marry and produce babies because we need to belong. Maybe he's trying like everybody else to make sense out of life." Then, distractedly, she discovered a cache of computer image prints devoted to athletic movements—everything from shot put to ice-skating. "What are these?"

"Alex used to work with movement imaging at the Olympic Training Center in Colorado Springs. Remember? You told me about computer imaging applications in your rehab labs. Another power thing for Alex, now that I think about it. What could be more exacting of him than to find ways to increase the power and efficiency of Olympic athletes?"

"I wouldn't have called it an obsession, Nick. Any more than you're obsessed with brain surgery, or—"

"Any more than your becoming obsessed with Alex?"

"No!"

"No? You aren't going to give me chapter and verse on the Alex Petrakis you've come to know so well?"

Vanessa felt herself trembling inside. Somehow she knew there was no evidence of it in her body language. She tossed her purse onto a chair she imagined still held the warmth of Alex's body. "Why are you badgering me, Nick?"

"Because I called to talk to Papoo this morning and from what he tells me, you've gone off the deep end right along with him!"

Straightening, willing herself not to agree with his assessment and spill her anguish, she cast about for a distraction for them both. "Did you bring the hyperalimentation supplies?"

"Of course. I already transferred the boxes into the VW."

"Papoo said you'd know where the wall safe is." In fact, Alex had told her precisely, but feeding Nick's doubts with such a truth seemed foolish when Papoo had said Nick could show her.

"Yeah. Why?"

"Because there's stuff in it I need to get."

"Such as?"

"Just show me, Omega Man," she demanded. *And please, please. Don't ask any more questions I have no earthly answer for.* She'd start talking a mile a minute and admit her incredible folly. "I don't have all day. I need to get back."

Casting her a "this isn't over" look, he turned away. "It's in Alex's bedroom. Did Papoo have the combination, too?"

"Yes."

She kept a tight rein on her emotions, on the contrary need to explore Alex's bedroom, and followed Nick straight to a Georgia O'Keeffe original. The gilt-framed painting swung aside at Nick's touch, and Vanessa forced herself to work the combination. Inside were three manuscripts, bound with leather but unlabeled. Nick reached for them when Vanessa stood aside, unwilling to see what Alex wanted her to bring back.

He flipped open the cover on the top one, and his jaw dropped. "Well, I'll be a son of a—"

Wanting in spite of herself to see, Vanessa touched Nick's sweatshirt sleeve. "What? What is it?"

He tilted his hold on the bound sheaf for her to see. The cover page, stamped with Draft read *Cold Sabbaths* by Alexander C. Petrakis. "This script. Alex wrote it!"

Vanessa felt the blood rushing from her head. *Cold Sabbaths* had won an Oscar—was it for cinematography?—several years before. Cited for the pure Greek scholarship and the first-ever use of high-tech holographic images, the surprisingly powerful drama of a mythical love story had been too artsy to garner Best Picture. Even Vanessa knew Alex had produced it; no one knew he'd written it.

Flipping the page, Nick pointed excitedly to a quotation in the original Greek. "Look. *Esti kai en psukhrois sabbasi thermos Eros.* 'Love burns hot even on cold Sabbaths,'" he translated.

A curious weakness gathered at her knees. "Who did he credit with writing it?"

Nick shook his head, trying to remember. "A consortium, I think. Like a group of writers."

The next script, a draft of the movie *Thrice a Brigand*, she remembered very well. Set in medieval times, the movie depicted a fantasy love accursed by an evil priest, and had been mimicked far less successfully many times. The title here was explained in a Greek quotation as well. Translated, it read "Truly love can be called thrice a brigand—he is wakeful, reckless, and strips us bare."

Vanessa paled at the memory of Alex, wakeful and reckless, stripping bare her soul. That and the awful aptness of his calling her Caterpillar, bound up against any expression of her sexuality.

Her knees buckling, Vanessa sank to the king-size water bed in Alex's own bedroom.

"There's another one, here, Van. One I don't recognize," Nick said. "*Demon Alone*." He glanced down at her to see if the significance had sunk in. "Alone. *Demon* Alone. Didn't I tell you?" Only then did he seem to take notice of her pale, stricken expression. "Van?"

She barely heard him, because in her mind she was hearing her conversation with Alex again. What am I looking for, Alex? *You'll know it when you see it,* harato mou.

These were his life. These sheaves of bound paper and words, words that came brilliantly to life on the screen, were his. He would share them with her, in spite of having kept his authorship a secret all these years. And here she would find him. Not in the facets and hues of his home or the depths of his closets or the reflection of his shaving mirror.

Alex, the real, intimately unique *alive* Alex lived through these scripts. Vanessa wanted nothing so much as to snatch the bound volumes from Nick's hands, hurl them back into the wall safe and slam the door on them. She'd caused Alex pain and would cause him a great deal more, because finally she'd have to leave him.

She'd accused him of cruelty, of holding out against Papoo, of offering what he couldn't deliver. But it was herself she had to blame for offering the promise of herself as though she were woman enough, when she knew, *knew* that she wasn't.

She would devour *Demon Alone*, later, when she could be by herself. Now she had to get rid of Nick before she crumbled into a thousand shards of guilt. Alex had always lived with loneliness. If he saw in her a cure for it, he was wrong, for after him would come others who needed her, others who would take from her all she had to give, and then take more.

Curing *alone* wasn't in her bag of tricks.

Chapter Six

"THANKS FOR BRINGING out the supplies, Nick. I know you're busy, so you might as well go." She shrugged out of her coat and took the scripts from his hands to put them with her purse. She waited for him, rather pointedly, by the front door.

One elegant, sandy eyebrow quirked up. "You're staying?"

Her chin rose a bit as well. "For a little while."

"I thought we'd go have a bit of tea, Van. I need to talk to you. I think things are getting out of hand."

She'd been operating on instinct for weeks. It let her know now that Nick wasn't referring to anything or anyone but Alex. Her nerves were already worn ragged, and the concern in Nick's hauntingly Petrakis eyes made a wreck out of her control. In another minute she'd break down and admit that Nick was right. In another minute, she did.

Her voice shaking, she whispered, "I can't go back there, Nicholas."

Nick stripped off his Levi's jacket, left it in a heap on the floor and took her in his arms. "Van, my God! What's happened?"

Tears were beyond her. She backed away from the comfort his arms offered because comfort was the last thing she deserved.

"I'm going to brew some tea." Turning on her heel, her whole body brittle with tension, she went to the kitchen. She found a small teapot on the back burner of a Corning stove top and turned the hot-water tap on full force, as much to drown her own guilt as to fill the pot.

"How is he?"

"Fine. Until this morning. He'd been making great strides...." Her knees would buckle, she knew, any minute now.

Nick dragged a chair from the kitchen table and straddled it. Pushing a suddenly nervous hand through his hair, he took a breath to calm himself. "Tell me about it, Van."

What had Papoo already told him? Romantic old codger that he was, he'd probably baited his patently unsentimental, devil's advocate grandson with an embellished version of the truth—Alex's truth.

"I hear things, Nick. I hear Alex as clearly as if he were talking, which he's not. Whole conversations with him! Papoo is an old man, it's understandable that he...but I'm supposed to be a professional. It's not possible, is it? Is it, Nick?"

His expression grew thoughtful. It shouldn't be possible—she knew he knew that. "I've seen too much happen to you to doubt the possibility. If you think you're hearing him, you must be."

"I do, Nick. Even when I know for scientific, incontrovertible fact that it's not possible."

"Anything is possible, Van," he scolded. "You wouldn't be Vanessa Koures if you didn't believe that. If you're having a problem with it, maybe it's because you're trying so desperately to be someone else. Why? Who are you fighting? Alex? Yourself?"

She turned away from the unexpected acceptance in Nick's eyes to search for tea bags. "Both, maybe. You, maybe, for believing in this claptrap! It's bad, Nick, and getting worse. I'm a professional, a scientist, but none of that alters the fact that I hear him."

Nick hung his arms over the top of the ladder-back chair. "How, do you suppose?"

"I don't know how."

"Okay. Suppose for a minute it's your imagination. You're incredibly intuitive, Van. Maybe you're just tired of talking to yourself, or talking to him and getting no response. Isn't it possible that you're just feeling what he must feel and putting it into words you think he might use to express—"

"No." She found the tea bags in the nearly empty freezer, dropped one into a cup for each of them and turned to face Nick. Leaning against the tiled counter, she continued when she hadn't meant to. She hadn't meant to do a lot of things, lately. "I thought that was it for a long time. But that first night, when you and Constantine and the nurse were still there and I said I was moving in with him—"

"A stroke of pure genius, Van—"

"I heard him. 'Over my dead body,' he said. I would never have used that phrase, Nick. I don't think it's funny, I don't like it, it goes against the grain. So you explain it, if you can."

"A feeling. When you got those headaches three years ago, they weren't your idea, you didn't think they were particularly great, but you got them...."

"It's not the same." Stymied with his calm, unruffled explanations, she tried another tack. "I was supposed to make him uncomfortable, angry with me being there, angry with my intrusions and my therapy. Alex hasn't really been angry since that first night."

Not strictly true, an inner voice insisted. She remembered to her most private feminine core the heated accusations Alex had made in defense of calling her Caterpillar. But that anger had nothing to do with anything she'd wanted or intended to arouse in Alex. She'd abandoned her original plan very early on.

"Papoo says Alex is very close to you, Van. That he's very likely in love with you."

"No." Vanessa's throat constricted with disbelief. *"Exo tou pragmatos." Beside the question.* How many times had they shared that insight in diagnosing a particularly difficult case? Alex wasn't just another case to her anymore, nor could she easily confess her feelings for him to his cousin.

"Maybe it is the only question," he argued. "You hear him. You know him. Truth is truth, Vanessa, no matter how unbelievable." Strangling his tea bag with its string, Nick gave her a long, steady look of reassurance. "What does he say?"

"He calls me Caterpillar. *I* would never call me Caterpillar."

"Are you trying to convince me, or yourself?"

"Why do you believe all this? No person in their right mind would believe a word of it! It's like some black fairy tale!"

Nick covered her now shaking fingers with his hand. "Will it take migraines or a heart murmur to convince yourself? This is no different from anything that's already happened to you over and over again." He smiled, trying to inject a fragment of humor. "If I hauled out my stethoscope, Vanessa, would I hear your heart doing tap dances to beat the band?"

Yes. "Dammit, Nick, I'm trying to tell you that I'm... in love with him! With a vegetable!"

His jaw tightened. "You don't believe he's a vegetable, Van."

"I'm supposed to be a physician, not some crack-brained, lovelorn mystic hearing voices no one else hears!"

"Not voices, Van. Just one. Alex's. And no, you're not a physician anymore. Remember? You couldn't handle it. You're special, lady. And special can't argue with itself."

Her empathetic responses weren't any of her choice, but she'd been stuck with them since her father had landed in the hospital. After the first terrifying demonstration he'd seen of her misbegotten talent, Nick had believed. He wouldn't be shaken from it now, either.

"I slept with him last night."

Nick choked on the tea. "You did *what*?"

"I slept with Alex last night. Do you think I can tell you why? Well, I can't." She looked beyond him, out Alex's kitchen windows toward the snow-laden branches of a spruce, and felt her focus go soft and blurry as tears welled up. "Why, Nick? Why did I do that? It didn't prove anything, didn't accomplish anything but pressure sores on Alex's backside...."

"Sores heal, Van. Are you interested—" Nick's voice broke, and when Vanessa looked at him, wonder and admiration shone through tears she'd never thought to see in his eyes. "Do you want to know what I'm thinking? I'm thinking...no, I'm feeling jealous as hell. I'm thinking if Alex *isn't* in love with you, he's a fool. Some things a person does just because they're the right thing to do. Whatever you did, it was right, Van. Sleeping with him was right and beautiful and the most generous—"

"Nicholas!" she croaked. "Can there be such a thing as *right* in all of this? He's in a coma he may never come out of!"

"Exo tou pragmatos, koukla," he chided softly. "The question is not whether it was right or wrong, but what else you could have done. He asked you to sleep with him, didn't he?"

"Yes. He just asked."

Both of them remembered, then, the humbling wishes of a ten-year-old. Sarah Gilles wondering, *Why don't you just ask?*

"It isn't in you to refuse. It just isn't there to do anything less. You are Vanessa Koures. You will always be special, *koukla*, you have no choice. If Alex has the heart God gave him, he'll wake up before he loses you."

VANESSA DROVE BACK to the compound in a blur of tears. In the end Nick had held her, accepting the inevitable fact of her emotional attachment to Alex as if it were a sane, sensible, reasonable thing.

It was none of those, but he'd made her see it for the far greater thing it was. She realized with a sudden clarity that for all she'd done to facilitate Alex's recovery, he'd begun to slash through the tangled woods and brambles of her own prison. He'd reminded her of her own passionate, sexual nature. He'd given her back everything feminine in her feelings. He'd given her life as she'd never been free to accept it before.

And all this while he slept. The bitter irony of it brought a fresh bout of tears that forced her off the road. She fled into the forest, and though her boots weren't high enough to avoid getting snow inside, she barely noticed.

It took Nick's acceptance to bring her back to her own realities. Among towering, age-old pines her tears only got worse.

It was a long time later that Vanessa soaked up her tears with the sleeve of her sweatshirt. Standing there in the streaming sunlight, she relaxed a little, only to confront a sudden sense of guilt. She'd been gone far longer than she'd said she'd be. Alex needed her.

She needed Alex.

The realization scared her. She had no business needing him. He had no business understanding her needs, or answering them. They were worlds apart.

In real life Alex was an international star—maybe not meteoric, maybe not an aurora, but a recognized, up-and-coming producer nonetheless. What did it matter that the world saw a rich playboy and didn't even know he'd written the scripts to his films, too?

Vanessa Koures was a little fish in an even smaller pond and fiercely proud of it. She'd never inspire such acclaim in rehab medicine, even if she actively sought it.

Alex Petrakis yachted in the Mediterranean whenever it suited him. Vanessa Koures would pay off her medical and grad school debts in 1999 and maybe, just maybe, see the Mediterranean in her lifetime.

Superficial differences? Vanessa wondered. Yes. The real kicker was that Alex Petrakis slept while Vanessa Koures struggled for his life.

She felt a chill go through her as the sun passed behind a bank of clouds. She wouldn't be the first doctor to fall in love with a patient, Nick had said. But daring to love a man she didn't even really know? One who had never spoken aloud or whispered endearments in her ear, who had never looked at her like a man looks at a woman or made love to her?

She turned in the deep snow and trudged back to the VW. At least she had the small comfort of knowing in advance there was no hope for her.

When she reached the circular drive of the compound and turned off toward the garage, she knew she wouldn't be doing any reading very soon. Parked directly in front of the house was a white Jaguar. Without remembering how she'd acquired the trivial detail, she knew. The car belonged to Alex's fiancée, Elizabeth Pederson.

Vanessa shut off the backfiring engine of her out-classed German bug and crammed the knuckles of both fists against her lips. All she needed now was a face-to-face encounter with one more reason she truly couldn't have Alex. When all was said and done, there was still Elizabeth Pederson.

Vanessa slipped out of her coat and buried the screenplays deeply within its folds. Elizabeth might lay claim to Alex; she had no stake in the treasures he'd offered Vanessa.

Defiantly, she walked through the front door.

Nanny Bates practically flew at her. "Doctor Koures, Miss Pederson wants to see Alex. She says his father gave her permission, but I don't believe a word of it."

The poor dear was headed for apoplexy. Vanessa felt herself hurtling down the same path as Nanny, but she placed a gentling touch on the old lady's shoulder and gave her a smile neither of them believed for a second. "It's all right, Nanny. It must be true if the guards let her past. Why don't you go heckle Papoo into cutting some fresh flowers for Alex?"

Gratefully Nanny Bates hustled out, casting Alex's fiancée a murderous glance as she went. Vanessa turned to face the woman standing at the foot of the stairs.

Wealth swathed Elizabeth like a cloud of perfume. The scent of it reminded Vanessa with a brutal clarity of the disparity in the worlds they occupied. Elizabeth held herself with an air of aloofness that Vanessa suspected was gained in the most exclusive of finishing schools. She wore a casual wool skirt with an extravagant cream-colored silk blouse. Her blond hair was pulled into an elegant French braid, and her earrings were surely a carat each of the clearest green emeralds known to man. Caught in cords and a sweatshirt Elizabeth wouldn't know from rags, Vanessa was consumed with envy. Elizabeth clearly suited the world Alex had been born to.

"I'm Alex's doctor, Vanessa Koures. Can I help you?"

"He's...alive, then."

"He's alive."

"And well? No...I suppose not if he needs you. I'd like to see him.... Now."

Why now, Vanessa wanted to needle. Why not last week, or last month? "All right."

"I should have come sooner...I have been...upset, myself."

Vanessa wondered nastily if the woman was capable of speech without the high drama of her oh-so-elegant pauses. In the same moment, Vanessa sensed a panic growing in the other woman that felt all too familiar. Contrite now, she asked if Elizabeth knew her way.

"Please...show me—and stay."

Carrying her coat and the precious hidden bootie of Alex's screenplays, Vanessa climbed the stairs ahead of Elizabeth and led the way to Alex's rooms. The woman was hurting, but whether for herself or in guilt over Alex, Vanessa couldn't tell.

ALEX WAITED for what seemed to him an extraordinarily long time. He heard the arrival of one car which he knew wasn't Cat's, and then maybe ten minutes later, the distinctive rattling of her little VW.

Thank God. After she'd discovered the pressure sores on his backside, he'd had more faith than reason to think she'd come back. His wait made him more aware than ever of the way time was beginning to matter to him. He wanted Cat to read *Demon Alone*, and fancied she'd already had the time to do that.

The script had all the earmarks of a commercial success. It was not only a love story, it was also set against the backdrop of time travel—a concept especially suited to the high-tech movies the public adored. It had plenty of action as well. Richard and Catherine had only each other to count on while they confronted dangers in the present and in the past. In the process of learning that being together was better, the pair fell deeply in love. It was Catherine's willingness to take emotional risks with Richard that Alex wanted Cat to notice.

But when Cat entered the room, her tension filled the air. He heard it in her rigid voice, felt it in her business-like approach—just before he caught the scent of Elizabeth.

Compared to the simple, uncomplicated aura of soap and water and the delicate shampoo Cat used, Elizabeth's overdone, overly sensual perfume displeased Alex, and he'd given her the stuff.

Elizabeth.

Cat.

The woman he'd thought to marry spoke first. "Is he sleeping...or what?"

"Or what," he heard Caterpillar answer quietly. "Alex is awake. I'm certain he knows you're here, but he's still in a light coma."

"A coma?"

A coma. Yes. As in unconscious, Liz. As in critically injured by your stupid little games in a jet-powered boat you had no business fooling around with!

Cat stayed silent and sat at his desk, ignoring the unfolding antagonism.

"Does he hear me?"

Alex had heard the electricity crackling when Cat brushed her hair; he'd heard the quiet, gentle sough of her breath as she'd exercised his body; he'd heard his own blood rushing as his sex swelled with the need of Cat in the dark of the night. He'd never been more attuned to subtle inflections. The fear and disgust he heard in Elizabeth's voice blared through the camouflage of whatever else she was trying to convey.

It was perverse and contrary to enjoy her horror, Alex thought, but . . .

"Miss Pederson," Cat said, "have you ever accidentally overheard someone talking about you?"

"Of course," Elizabeth said. "What does that have to do . . . with anything?"

"Alex doesn't appreciate it any more than you would."

He heard the clatter of a half-dozen gold bangles as Elizabeth gestured with her hands.

"That's . . . impossible."

Her tone said it was worse than impossible—that it was absurd, sick, even. *You can't even imagine it, can you, Lizzy?* He wished to God she'd hear him now, but even if she could, *he* couldn't even begin to express his anger toward her, or the agony she'd caused, or the time she'd cost him.

"It's not impossible."

Quiet certainty, Cat's voice. She truly believes, Alex discovered, that anything is possible.

"Do you talk to him?"

Cat didn't answer the question, at least not directly. "I'm supporting Alex any way I can until he decides to come out of it."

"Until...he...decides? Are you telling me he's actually chosen to be...to stay like this?"

"The decision is not a conscious one," Cat explained carefully. "His coma is a subconscious mechanism to protect him against the horror of the accident."

"Oh, so it's *my* fault he's like a vegetable...is that it?"

Damn straight it is! He'd take exception to her label, only he knew it wasn't true.

"No. He loved you, Miss Pederson. I'm...maybe he still does. But you've stayed away a long time. He resents that."

Had he loved Elizabeth? He'd thought he had; now he wondered if he'd ever had the least idea what it was he'd felt for her. He'd never shared his scripts with her.

"Alex did love me," Elizabeth claimed now. "But *this*...this isn't him. The man who loved me is dead."

Her words echoed through the room. *The man who loved me is dead. Dead.* Insight hit Alex like a ton of bricks. Elizabeth flitted carelessly; Vanessa cared. Elizabeth contrived; Vanessa coped. And real compassion was as foreign to Elizabeth as Papoo's orchids were to the harsh winter climates he defied with them.

Alex suspected what it was he'd seen in Liz, what he'd finally settled for. A woman whose demands were so simplistic they could be met with his money and his sex. A woman who didn't require the commitment of emotion because she was incapable of it herself.

He'd been wrong. Horribly wrong. The texture of his life, even this half life he was condemned to, had changed with Vanessa, become rich and passionate and worthwhile. Vanessa knew his most private needs in a way Elizabeth never would, could never imagine.

It was no wonder he hadn't written a solitary line since Elizabeth.

He knew Vanessa's most secret heart of hearts. It occurred to him that he'd achieved a perfect understanding with her while he slept. *Because* he'd slept. He was caught in the most terrible irony of all. He hadn't woken because waking would destroy something precious between them, something rare and exquisite. Something blooming most unexpectedly, like a delicate fern in the harsh, relentless Rockies.

Vanessa. Papoo had said her name came from the Greek for butterfly. He thought of butterfly kisses—and ached for a moment, for the lightest touch of his grandmother Eleni's eyelashes, like butterfly wings to his cheek.

Vanessa. She'd given him back his child's capacity to wonder. To believe anything was possible. To see the gentleness in strength and the desperation in power. To appreciate real risk. She'd come to his bed when he couldn't even assure her with his eyes or with his touch that her caring was returned.

Elizabeth wouldn't so much as speak to him. Vanessa had countered his desperately selfish need with the most generous, compassionate, uncontrived of acts.

Alex discovered love, and knew what he'd had with Liz wasn't it.

FOR A LONG TIME after Elizabeth had gone, Vanessa worked with Alex, now scolding, now encouraging. Every joint, every major muscle group, every tendon. Slavishly she worked on and on into the deepening twilight. Tomorrow, on Christmas Eve, Advent would be over. Alex thought he'd put Vanessa through more than enough penitence. He ought to end it, ought to wake up. Now.

Any time now, sports fans. A rage at himself for this unending self-indulgence of sleep began to smolder.

To fill the silence and the hours, Vanessa told him about Christmases spent at her Aunt Chloe's. Her father, Georgiou Koures, had thought Chloe a crazy old woman, but he'd not had much to say about where they went for Christmas.

She told Alex that that was the worst part about her father's illness—the loss of his manhood, the seeping away of his control. Girls thought their dads were invincible. Vanessa learned too early that dads were as mortal as pet turtles and lame birds.

But then she'd had to explain. She realized, she said, that she'd never told Alex about her dad. The telling was almost mechanical. Almost. But finally Alex understood what was truly at stake for Vanessa in the bargain she'd made with his father. She wanted nothing so much as to redeem herself. She hadn't been able to help her father, so she'd put everything she had on the line to bring Alex back from his endless sleep. Had she traded in one lost cause for another?

You can't last against it, Cat. You can't save the world. It's been tried, you know. There are just too many people, too many souls who are no better off than lame birds.

"Yes, there are too many. But don't you see that's why I have to try?"

He didn't. But then, he didn't have her passion for redeeming lives.

He listened to her talking. Listened for the nuances that would reveal what she was feeling right now. But she massaged his fingers and worked with his knuckle joints, and oh, did that feel like heaven on earth and sometimes he couldn't focus on what she was saying at all.

She touched his hands, stroked at his palms and the hair at his knuckles, thinking she could turn her thoughts away from the masculine perfection of his thighs, the swell of his broad shoulders, the rise of his pectorals, scattered with stiff, blatantly sexual honey-shaded hair. But ever since she'd touched the granite hard length of his sex, every other part of his body triggered a feminine panic in her.

She refused the dinner Papoo brought, but encouraged the old man to tell a few stories, and after Papoo left, she began to work again.

She concentrated on Alex's feet and explained to him the monumental difficulties he'd have just standing when he woke because for all the therapy, nothing she could do would stimulate the thousands of subtle adjustments that feet make in maintaining balance.

He wondered if she'd be there to support him then, too. His icy anger at Elizabeth was as nothing compared to his blistering need of Cat.

He'd grown adept at cataloguing in his head all the ways he admired her, all the reasons he'd discovered to love her. Alphabetically, chronologically, in order of importance. No matter which way he arranged them, like Papoo his flowers, it was her daring that drew him to her like a hummingbird to nectar. She'd dared to defy his coma. Dared to hear him, dared to bare her soul, and then, dared to touch him, woman to man.

She was a defiant soul who dared love a man who couldn't even touch her.

She told him how the Christmas lights looked from his window, and how her research was progressing, and how she still had piles of reading to do for her postdoctoral paper, in spite of the fact that she sat for hours every night reading.

And at last Alex understood. Elizabeth was still in the room with them, at least in Vanessa's mind, and because of Elizabeth, Vanessa wouldn't read the script, or come to his bed again, or touch him with the intimacy he craved.

Harato mou, *stop it. Now.*

She refused to hear him, as she had all afternoon. Or, at least, to answer, for he knew better than to think she could shut him out.

It's too late for games between us, Vanessa.

She liked it better when he'd called her Cat. What had started out to be an insult had become an endearment she wondered if she could go without hearing the rest of her life. But it would never do to tell him so.

Cat?

"Alex!" Could he read her thoughts now, too? The longings of her heart, the cravings of her body?

Elizabeth is gone, Cat. Gone.

"She'll be back when you wake up."

When all the world's evil is stuffed back into Pandora's box!

"Sooner, I think."

I love you.

She missed a beat in stroking his heel. Maybe two. Or maybe it was her own breathing she missed. "Chalk it up to the family talent for exaggeration, *andras*. A simple case of loving the one you're with if you can't be with the one you love."

No.

"Yes. You love whoever's handy, Petrakis. I'm not handy on yachts."

He smiled at that.

She could've cried; handy at setting herself up for the big fall was another thing altogether.

She's not worth your jealousy, Cat.

"She was worth your anger, Alex. You hated her this afternoon, but you know what they say. Hate is just the flip side of love." And pain the opposite edge of ecstasy?

Read the script, Cat. Please.

"I can't."

I love you, Cat.

"You don't know me."

I know you.

"You know nothing, Alex! Nothing. You don't even remember how to talk!"

The pain in his gut felt like a small conflagration of flying mortar. *Cheap shot, Cat. Why should I talk when—*

"Because it's a cheat! Because I don't...can't...we can't go on like this—"

Because we understand each other too well?

She hated him, despised him for his intimate glimpse at her naked soul. "What do you think you understand, Alex? Do you understand how Elizabeth feels?"

He hated her hiding from him behind a woman who'd written him off for dead.

I'll tell you what I understand—our time is growing short. That it'll be Christmas before I've had time to put up the lights and I wish I'd gone shopping for you but, dammit, I've been kind of tied up and I thought maybe I'd give you what I haven't given another living soul. Of course, it's just a script—

"Damn you, Alex! Wake up and tell me for yourself, whatever it is!" She was scared now. Scared of hearing what Alex wouldn't say aloud. Scared of having fallen hard for a man half alive and what he made her feel, anyway.

Tell me you know I would if I could, Cat.

But would he, afraid as he was now of losing Cat?

"You can, Alex," she whispered. "You just won't."

You know why, Cat. Tell me how else I could have fallen in love with you when I haven't even seen your smile or your eyes or your hair, or touched my lips to yours or your breasts or—

Vanessa clamped her hands over her ears. Of course that made no difference. Her breasts ached for want of his lips. "I'm going to bed, Alex. My bed. To sleep. Alone."

I love you.

She stripped off her sweatshirt and scooted out of her jeans and undies. She peeled back the covers on her lonely bed, turned down the lamp and drew the covers up over her head to shut him out—just before the tears stinging her nose and burning her eyes dribbled helplessly onto a Petrakis pillow.

Alex felt his breath desert him, felt for the first time in months his fingers tightening of their own volition into fists of utter frustration, felt his soul shrivel.

He had to touch her, had to get out of this bed. His fingers loosened and tightened again.... Had to...had to. That he could control his hands gave him a burst of hope, the kernel of certainty that he could, had to, would go to her.

His eyes opened. Wouldn't focus and then did, on the ceiling in the darkness.

His wrists flexed at his will, the most extraordinary feeling. His hands groped at the bedrails at his command. He swallowed, and swallowed again, scared that he could make it, scared that he couldn't.

He rested a moment, more to listen for Vanessa's tears soaking into the pillow than because he thought he needed to. Her tears. God in heaven, he'd driven her to tears.

His eyes were focusing. Slowly, so slowly, he flexed his neck and saw her small shuddering shape beneath covers on a bed far lower to the floor than his own. But the effort robbed him of everything, sapped his new strength, devastated him with his limitations. His gaze lit on the IV pole and the bag hanging from it, followed the tubing to his upper chest. He couldn't see where it invaded his skin.

His eyes fell closed again and no matter what he did or how he berated his limitations, they wouldn't open. Nor could he let go of the bed rails.

Panic tore through him.

In spite of herself, in spite of her every effort and her tears and her longing to shut him out, Vanessa felt his rage, knew his panic. There was nothing she could do.

Alex couldn't fully wake, couldn't touch her, either, but his panic wouldn't stop him or the one thing he had left to give her. His mind could touch hers, and with his mind his loving her was still . . . possible.

Follow me, zoe mou, *my life. Follow me.*

In his mind he drew near and lay with her. Inhaling her sweet chaste scent, he reveled in it. He pulled her into his mind, into his body, and though he couldn't know for sure that she followed, he believed.

Follow me . . .

In her dream, Vanessa felt the sunburst warmth of his breath at her neck, the knowing touch of his hands at her throat, the kiss that took her lips, sucking greedily at her tongue, leaving her mindless and forgetful of the emptiness that would linger like the precious earthy scent of loving.

In her dream his hands cradled her breasts. Soothing and stoking the swelling need, he suckled at her love-hardened nipples. Pure skin-tightened sensation followed as surely as the bloom follows the bud.

Follow me, zoe mou . . .

In her dream, he treasured her, worshipped her, needed her. His need was more real to her for having touched him herself, than her own. Thick and swollen it was, turgid with the gathering of his life's blood at his male flesh.

Follow me, Vanessa . . .

He recreated for her the imaginary moment in time when *The ManWoman* happened. The man was him, had always been him, but before Vanessa, the woman had only been an illusion, a dream of completion.

In her dream she felt the gathering of her own fluid heat, felt the swelling of her own tender, needy flesh, felt the flower named Desire budding, the petals of her woman's body blooming in exquisite preparation to take him inside her.

But she'd never known that taking in, and her dream couldn't create for her what she had never known.

She moaned in her sleep.

Her body fought off the dream and she woke, but the remains of her fantasy lingered. Her dampened thighs quivered. Her breasts ached. Her heart thudded heavily, relentlessly. This was the emptiness she knew so well.

And by the gentle, sweet, torturously perfect communication he was afraid to give up, Alex knew her body's hollow need.

Vanessa hadn't meant to come back from Alex's errand at all. She'd meant to use it as an excuse to leave and never return. She remembered, now, wanting desperately for Nick to tell her she had to get the hell out before she destroyed herself. Instead he'd looked at her with eyes that said, "Alex is the luckiest son of a bitch in creation for having a woman who would do for him what you have done."

He'd made sure she would return.

In the end Nick was more what he was than who he was—more Petrakis man than her dearest friend and mentor.

In the end she'd known, herself, that she had to come back.

Hours passed. In the cold, cloudless dawn of Christmas Eve morning she knew she had to leave Alex. Not today. Not tomorrow, for leaving him on Christmas was unimaginable. But the day after, because for all that she loved Alex, for all that she'd given and done and said and promised, he slept on.

There was nothing left for her to do.

Chapter Seven

CHRISTMAS MORNING it snowed. Huge, moisture-laden flakes drifted toward the frozen earth in no particular hurry to end their peaceful, weightless fall. But when they lit on trees or spruce needles or even utility wires, they clung faithfully and managed to create something altogether new and wonderful. Tepees of snow, icy fingers, strands of diamond dust. Peering out the windshield of Constantine's Cadillac, Vanessa pushed aside her fanciful thoughts. Fancy had gotten her nowhere in her quest to bring Alex back.

It was a heavy, wet snow that made driving down from the foothills dicey, but Constantine had asked that Vanessa accompany him to the early church service. He drove a white Fleetwood with a burgundy leather interior. Vanessa watched the mesmerizing motion of the wipers sweeping back and forth and tried to imagine what she was going to say to Alex's father. What possible hope could she hold out to this man? Maybe he wouldn't ask for any of her reassurances; maybe he'd send his prayers where they belonged.

She started a couple of times to bring Constantine up to date—he'd been in Palm Springs for a few days—but each time, he gave her a look that indicated he really didn't want to hear. The time was past for placing faith in the miracles she should have delivered by now. In spite of that she grew more certain with each mile that he had things he wanted to say to her.

The archbishop conducted a passionately joyous, humbling service. Constantine's eyes filled often with sparkling, unshed tears. The Son of God was born this day; the son of Constantine Petrakis languished.

Vanessa's own tears never quite dried. It had been years since she'd attended, for she'd not been a good Greek girl in a very long time.

Introducing her to the archbishop and another priest, as a daughter of his heart, Constantine again revealed himself for something less, or more, than the powerful, demanding magnate he presented to the world. Here was a simple man with a very fragile soul. Here was a man with every earthly pleasure and possession at his fingertips, and he couldn't regain life for his beloved second son.

His gesture in claiming her as a daughter of his heart thawed Vanessa's own frost-encrusted heart.

In the midst of offering His Eminence, the archbishop an opinion on the state of the world this Christmas, Constantine saw his eldest son. Matt had taken possession of Vanessa's arm.

"Pop... Your Eminence. I drove up to see Alex this morning. Nanny told me you'd come to early services."

His father was pleased to see Matt here. "Have you brought Beatrice and the boys?"

Matt shook his head. "We're not on very good terms right now, Pop. I thought she'd bring them out for the holidays, but ... she didn't."

"Divorced or not," Constantine scowled, "a man should have his family with him at Christmas."

"I know, Pop," Matt admitted. "I know. Things just aren't that simple anymore." He turned to Vanessa, then. "Can I talk to you?"

Vanessa nodded and begged the archbishop's leave, which he granted. Knowing Matt and Vanessa would discuss Alex, Constantine agreed as well. "We haven't much time."

"I'm aware of that, Pop. Vanessa needs to get...home, I'm sure."

Matt led her to a far distant corner of the community room. Older than Alex by only one or two years, he reminded Vanessa more of his father than of Alex. The same dark, demanding eyes, the same broad, commanding body shape. She said nothing, but waited for him to decide exactly what he wanted to say.

"We're all very concerned, Vanessa. Nothing seems to help. No matter how long you're with Alex, no matter how often one of us drops by to see him— He's not coming out of it, is he?"

Vanessa took her hands from Matt's warm grasp. "It's very...complicated. He's improved a great deal, but...he's still not conscious."

Matt swore softly. His expression told Vanessa he thought she must also be at the end of her rope. "Liz came into The Apollo the other night spouting wild stories about Alex refusing to wake up. She even said you think you hear Alex?"

"They're not so wild, Matt." Vanessa's hands opened wide and then came together as she tried to think of a way to make Matt see what Liz Pederson had not. "She misunderstood me. I told her that Alex could hear her, not really that I could hear him. But...people usually don't understand. I said I was supporting Alex any way I could until he decides to come out of it. I tried to explain that it isn't a *conscious* decision. His body must need this coma to recover, Matt, or it wouldn't be forcing it on him."

"So he's not really... refusing."

"No. But I feel very badly that I haven't been able to bring him out of this—"

"Don't, Vanessa. We all knew from the start that the odds were against it."

Her throat began to ache from holding back her tears. "What about Liz? I know your father gave her permission to visit Alex, but I don't know why—not after he told her to stay away."

Matt nodded. "But remember, he'd asked her to come—to see if her being there wouldn't help Alex. I think she feels guilty as hell, now, and besides, she wanted to come home. She called me again last night. I guess the *Post* caught up with her at her parents' home yesterday. She managed to squelch whatever story they thought they had, but she wanted us to know she isn't going to put her life on hold for Alex's sake anymore."

"I guess we have nothing to worry about, then." *Only Alex. Oh, God. There's only Alex to worry about,* she thought, *and I've done everything I know to do.*

"Only Alex." Matt echoed her thoughts. He took her by the shoulders. "If I'm understanding this at all right, the ball is in Alex's court now."

"Yes," Vanessa murmured through her tears. "The ball is definitely in Alex's court."

"Will you do this for me, Vanessa? We'll still be around to visit, but will you let him know that we're all calling in whatever markers we have in heaven?"

Did heaven keep accurate records? Vanessa hadn't been to church in years, and God owed her nothing. "Thanks, Matt. I'll tell him."

Constantine helped her back into the car afterward and drove in silence back out to the foothills. He passed the turn to the family compound and drove higher up into the mountains. Finally he pulled to the side of the road next to a clearing, a plateau far above the far-flung city of Denver and the villagelike Evergreen. The peace of Christmas fell over them when Constantine cut the engine and pulled off his driving gloves.

At last Vanessa spoke, because Constantine expected answers even when he asked no questions.

"Matt told me about Liz being back—and that they're all praying for Alex."

Constantine nodded. "She went to Matt."

"Yes. Apparently she's promised him to keep quiet outside the family. She won't wait for Alex anymore, though. I guess that's what she went to tell him in the first place."

His expression told Vanessa the loss of Liz was no loss at all. And again they were quiet for long moments.

Vanessa could see forever toward the east in spite of the gentle snowfall—the Denver metropolitan skyline and the plains beyond in the background. Up here in the foothills were stands of winter-denuded aspen, and beyond them ageless evergreens surrounded the clearing.

A doe stepped tentatively out of the camouflaging shelter of trees. A buck, with his spectacular five-point antlers raised and still, sniffed at the pure, crystalline air. The doe tossed her head and the buck snorted, pawing at the ground.

Vanessa felt a stab of recognition for the pair. She sat transfixed by their presence.

"My sons brought their girls here," Constantine said wistfully, as if a father *should* know where his sons made their first conquests. "In the summer, when the snow is gone, there are well-worn car tracks. Prairie grass is beginning to overtake them."

She thought, *a father should know,* and then she knew: Constantine's instincts were no less unerring than his son's, where her heart was concerned. She tore her eyes from the deer. "I'm sorry. I should have told you."

His hand, warm as the deers' breath in the frozen air, took hers. "I have no need to be told what I already know, Vanessa. The question I need answered is what you're going to do about it. You can't go on like this. Nor can my son."

The cold slowly seeped into the Cadillac. Her wretched breath began to make frost on the window beside her before she'd formulated a single coherent thought. "No, Alex can't go on much longer. He's lost a little weight in spite of me, and with only the hyperal IV, he'll go on losing. His body has reached a point of no return and there's nothing I can do to stop it."

Constantine's fingers pressured hers. "Is he so stubborn, then?"

Vanessa understood the real question very well. "Stubborn? No. In the beginning his coma was very much a matter of self-preservation. Now...I think it's what is between us that he's afraid to give up."

"What...exactly is between you?" he asked. "I know there's something most extraordinary going on—I see the evidence of it in both of you. But I don't—I can't understand it."

"It's beyond understanding. Like nothing either of us has ever known. In the beginning I thought that I could feel what Alex felt. Now—" She hesitated, for the moment had come to admit she was hearing Alex's every thought, and she didn't want his father to misunderstand in any way. "Now, he still doesn't speak aloud, but I hear him. Sometimes, when I don't say what I'm thinking, he hears me, anyway."

She paused again. "Maybe the message is just beginning to get through to me. 'Vanessa Koures, it is not given to you to create miracles.'"

"So." Constantine stopped to clear the emotion from his throat. "You believe Alex is afraid that if he wakes, this...understanding between you will cease."

Vanessa could only nod.

"Then you have only one course left to you—to us."

Leave Alex.

The words remained unspoken between them. She'd made the choice at dawn, and still it was no easier to say.

"Vanessa, what will become of you if he's right, that what is between you will...disappear?"

The deer will still mate. New fawns will still be born, she thought. "I don't know. I'll...I don't know. Did you know, did Papoo tell you that I promised Alex once that I'd be his forever if he'd only wake up?"

Again Constantine cleared his raw throat. "Yes. My father told me."

"If...if it takes leaving Alex, never seeing him again to make him wake...I'll do that instead."

Constantine's eyes watered. From his pants pocket he drew a handkerchief and daubed at his nose. "I beg of you, daughter of my heart, forgive me. The burden was too great, the price too high. If I had it to do over again—"

"Don't!" Vanessa cried. "No price is too high." If she had everything to do over, she would do again exactly what she had done, even knowing, now, the outcome.

The expression in Constantine's eyes was the same she'd seen in Nick's, admiration threaded with belief and disbelief and gentle envy. A look that said "I've spawned a fool for a son if he manages to lose you."

This time Vanessa couldn't handle it. She'd done nothing half so self-sacrificing as Nick or Constantine wanted to believe. If she'd heard Alex it was because she had no choice. If devoting her every moment to him had managed to bring him back, it was because *she* needed to redeem herself and her papa's misery. If she loved Alex, it was her own selfish need, and futile at that for though he claimed to love her, he hadn't exactly leaped at the chance of a forever with her.

Slowly, she shook her head. "You've not raised a fool."

"Thank you, little daughter. Whatever happens, thank you for that." Drawing a deep breath, he gestured toward the clearing. "This is the place I had in mind for your rehabilitation center."

Surprise clamored in her heart. "But—"

"No buts, Vanessa. Before she died Alex's mother had intended this land for a charity cause in any case."

"But I've done nothing—"

"On the contrary. You've done everything humanly possible—more. It's up to my...to Alex now." When words wouldn't come to her, he continued. "I've spoken with my sister's son in Palm Springs about drawing up some plans. Mike is a commercial architect, but he wants to design your center, if you agree.

"We'll break ground as soon as possible. Mike thought it would take no more than three or four months to build, but drawing up the plans and getting the necessary permits could take even longer. You like it, then? It will serve for your purposes?"

The words didn't exist in any language but that of the heart to express her feelings. She clung tightly to Constantine's hand until the deer had run off and the cold forced them to leave.

ON CHRISTMAS NIGHT she replaced *The ManWoman* above Alex's desk.

He sensed the withdrawal in her, the submission to something beyond her control. The fight had gone out of her, and though he didn't understand exactly why, he knew he was the cause of it.

He wanted to reach out to her, but he didn't know how anymore. Several times more he'd been on the very edge of waking. Cat had all but ignored it, like so many empty promises. She never said "Wake up, Alexander *mou*, and I'll be yours forever."

Whatever near-perfect communication they had shared wavered precariously now, like the flame of a candle in an evil wind, and waking up seemed a whole lot less frightening. He was losing her, and he didn't know how to stop it unless he woke up.

It didn't happen. Instead he slept on, and she came to sit in the Petrakis rocker beside him and took his hand. The cold of her fingers chilled him to the marrow.

Why? Why did you replace The ManWoman?

"Because it's Christmas, *andras*, and I have nothing else to give you."

You're here, harato mou. *That is enough.*

From your lips to God's ears, she prayed silently. But although she knew that being here had been enough in the beginning, that was no longer true. Now, the longer she stayed, the more she imperiled his already unbearably slender chances.

She had it in mind to tell him straight out that if he couldn't take her, all of her, in more than their dreams, she couldn't stay. She meant to tell him why she'd put *The ManWoman* away in the first place—because after the beauty of it seduced her, the consummation of it left her empty. That she wouldn't *be* a virgin if she'd had her way.

Telling him straight-out was what she'd intended.

Straight-out was impossible. It would sound pathetic and self-pitying and melodramatic. Her leaving had to mean *something*, had to accomplish his waking if anything could. He had to understand exactly how badly what they shared had hurt her, even if it meant peeling away from herself the last vestige of her fragile armor.

"Red thread twisted well,
Neatly wound upon the reel;
Set the reel a-spinning, do,
And *paramithi* I'll tell you."

Alex's heart knocked painfully in his chest as Cat's sweet voice echoed the centuries-old once-upon-a-time formula Papoo most favored.

"There was once a girl, and a boy named John," she continued. "Eldest son, first generation Greek-American. His father was a pilot for United when it was headquartered in Cheyenne, Wyoming. Did you know that, Alex *mou*? Years ago, when planes didn't have the power they do now, the easiest way across the Rockies was through a pass in eastern Wyoming."

Alex couldn't fathom why she'd begun talking this way, distantly, as if recounting an ancient tale, but he was himself a storyteller and he recognized the awkward beginnings that sprang from not knowing exactly where to start, just as he recognized the traditional opening.

Instinct told him the story was not without purpose, and that purpose scared the hell out of him.

"John's father was as traditional as they come. His mother, Sophie, made the lightest *phyllo* dough the girl had ever known—and she'd spent not a few hours in the kitchens of her grandmother, her aunts and her mother. But this *phyllo* was the pride of Sophie's life. That and her son, John. He was her only child, and she was bitterly disappointed when he brought the girl home. She was one of *those* girls, college girls, surely loose, and without morals or any understanding of her place as a woman. Sophie refused to think why *phyllo* and a man like her son and raising her grandchildren wouldn't be enough for the selfish girl.''

Vanessa sank into the quagmire of her past. Words she'd never spoken aloud, she spoke to Alex. Pain she'd never given voice to, she shared with him, for the story she told was her own. She'd exhausted anger and humor and love in trying to wake him. Pain was all that was left to force him from his sleep.

She touched her tongue to her lips and continued.

''John . . . John wanted to marry the girl, but he also wanted to become a lawyer, and his parents told him flatly he'd be on his own, disinherited and cut off from their emotional support—if he married the girl before he graduated. It might have been different if the girl had agreed to settle down to producing their grandchildren.''

The suggestion, the fleeting image of the girl's body nurturing any other than Petrakis babies—his babies—made Alex shake, for he knew, inexplicably, that the girl was Vanessa.

''She couldn't. She needed to go to medical school. She needed to think there would be something she could do to get back her father's life for him. He was so sick, Alex. Most of my . . . of her life, her father was just so sick and weak . . .''

Alex felt his world cracking apart. His own father had been so vital, so full of life and love and the devil, as the

Boston Irishman in the Senate had been so fond of saying, that Alex couldn't imagine a life devoid of that paternal strength and guidance. He felt a tremor of foreboding, and he wanted her to stop.

"So. John and the girl didn't get married. They got engaged, but that compromise wasn't good enough for Sophie. She prayed hourly to all the saints in heaven that John would come to his senses.

"His father was another story.

"John would come home from a weekend with his father and just shut the girl out. His conscience wouldn't let him go find sex elsewhere as his father suggested he do, but he couldn't marry a nonvirgin, either. So they slept together, but nothing ever happened.

"They kissed, of course, and petted. They did everything." Her voice withered to a whisper. "Everything . . . but destroy the girl's precious virginity."

Silence fell, like ice forming over the eddies of emotion. Alex cursed the hypocrisy of the man. Virginity was still an honored, essential commodity to too many men of his own heritage. And there were still those who sent away to Greece for wives, because American girls would never know their place or be the docile, subservient woman such men required. Though Alex knew personally of no man as consummately stupid as the one in Cat's past, he didn't doubt her for a second.

In the deepest recesses of his heart, Alex knew he was no better. He'd taken his share of women, and if he'd not chosen to make virginity an issue with Elizabeth, it had far more to do with her not being Greek than with his honor.

The worst was yet to come. In Cat's own time, he thought, but pain sprouted in his gut that she told her story in the distant third person, as if *her* pain, her tears belonged to someone else.

The Petrakis rocker began its gentle creaking as she sought small comfort in its primal motion.

"As a Greek girl, of course, she could not grow up misunderstanding the cultural mandates. Good girls don't. Even most of her *xenoi* friends had been raised that way. She understood, and she thought she could deal with it."

"At first the casual sex was enough, but as time went on, the hot and heavy petting only left her cold. The girl wanted him, she thought, and begged him, even tried seducing him."

"He...he was flattered in the beginning.... Strutted like a peacock just knowing how desperate the girl was. But in the end he turned on her.

"She shocked him, he said. She must be loose, he said, just like his mother always believed. At least *he* had the strength to be decent. And then he began lording it over her. Why couldn't she wait? Didn't she think he wanted it? Did she think he had so little respect for her that he would take her before they were married?"

Obsessed now with getting it all out, Vanessa hurtled on. "The girl couldn't leave it alone, Alex. She just couldn't. She thought, you bastard! How can you touch me and taunt me and make me beg you? She told him there was no difference between what they were already doing and what she wanted. 'Semantics!' the girl cried. Splitting hairs. That's all it was, for all the sake of a piece of fragile, useless tissue. Chastity? This was chastity?"

Vanessa clamped her knuckles to her lips to stop their quivering, and the tremor in her voice. "I...the girl tried reasoning with him. She told him girls used to take candles to themselves in the middle ages, in the *dark ages*, to be rid of their damned virginity before they married.''

"He broke every candle in the off-campus housing she...she shared with her roommates. He...told her she'd better get out of premed if that's the kind of trash she was becoming.''

"Becoming. He meant *learning*, but he said *becoming*...''

Alex died a small death for the girl Cat had been. With all his ugliness, the man in her story hadn't been able to drown her instincts for loving and giving, but he'd punished her passion and driven it from her.

There would be no "happily ever after, and we are even better.''

He'd done no better by her than the virginity-obsessed bastard of her story. Loving her in his dream should have been a gift more precious, even, than the script she had yet to read. Instead he'd brought her to the same raw chasm of need.

Instead he'd driven to the hilt the dagger of unfulfilled longing, and none of his good intentions changed any of that. She'd be gone by morning, and he'd be left with his overwhelming guilt.

Guilt. He'd swiped whole plates of Grandma Eleni's golden-brown wine cookies, *tsourekakia*; he'd bloodied more than his share of noses; he'd squandered time and money and lied on occasion to his mother. He'd used and left more women than he cared to admit. But this...

Who'd have guessed guilt wounded in technicolor crimson?

Vanessa let her head sink back to the headrest of the rocker. For a long while she sat in the generations-old chair, listening to its gentle creaking.

She would miss this old rocker, the hours she had spent reading here, the unexpected comfort of it, next to the bed where Alex's spirit lived and his body languished.

She endured the burning of unshed tears behind her eyelids, and the bite of emotion at her throat—the inadequacy, the guilt, the sorrow.

An insistent rapping at Alex's door finally drew her attention. Vanessa's lungs dragged raggedly at the air, and a shiver passed through her body. Hands still shaking, she pushed herself out of the rocker and somehow, she would never know how, she reached the door.

Mrs. Hancock, her expression forcedly blank, her posture a dead giveaway of disapproval, moved through the open doorway.

"Mr. Petrakis has given me to understand that you must leave for a while. A family emergency, I believe he said?"

Vanessa moved away disjointedly. She hadn't spoken to Constantine about the mechanics of her leaving, or said in so many words that she'd prefer someone other than the disingenuous Hancock to come. The woman didn't buy for a second the excuse he'd handed her, but Vanessa wouldn't contradict him.

Nor had she expected anyone to show up tonight.

"Yes. My mother..." She trailed off, leaving Mrs. Hancock's impression intact.

The nurse tossed her coat aside and then noticed Vanessa's bed. "Or is it that your unconventional methods haven't worked any better than mine and you needed a plausible excuse to leave, *Doctor*?"

Inside Vanessa, rage flared. Throwing the nurse her coat, she pointed to the door. "I would like another moment alone with Alex. I'll speak with you downstairs. For now, *get out*."

Sniffing haughtily, the nurse flounced out and left the door wide open. Vanessa wanted to slam it shut. Instead, she quietly pushed it closed and forced herself to gather her essentials. The draft of her paper and the handwritten notes she'd garnered over the weeks. Alex's screenplay. Her purse and a few toiletries, very few. Moving like a robot, she dumped the armful on her bed and turned at last to Alex.

Goodbye. Farewell. How did one say those things?

If you're hurting, Alex *mou*, that's good. How could she possibly say that, when pain was the last thing she'd willingly inflict?

She approached his bed and stood watching him. The first thing she'd ever asked of him was a swallow. The last of him she might ever see was the convulsive, pain-wracked bob of his utterly masculine Adam's apple.

Unable to stop herself, she threaded her fingers through his hair with no other purpose or thought than to touch him. And she swallowed, convulsively.

Don't, Cat, he wanted to say, don't leave, don't do this to us. But his lips weren't moving and his mind was no longer touching hers.

Bending closer, she stroked his honey-shadowed cheek, whiskers soft as goose down in one direction, prickly as one of Sarah Gilles's cactuses in the other. For all these weeks she'd thought of his beard and his hair as the same color. Sandy, tinged with smooth, brilliant sunshine. His whiskers truly were darker, she thought now. Like honey, yes, but not any ordinary honey. Whiskers the color of Symian *meli*.

Her papa had been a connoisseur of the best honeys, and in Greece, autumn honey was the rarest. This honey, Papa had said, was thick because there was no water, and scented with thyme because *thrubi*, the most aromatic of flowers, survived the endless, hot summers.

Whiskers the color of Symian honey. She would remember...

"There are worse things, Alexander *mou*, than being alone."

Please, Cat. Read the script. Please.

Her eyes were drawn to his full lips, and slowly, though it killed her, she pressed her lips to his. She meant to draw back, meant the touch of her lips to be no more than a farewell she couldn't put into words, but she craved the taste of him, just one to take with her, to store and treasure in her memories. Her tongue traced the generous shape of his lips and dallied over the tiny crevices.

She ached. Fluid heat flooded her—everywhere.

He ached, reacting instantly, rigidly to the delicate wet heat of her lips and the fragile, woman-scent of her. Precious, more precious to him than memory or imaginings, for unless he woke, he would never know or remember so exquisite a feeling, or imagine it, either.

The bittersweet sough of her breath at his cheek was the last he knew of his Cat.

IT WAS DAYS before Alex would let Mrs. Hancock come within slugging distance of him. He found that he could move his arms and torso and legs sporadically, enough to give her fits, enough to make her threaten to leave.

It was days before Vanessa would enter into even the most trivial of conversations with her mother or her aunts in Chicago. She met Althea's "What has happened, *koukla*?" questions with an emotionless mask.

Constantine doubled and then redoubled the nurse's wages.

Althea tried and tried again to break into Vanessa's emptiness.

Alex jerked the IV from the vein beneath his collarbone and let it run itself dry onto his bed.

Vanessa refused the nourishing *avgnolemeno*, Aunt Chloe's version of lemon-chicken soup, and the tempting *baklava* her mother slaved over.

Papoo despaired. The orchid plant died in Alex's window, and the hot-house hybrids in the greenhouse wilted from a dearth of attention or even water.

Nanny Bates decided to take matters with the old fool, His Greekness, into her own capable Scots hands. She marched up to his room one day, drew out his suitcases and opened them onto his bed.

"You'll be packin' y'r bags for Greece." Her voice shook, but she finished her threat.

He slammed them shut again, and wisely, Nanny withdrew.

Aunty Ennea told the ladies at church that her niece had come home with a malady as yet unknown to man. The ladies nodded, and thought to themselves that the girl was truly done with her rebelliousness.

Alex discovered his voice and a vocabulary suited to a stevedore. Mrs. Hancock thought she'd heard it all; she'd worked postop most of her life and knew that patients still under the effects of anesthesia could swear a blue streak. She earned every penny of her inflated salary for the blistering her ears took. Constantine began searching for Vanessa, but even Nick's calls to Chicago were refused.

And still Alex lingered in a coma. Lashing out at any attempts to help him, he didn't give a damn if he starved himself slowly to death. That didn't work, either, any more than trying to wake worked.

If Vanessa sensed Alex's turmoil from across the thousand miles she had put between them, it wasn't apparent to her mother or her aunts. What was apparent was that the girl was either anorexic—God forbid!—or broken-hearted. The spinster Ennea knew that one well, and Vanessa would survive it. Not happily, perhaps, but she would survive.

Then came the day, by Vanessa's reluctant but strangely imperative calculations the one-hundred-and-twentieth day of Alex's coma, that everything changed. The world went on its merry way, Aunt Chloe and Aunty Ennea chattered and Althea fussed. Vanessa began to read *Demon Alone*.

She read for hours, sensing from the spare narrative the hostile mood of the environment, the frozen ambience of *alone* Alex had created of the hell into which he'd plunged Richard and Catherine.

Until Catherine and Richard had captivated her imagination with their desperate, separate bids for survival.

Until, in spite of themselves and the harsh impossibility of escaping their ordeal, they fell in love.

Until the end of ACT II when Vanessa finally discovered Alex's meaning, the message he'd meant for her. Richard knew his way out.

Alex knew *his* way out.

Hope, then certainty, flared in Vanessa. Alex knew his way out, just as Richard did. Was he waking, even now?

Hope gave rise to doubts and fears that were as inexplicable as the day Alex had asked her, *"what if,"* and *"why,"* and *"why won't it work between us?"* He could make concessions to her world, and she could make concessions to his.

She was confused about her ambivalence, but supposed that when she'd step into the fantasy of Alex's love for her she had already lost a piece of reality. Now reality perversely insisted that she'd never been there at all.

They'd never survive the transition to here and now together. She couldn't read to the end of *Demon Alone* suspecting—no, *knowing* that Catherine and Richard must surely escape and live on. Together. Happily ever after. Fiction, fantasy was too easy.

Even so, Vanessa booked a flight to Denver.

ALEX GAVE UP FIGHTING. Mrs. Hancock rejoiced, thought about injecting sedatives to make the peace last a few more hours, and then thought better of it. Constantine and Papoo and Nick were worried, and worried sick.

Alex went to that place in his head where before he'd found nothing but the demon alone. And found that Vanessa had moved in, painted in it dimensions of herself and left impressions of her being he would never be rid of.

She had believed in him, believed that he'd come back.

She had slept with him, when a more rational, less generous woman would have turned away.

She had touched him. Even now a heaviness wedged in his loins, for he had known satisfying sex, and Vanessa's brief touch was neither as skilled nor as intense nor as practiced as even the most naive of the women he'd had, but it was without doubt the most precious, vulnerable, erotic touch he'd ever known.

Her kiss was a treasure beyond any value he knew, and because of that kiss, Alex swallowed and began the journey to awake.

Chapter Eight

BETWEEN ONE RAGGED BREATH and the next, he woke. Instinctively he warded off the surge of urgency. He'd come this close to waking fully before, only to sink back. He shivered to think of being dragged back down. Without Cat around, he'd even lost the ability to communicate with Papoo. The charm of sleeping off the accident had worn unbearably thin.

Alex missed her savagely.

Nor would he give in to the elation crowding his senses. If this awakening were real, he'd know it soon enough, and have the rest of his life to savor it. If not . . .

He wouldn't open his eyes yet, or tempt fate with the slightest movement. He let the pleasure of waking and the resurgence of power wash over him. His internal clock had become finely tuned. He knew Hancock would be back in moments to turn him for the last time before morning dawned. He would allow it one more time, and once only. His waking would be his own until the sun rose.

It would be his own after that, too. Today was Sunday; his father and Papoo had begun going to church and sitting around with the men for hours afterward.

He feigned unconsciousness for Hancock when she came. By that time he'd risen onto his elbow long enough to see for himself what he'd already known. Cat's bed was still there.

God in heaven but he missed her! Wanted her, needed her, craved her touch. Or the touch of their minds, or the scent of her, or the sound of her. Hancock had all but eradicated the traces of Vanessa.

Cat would be back. Did she know he'd awakened? He'd bet the truth of his waking on it. She'd be back.

Then elation filled him to overflowing. He would look at her. He would walk with her, hold her, drag his hands through her hair and kiss her until her lips were swollen and her need was as violent as his own. And take her. He'd known a need in her since the moment she'd walked into his room three months ago, and had been half crazy with it since the night she'd summoned the guts to touch him. He forgot that he hadn't wanted power of any sort over her and willed her back to his side.

He eased himself up as sunlight blazed over the horizon and into the room. His eyes reacted to the unfamiliar brilliance with stabbing pain. For the first time in four months he squinted against the sun to see the matchless azure of the Colorado sky.

He started to swing his legs over the edge of the bed, only to encounter the railing. He slammed the heel of his hand into the metal guards in his anger.

Hancock, still in hairpins and housecoat, stormed into the room. If she was surprised at his Lazarus act, she didn't show it.

"Lie down this instant! What do you think you're doing, anyway? You've been bedridden for over four months now, and you've no bloody business thinking you can just get up and go take a leak!"

She stamped across the room in outrage and thrust a urinal into his hands, then crossed her arms across her sunken chest and glared at him. Alex felt an uncontrollable urge to laugh but when he would have told her to get the hell out, he choked and coughed.

"What did I tell you?" Hancock sniffed. "You shouldn't be thinking you can talk, either. It's a whole different matter to carry on a civilized conversation than to snarl obscenities. Your vocal cords will be weeks coming back."

She reached out to push him back into a supine position, but he surprised her, caught her wrist and shoved the unused urinal right back at her.

She was right. He hadn't the least intention of carrying on a conversation with the old biddy, but his throat hurt and rasped badly. "Take this . . . put down the bed rail and get ou-out."

Whether it was the fierce determination in his eyes or her own knowledge that he'd soon find out for himself how indispensable she was, he didn't know. Either way, Hancock dropped the bed rail with a clang and backed off.

She huffed out of the room with dire don't-blame-me-when-you-fall-on-your-face warnings.

Alex collapsed, laughing silently. If Cat could only have seen that! But the effort it cost him to get up and stand made him glad she wasn't here. His legs shook like aspen leaves in a brisk wind. He grabbed for the unused IV pole and nearly fell in the attempt, but he was damned if he'd lie back down.

No way would he be lying in that bed when Cat returned.

He clung to the pole, transferring his weight to his arms—and gritted his teeth against the weakness he was only beginning to discover.

Hanging there, just trying to breathe, he felt as if he'd climbed Kilimanjaro or dived so deeply the bends would kill him. His head throbbed, and he couldn't drag in enough oxygen to fuel his arms. God, but they ached.

He broke out in a cold sweat with the exertion of taking a single step, such a sweat that his fingers kept sliding down the metal pole. He'd been an ass or worse for jerking out his IV. His body craved liquids and calories, his lungs craved a shot of pure oxygen.

Maintaining his balance was a nearly insurmountable task. Conscious thought left him within three mincing, tentative steps toward the bathroom, dragging the IV pole over the thick pile carpet for a modicum of support. Step... drag. Step... drag. Step... drag.

He knew only that Cat was coming back because he willed it so. Damned if he'd be wallowing in that bed when she returned....

He made it. Afterward he never remembered quite how. He braced himself against the doorjamb. His legs were on fire, and his arms... he'd lost all sensation. His hands felt like dead weights at the ends of his cramped wrists, and his wrists like putty. He stood there for an eternity, because if he moved now he'd go crashing to the ceramic-tiled floor and crack his head open. If he could just reach the mirrored wall... the shower door.

The ceramic tiles beneath his feet were cool and hard, another texture altogether from the acres of plush carpeting he'd crossed. He might have reveled in the new sensations. He wanted to, would have given anything to heighten his newfound awareness, but his brain sent ten thousand conflicting messages to his wobbling ankles, correcting and overcorrecting for balance. Cat had done her job; the strength was there, but somewhere along the line his feet had lost contact with the reality of standing. One more step. One more.

He stood over the toilet, his arms planted against the wall behind it, and relieved himself. Tears sprang to his eyes over the sheer satisfaction of taking care of his own bodily needs.

He knew without question that Cat would be back at his side. A matter of hours, perhaps. He also knew if she walked in now he wouldn't have the strength left even to touch his lips to hers. He wanted to believe he had that latent strength. He wanted to believe that Alex Petrakis would have it left in him to make love to her if he'd been sleeping Rumpelstiltskin's ninety-nine years. He wanted her.

This was no fairy tale, and Alex was bone tired. He blotted the sweat and tears on his pajama sleeve, and rested his head on his outstretched arm.

He stood there a few seconds longer, gathering the fortitude to venture back.... He'd been a fool to jerk out his IV and deprive himself of the nourishment. He'd been in that bed for months, and the awful irony of needing sleep now all but crushed his spirit.

Alex made it out of the bathroom the same way he'd gotten there, dragging the IV pole along, using his arms to carry most of his weight. He took one look at his bed and turned toward Cat's....

Alex slept for hours, deep, dreamless sleep, and when he woke the sun was still shining. Hancock sat penning notes at his desk. He swallowed his pride and asked politely for food, water and to see his father and grandfather. Clearly Hancock didn't trust his good manners. She supplied the water, heated some broth because Mrs. Bates was napping, and announced that Mr. Petrakis and his father had departed before she could advise them he'd awakened.

Alex's manner deteriorated. He'd have preferred a three-inch steak but he would spoon the soup into his own mouth, thank you. And unsteady as he was, he managed it. The triumph fed his soul as much as the broth replenished his body. But he slept for several hours more, and when he woke this time it was pitch-black outside. His first thought was of Cat, and his second, of taking a shower. A curious sensation curled through him—an awareness that Cat was on her way to him, closer every moment. Elation.

He made it to the bathroom, and the effort required wasn't half what it had been the first time. The hot, delicious, indescribably wonderful needle spray of water cascaded onto him through the damnable hospital pajamas to his skin.

Alex leaned against the shower wall, ripped aside his pajama top and laughed until he cried.

VANESSA FOUND HIM THERE. The sweat of his incredible exertion and stray droplets of water mingled with his tears and clung to his beautiful, unkempt, days-old beard.

She stood at the door of the bathroom for endless, silent moments. Time was suspended. Enjoying the miraculous piece of heaven he'd achieved, his eyes closed, Alex moved no more than he had to to breathe. The force of the water plastered the flimsy pajama fabric to his body. It clung faithfully against every muscle and sinew of his flesh, leaner now than her hands had known, but no less masculine or dominant or virile.

No detail—not one—was left to her memory. In that moment, she discovered the rapture that Pygmalion himself must have known. Marble brought to life because he had fallen hopelessly in love with his sculptured Galatea and wished so hard in his heart. Willpower, the force of Pygmalion's strength, had nothing to do with Galatea's coming to life. Only love had accomplished that miracle.

Alex's shoulders flexed forward. Vanessa mirrored his motion. His breath came in labored, heaving gasps. She ached to support his weight for him and knew that she daren't, for he'd earned the privilege of controlling his own body.

He doesn't know I'm here, she thought. He wasn't aware of her presence. He'd always, always been aware of her.

But not now. The incredible realization bashed into her heart with the welcome of a viper in the Garden of Eden. The rapport between them already diminished, pain shot through her with the lightning speed of a striking snake.

And still, she knew *his* trembling anxiety as though it were her own. Muscles that had only worked with and against her counterweight for weeks, he now expected to function as if he'd just wakened from a single night's sleep. That he had made it from his bed to the shower said more to her about his will than about his strength.

He couldn't move; her empathy, her body told her so.

Tears of powerlessness gathered on her lashes, mirroring his own. He doesn't even know I'm here....

But when he opened his eyes, almost as if in response to her thought, her heart leaped into her throat and hung there. His eyes, filled with the agony of simply maintaining his upright posture, gradually focused on her. He blinked and squinted and blinked again as if to reassure himself that she was really there. Beautiful, expressive gold-shot hazel eyes. She couldn't name the expression in them. Whatever empathy she possessed deserted her in the space of a heartbeat.

Alex forgot how to blink; his eyes feasted on the small, delicate form that was Vanessa Koures. Papoo had understated her beauty. Her hair, a darker, more vibrant hue than a fox's coat, silhouetted her heart-shaped face. And fair, lush lashes framed the most compassionate, depthless hazel-blue eyes he had ever seen. And her lips; he'd memorized their softly pliant texture with one kiss, and measured long hours against that instant of bittersweet joy. He forgot how to breathe.

He tried to smile, but even those small tremulous muscles—whatever the hell Cat had called them the first time he'd smiled for her—quaked.

She smiled for him, at him, and the curve of her lips was everything radiant and female in all creation.

He dared to take one supporting hand from the shower wall and offer it to her.

A strangled, jubilant sigh escaped her throat and mated with the groan issuing from deep in his chest. She kicked out of her pumps and stepped into the shower, oblivious to the water spray and her emerald mohair slacks and the sweater that molded gently to her breasts. His arm went almost desperately around her shoulders. She leaned into him; her forehead sank against his chest. She'd never felt anything half so wonderful as the weight of his arm around her or the scrape of his whiskers against her scalp.

Stunning, sensual images of a mountain buck nuzzling a doe raced through her body. Her hair caught in his unshaven beard, as the thick hair on his chest abraded her cheek. And she'd never known anything half as powerfully sexual as that, either. She smiled foolishly.

Certain of her support, Alex wrapped his other arm around her, too. He clung to her, all thought of proving his strength to her washed away. His power at this moment lay in having drawn her back, inexorably back to him, and that was enough.

"Vanessa," he croaked.

"Alex *mou*," she murmured.

His hands splayed across her narrow shoulders. He couldn't get enough of her back, and one hand found its way under the sodden, clinging sweater. Her bare water-slick flesh excited him more than anything he could remember. Ten minutes ago he hadn't the strength left in him to spit. Now, ancient primal reflexes granted him a certain strength and ignited his loins.

His stance widened subtly through no intent but to bring her closer to the throbbing, rigid length of his sex.

Vanessa knew every dimension of his body, but she'd learned it differently. She'd known he stood six-one and weighed a hundred ninety-eight pounds. The knowledge hadn't prepared her to stand nose-to-sternum with him. The simple reality of his size to hers was something altogether mystifying. Nothing in her experience had prepared her to feel so utterly female, so protected by the man whose body *she* had preserved.

Her pelvis rocked toward him with no conscious intent. She wanted closer. She would willingly burn in that pyre, and no amount of pounding water could extinguish that heat.

She lifted her head to look into his eyes. If she lived a hundred years she would never, ever forget the moment his eyes regained their gold-streaked luster. Or that she had discovered passion was hazel-gold.

He managed a smile, and the twist of his lips was everything radiant and arrantly male in creation.

When he lowered his head, the thought of taking her, taking only her precious mouth, tore a raging groan from him.

When his tongue licked the gathering of water from her lips, she thought she'd die.

His eyelids closed and hers fluttered shut. The rushing heat of her breath and his was a desperate thing. He dipped closer, and suckled at her lips. The exquisite sensation echoed on her breasts with the play of his fingers, and echoed again in her tremoring womb.

Her pelvis fell into a gently grinding rhythm that tortured his rigid flesh. His hands dropped to her hips, and her undulating motion triggered something so primitive, so timeless neither of them could get close enough.

The warm and healing humidity in the shower worked its magic on his voice, enabling him to whisper, "I want you, Cat.... All of you."

Her emotions whirled with the husky, almost threatening sound of his voice. But he took one unwitting step forward, and without warning his knees buckled. Unexpected as it was, Vanessa reacted reflexively. Using the strength of her legs, she caught him and levered his superior weight against the side wall of the shower.

Alex uttered a short, succinct curse. He didn't want her here catching him, watching him stumbling around like a drunken sailor.

"Alex, sit down. Just slide down. You've got to get your weight off your—"

"No, dammit! No!"

"Alex, stop playing macho man for one second and listen to me. You can't just—"

"Playing?" he lashed out, his voice strained to its very limits. His features twisted with pain, but the greater pain lay in the blow to his pride. He gritted his teeth against the treachery of his body and laid on the sarcasm. "Am...I...having fun...yet?"

Again, one knee buckled. Vanessa wanted desperately to make it all better, to blink away the days or weeks a full recovery would take him, to take his head against her breast and soothe the insults to his male self-regard. Instead she forced herself to remember all the sound psychological reasons she shouldn't baby him now.

She anchored her shoulder under his armpit and lashed right back at him. "I don't know, *andras*. Are you having fun? Am I?"

The old Alex Petrakis had a dozen quick, biting comebacks designed to put a woman in her place. But he'd lain in that bed for weeks, and though he'd let Cat have it any number of times, a more gentle instinct insisted, *Don't blow this, Petrakis.* Don't ruin this moment—Cat deserves better.

Even now, when the look in her eyes told him she'd rather give in to his petulant whims, she stood her ground, forcing him for his own sake to be another kind of man, a better man. If he'd thought he had nothing left to learn, he knew better now. She made him more of a man every time she looked at him, every time she refused to let him be less.

He drew a ragged breath and lifted a hand, touching her hair. But the need in him returned, fierce and hot and more compelling than he'd ever imagined. He thrust his fingers into her heavy, wet tresses, buried his hand there and pulled back. Cat let out a tiny whisper of pain and delight. Unpracticed and jerky, his thumb stretched to caress the sensitive length of her throat. His eyes followed the course of his thumb to the throbbing of her heartbeat.

He hadn't seen anything in months; in his whole life he hadn't seen anything so dear or so poignant or so erotic as the wild beating of her heart in her throat. His hand shook violently, and the only thing he knew to stop the trembling was to clamp his fingers to her head and kiss her until they were both numb.

"Yeah, *harato mou*," he admitted, his voice no more than a rasping murmur. "We're having fun."

His lips captured hers in a frenzied consuming embrace more fierce than loving, more desperate than a man should be.

She answered with a desperation all her own. There had to be an end to his endurance, but his tongue stroked in and out of her mouth in a seductive promise of the act she'd never before completed. She wanted more, all of him, all that thrumming hard need against her skin buried deep within her instead.

His unshaven jaw trailed a sweet burning path down hers to the lobe of her ear but he could bend no farther. The exquisite stab of his whiskers on her neck only intensified the touch of his tongue to the hollow above her collarbone.

If he couldn't taste her skin, take her naked breast into his mouth and feel on his tongue her tight puckered nipple, he'd shatter into a thousand pieces.

"*Andras mou*, I don't know if I can take any more of this fun," she whispered.

Alex's head lifted until his eyes could search hers. *Andras mou*. Had he heard her right, or was his imagination running as rampant as his desire? Perhaps she'd meant only to tell him that she needed a real, honest-to-God consummation.

Andras mou.. "My man," it meant, simply, but the impact, the status she granted him with that way of saying it was much, much more complex. Put together like that, woman to man, the words implied *husband*. He struggled with knowing exactly what she meant, for he'd never heard a woman use those words outside of marriage. His heart pounded painfully.

Vanessa only realized what she'd said when the doubt chased across his eyes, turning hazel-gold frenzy to dark anxiety. She flamed with embarrassment from the tightly aroused tips of her breasts to her cheeks. He belonged to another woman, or had, or might yet. Her fingers twisted behind him as she jerked her gaze from the hard masculine glitter of his and bowed her head. A battering stream of water punished her.

"I only meant..."

"Don't, Cat." Certainty sliced through him like a blade. Some desperate, unconscious part of her had wanted, by calling him *andras mou*, to accord him a husband's rights to a marriage bed—without the rings or blessings of the sacrament or the commitments.

She wanted him, and he'd have taken her here and now without her assurances. Without a mote of reluctance or guilt. If she took back her words, he wouldn't be able to do it.

If he stood in this shower much longer, he wouldn't have the strength left in any case. He anchored his thumb at her chin and forced her to look at him. "Now, Cat? Will you come to bed with me now?"

Her chin quavered in his fingers. "It's too much, Alex, too soon for you. You have only just—"

He stilled her protest with his lips. "We'll find a way, *zoe mou*, Cat. We'll find a way. Just help me get the hell out of here."

Promise and sweet stabbing anticipation bloomed in Vanessa's heart. Her experience told her Alex wouldn't have the strength left in him to make love to her, that his body couldn't possibly have left in it the energy to take her to bed. But the woman who was Caterpillar remembered well that *impossible* was nothing Alex had any close personal experience with.

There was far more at stake for her than the sexual innocence she still lived with.

She nodded yes, she would go with him, and smiled, and with her fingers, pushed his dampened hair away from his brow. She felt like a girl in the throes of her first sexual heat.

He reached for the tap handle and shoved hard to shut off the water. A lump settled in his throat. He felt like a kid taking his first girl for a stolen kiss and a quick, greedy feel.

Neither of them moved; both of them wanted to prolong the precious, poignant moment of awareness. She was expectant, and a little scared. He was ready, primed, hot and hard. And a lot scared.

There was far more at stake for him than the virginity he would steal. He'd thought he could make love to her without thinking twice, but he'd never before taken a virgin, Greek or otherwise. He needed control of himself to make it right for her, and he had none. He needed to believe that when the moment came, he would.

"Follow me, Alex *mou*, follow me." Her shoulder still supporting him much like a crutch, Vanessa urged him out of the shower. Murmuring softly, encouraging him to see each movement in his mind before he tried it, she made short, easy work of the journey out into his room. Of one mind, they turned toward Vanessa's much lower bed. Alex's body, warmed and supple from the heat of the shower, complied with every command of his brain. He had the control. Surely to God he could bring her to loving without hurting her after all she'd done and been to him.

At the side of the bed they sank together to their knees.

"Touch me, Alex. Please. Touch me," she murmured, but he needed no urging. Her eyes wide and luminous, Vanessa watched Alex's fingers approach her neck, watched as his knuckles traced a path of heat and raw, restrained power to the thrusting nipple of her breast. The sodden sweater clung to her shape like her own skin, and no subtlety of his touch was lost to her. Slowly, ever so slowly, his fingers caressed the side of her breast and sank to the bottom of her sweater, leaving in their wake a sensual contrast between the cold damp mohair and the heated, shivering echoes of his touch.

Then Alex's fingers were under the sweater, rising across her abdomen, over her ribs to the underside of her breast. A low growl of frustration came out of him. "Take your sweater off for me, Cat. Take it off before I tear it off."

Wild and primitive pleasure curled in her throat at the implied violence, a violence born of need reflected in the golden intensity of his eyes. She smiled tremulously, more aware of his lust than of her own, and crossed her arms in front of her.

As she pulled the water-soaked sweater from her skin it made a sucking noise that tore through Alex like a sudden squall.

So firm and delicate she needed no bra, the sweet, brazen shape of her breasts knocked him senseless. Her nipples, the color of a caramel confection, puckered in response to the cool air. To wake to this sight, now or ever again, seemed more than enough to ask of life.

His smile hurt.

Her movements, seductive, distracted him from the allure of her shape. She stripped the sweater to her shoulders; one arm pulled through, hoisted the emerald garment over her head as her neck bent gracefully to the side and her shoulders rolled in careless abandon. He'd never been more aware of the delicate beauty of a woman's shoulders as feminine muscle and sinew stretched and relaxed beneath alabaster skin. He'd been cheated for so long of movement himself that the motion of her body was more precious to him now than all the earth's treasures.

He watched her swallow and learned what a sensual promise swallowing was. And when she flushed under the passion in his eyes, he watched the color rising in her and knew the currents of heat, the coursing of her life's blood through her veins.

"Cat, are you sure?"

She ached for the touch of his unshaven beard on her breast, for the caress of his lips, but when he bent to suckle her breast, as his eyes had promised he would, she cried out. "Alex, my God. Alex, please..."

His tongue touched her, stroked her breast, and again he was enchanted by the tiny stirring of her nipple drawing tight. "Ah, Cat." His throat ached. His murmured endearments to her caused him such pain, but he welcomed it. Pain meant he was alive. "What if you hadn't come back to me?"

"I'm tired of your *what if*s, *andras*."

"I'm tired of your clothes *gyneka*, woman."

He leaned away from her and his eyes narrowed into glittering slits. He wrenched out of his pajama top, and the look he gave her said he wouldn't be accountable for the condition of her slacks if she didn't get out of them. Now.

She stood quickly to shed her clothing but her eyes were drawn to him stripping off his. The scorching knowledge that he wanted *her* this badly set up a wild fluttering in her breast. There was no way Alex would leave her unfulfilled. And that certainty lit a torch to her imagination and her own sexuality.

The scent of her flowing heat made Alex's whole body shake. His arms went around her legs and his fingers clutched at her bottom. She heard the pounding of her own heart in her ears, but it was nothing to the trembling of her legs or the roar of her blood when the stubble of his whiskers caught in the tight, sable-red curls at the juncture of her thighs. The husky sound in his throat was everything needful and greedy in a man's language as his fingers sought her most tender flesh.

The vibration of sound echoed again and again through her body.

"Alex." His name was both a plea and a caress. Her hands caught at his wildly damp, curling hair. And urged him, take her. His fingers traced light sensual patterns around the center of her swollen, spiralling need, and his tongue touched unerringly the very core of her, and stroked until her knees gave out and she sank onto the bed. The emotion that had flared through her the first time she ever saw *The Man Woman* returned to her with ten times the sensual power.

His eyes spoke of waiting longer still, of extending their mutually torturous pleasure, but her thighs parted for him and she tried to move farther back onto the bed and take him with her. He stilled her, and as he knelt at the bedside his thickened, near-bursting flesh touched the velvety threshold of her.

There should have been no strength left in him, nothing left with which to take her. He couldn't stand without her, or even crawl, but somehow, poised to enter and claim her, his mind and body tapped into ancient wellsprings of male power. He knew he couldn't hold off the rhythmic thrusting of his body much longer, but he did, because Cat was a virgin, and because he wanted to make it right for her.

He brought himself to the very brink of his control and hers as his rigid, scalding flesh probed hers in gentle, piercing motions until he felt the barrier of her virginal tissue. Her body arched toward him. She rose to her elbows and her tongue touched her gently curving lips. Again he found the core of her with gentle tugging fingers.

He stroked her slowly. Her warmth billowed. He increased pressure and tempo. Her hips fell into a rocking, silent plea of primal motion. Faster and harder he stroked her with his hand and body until Vanessa felt only the incredible force of fiery waves crashing over her, until nothing was left for her but to cry out in silence his name with every pressuring thrust.

And then the last vestige of his control went up in a flash fire as even the final barrier to his loving parted for him. He drove into her and stilled as much for himself as for her, because the full length of him lay buried in her, more tightly than any he'd ever in his life known.

The searing pain was but a moment's accent, a grace note heightening Vanessa's wild, uncontrolled emotion. She opened her gaze to the dark passion that burnished his eyes into shimmering gold. He watched the frenzied transformation of hers, silvery blue radiating in hazel like pewter. She reached for his hands and they clung to one another's wrists for exquisite leverage.

"Move in me, Alex," she cried. "I need you, all of you moving in me."

"So soft, *harato mou*, so hot."

I am yours. . . .

Give yourself to me, sweet gyneka. *Follow me and I will take you where we have never been*. He withdrew from her, easing past her fragile broken tissue and then thrust into her again and again until control was beyond either of them, and in oblivion they became *Man-Woman*. One in mind, one in body and in soul and in intent.

Chapter Nine

VANESSA ROUSED to the long shadows of late afternoon, the quiet, muffled sound of the door handle turning and the brush of oak opening against the teal pile carpet. Alex lay asleep in her arms, his lips at her breast, his legs entwined with hers, and the sheet barely reached the level of her hips. But there was nothing she could do, nothing she would do to wake Alex to the intrusion, and though her heart pounded, she closed her eyes again.

Papoo's knock she would have recognized. She wouldn't have guessed that she could tell the old man's step, and maybe she didn't. Maybe she just recognized the emotion for Papoo's, the tender, expansive swelling of his ancient chest, the restless, heedless joy of an old man.

Vanessa lay very still. The warmth of Alex's breath at her breast seemed to magnify a hundred-fold because Papoo drew nearer step by rugged step. At last he stood near the foot of the bed. And wept.

"Ornithon gala," the old man murmured. "She came to you. And you have awakened and done what a man does, after all."

Vanessa wondered dimly if Mrs. Hancock had stayed long enough to alert Papoo and Constantine to her return. Of course. The woman had had pointed comments to make about the convenience of family emergencies that allowed *Doctor* Koures to leave when the going got tough and return at will. Neither had she any qualms expressing her suspicions. She would surely have stayed long enough to warn them. Or perhaps Nanny had sent Mrs. Hancock packing.

Papoo stood for what seemed unending moments, his old heart unguarded. Vanessa felt the thickening of his throat in hers. Then at last he retreated.

When the door closed behind him, Vanessa's eyes welled over with tears of her own. She was without words even to think what it meant to her that Alex had taken her and managed to slip them both free of the bonds of time and earth. Alex who had brought her to the sense of completion, her womanhood and her passion given wings. And Alex who had found his own fathomless desire fulfilled by her.

But there could only be anguish waiting for her. Images of separation, like those she'd seen in the cold isolation of Alex's art passed through her mind. She was of another world altogether, the real world where little Sarah Gilles fought for the strength to undergo a second heart surgery, and happy endings followed nightmares if they followed at all. Vanessa couldn't not go back to it, just as Alex must return to his world. Soon.

She watched as he slept off the exhaustion of having made love to her, watched as dreams brought rapid movements to his eyes, watched as his mouth unconsciously sought her breast and his tongue dampened his lips. Pleasure ripped through her and intensified though she held back her answering cry. But he woke in that instant anyway, and the butterfly kisses of his lashes opening against her skin entranced her.

"Vanessa, *zoe mou*, my life," he whispered. "I love you."

And then misery shot through her because theirs was a love out of an uncertain eternity, born of his endless sleep and the things she could only have shared with a sleeping man. To speak of such love was to invite its ending.

She brought his seeking lips to her breast when he would have said again, *Vanessa, my life, I love you.*

"Papoo was here," she said, between waves of intense pleasure.

"Mmm," he murmured, while with his tongue and teeth he tugged at her breast. His fingers pulled at the soft curls between her thighs. "I heard."

"You did?"

"Yes."

"*Ornithon gala*—I don't know what that means. 'Bird something'?"

"Bird's milk," Alex answered.

"Bird's milk?"

"Bird's milk. Like . . . any marvelous good fortune." He teased Vanessa's nipple with the tip of his tongue. When he spoke again, his voice rasped with the unaccustomed strain. "Unlike a woman's breast, birds don't give milk, so if you happened upon one, it would be quite an extraordinary find. Papoo has been spouting 'bird's milk' good fortune for as long as I can remember. He believes in it, absolutely."

Vanessa struggled to rise above the sensations running along her nerves.

"He never spoke of it to me."

Alex swallowed. His voice was no more than a grating whisper. "He is old, *zoe mou*. Born to the ways and superstitions of a village that's existed for a thousand years. He made sure that each of my brother's wives held a child of each sex on her lap on the day of her marriage so that she would be blessed with many children. To him, to speak of extraordinary good fortune before it happens is to invite disaster.''

And to me, *andras*, she thought. Please, please speak no more of love where it cannot last, where it has no chance.

"He thinks you are my great good fortune." He pulled her down then, into his arms so that he could taste her lips. He took her face into his hands, and his mouth closed over hers and his tongue pressed hers until she couldn't think why such love had no chance anymore. Until she couldn't think at all, only answer him with her own hot, desperate-to-believe lips. His strayed away, dusting her precious face with kisses so needy, so poignant, so right. When he stopped, his lips settled against her fragile eyelids. "And that I have finally done what a man who is alive does with a woman."

Something so right, she thought, that it cannot be measured in mere moments, or pleasure, or by any moral standards.

Something so right, he thought, to withstand the loneliness of living in separate skins.

A little desperately Vanessa clung to him, her fingers deep in his hair. "Can anything so perfect exist in the real world, *andras*?"

He opened his eyes to hers, and discovered fathoms of pewter-blue in her eyes. He'd wake to another day, and another, just to discover the meaning of those gentle, absorbing depths.

"Ask Papoo if the vault of heaven exists. He'll discourse on the pros and cons for days. Ask him if good fortune exists, and he'll only nod." Alex wasn't a man to rely on luck or fate or good fortune. He believed in himself, in power and in operating from a position of strength. And yet he was beginning to discover the considerable charms of Papoo's bird's milk. How else could he account for Cat's presence in his life?

He had no answer for her. He only knew he was willing to settle for a lot less than *perfect*. Still, he sensed her doubt, and it scared him, and he wanted her off the subject of what was perfect and what wasn't.

"You weren't embarrassed when Papoo let himself in?"

"No. Papoo..." Her voice trailed off for a moment. "Papoo is...himself. Old and wise. He sees everything."

Alex could hear no shame in her voice, only acceptance and love for the old man who'd made her struggles here a little easier. But he heard something else in the fragile texture of her words, some fragment of unutterable sadness. "What does Papoo see, Cat?"

She shrugged artlessly and settled her head against the shoulder Alex offered. "Possibilities. He talked to you first, when no one thought it would matter. And...impossibilities." She drew a tight little breath and then another. "He sees passion, and because he's so old, he knows that it must pass."

An icy finger touched Alex's heart, and he refused to believe whatever Cat *thought* Papoo saw and knew. Defiant creature that she was, Cat had believed in him, in his ability to make it back for so long that her carefully camouflaged doubts now about the durability of their passion were like a talon at his throat. They had been as one for all the weeks that he had slept, of one purpose even when he fought her. Why couldn't she believe in its lasting?

He could barely speak now for the aching of his long unused vocal cords. "It doesn't have to pass, Cat. Sometimes it e-evolves, changing and growing into something special...something lasting and precious. Papoo had forty years with Eleni, Cat. Forty!''

But when his words weren't enough to silence her fears he rolled onto her and fastened his lips to hers to still their uncertainty and drove himself into her, again and again until she became one with him. And in the passion she'd only just discovered, her doubts were silenced once again.

ALEX WOKE TO DARKNESS softened by a wash of moonlight. His arm smarted, felt pin-pricked because Vanessa's head on his shoulder had cut off his circulation. But he was alive and awake, and stabbing pain was just a counterpoint to the ineffable joy swarming through him.

He supposed that with or without Cat lying here beside him, he'd have known joy. He might never again wake without it. But he might never have wakened at all without her. Without her promise of forever.

Forever. He remembered vividly his own uncertainty, his panic at the sincerity in her voice the day she'd said, "Wake up, Alexander *mou*, and I'll be yours forever." What did he know of forever, after all? Time without end seemed incomprehensible when he couldn't wake. Awake, forever was no less intimidating. But now he wanted Cat to be there with him ceaselessly, and Cat wanted him to accept their passion as a momentary, fleeting, here-today-but-gone-tomorrow thing. Such a thing as love discovered in a dream couldn't last, she thought.

He'd teach her otherwise. So help him, he would.

He eased his arm slowly from beneath Cat's head, as much because he couldn't move quickly as because he didn't want to wake her. He had to take a leak.

This trip to the bathroom was as desperate as his first. He thought to crawl, once, but the image of himself reduced to moving on all fours disgusted him. If a man had to crawl, how could he teach a woman the meaning of love that lingers a lifetime? He forced himself first to stand straight, and then to put one foot in front of the other. Again. Again. Again.

He accomplished his purpose in the dark. Then he sank naked onto the cool, glazed ceramic floor and wondered if he'd be able to get up again. Leaning his head back against the shower door he exhaled as sweat broke out on his upper lip. He ran a shaky hand through his hair and reached for a brush. The one he came up with was one of Cat's, not his.

He remembered her brushing her hair and the air crackling with electricity. The scent of her was there; the burnished, autumn red of a few strands caught and reflected stray moonlight pouring in through the frosted window. He put the brush to his head, dragged its natural bristles through his own thick, curling masses, and felt to the private core of himself the wealth of intimacy, his hair tangled with hers.

He never heard the approach of his father. Never guessed, either, that the powerful, respected man would lower himself to the indignity of a bathroom floor.

His voice gravelly, overcome with love and gratitude and uncertainty, Constantine gestured to the toilet. "Heard it flush." His eyes raked over Alex, again and again, as if to assure himself that a miracle had indeed been accomplished this day. "Hancock told us, of course. Then huffed out when Bates insisted 'Dr. Missy' would be taking over again."

Constantine offered his hand, Alex reached for it, and then threw his arms around his father's shoulders instead. Words, at least the manly words necessary to express their powerful ties and still more powerful relief, were beyond either one of them.

Alex was weak, knew he might be damnably weak for days, but he had no idea when his father's hug had grown so feeble, or just when the man himself had grown so old. Somewhere in his chest Alex felt wretched. "Pop."

Constantine sat back and flicked the tears from his eyes with a brush of his thumb. "She has come back."

Alex likewise leaned away, stretched out his legs in a slow agony and dispensed with a tear of his own. "Did you think she wouldn't?"

Constantine ignored the question, but his eye contact in the dark never wavered. "You slept with her."

Whether it was the sudden knowledge of his father's relentless aging, or the equally sudden gut-level feeling that he owed his father the truth, Alex nodded. "She is . . . was a virgin."

His father had lived too long, Alex supposed, to be startled. "Will you live with what you have done? With honor?" Alternatively, his father's eyes demanded, *Have you taken her virginity for nothing more than your own amusement?*

One might outlive surprise at life's vagaries, Alex thought, but Constantine Petrakis would never, should he rival the age and wisdom of Methuselah, outlive honor. Nor, Alex learned in that moment, would he. Slowly he shook his head no, he hadn't taken her with only his own amusement in mind.

"She is nothing like Elizabeth."

Elizabeth. Alex had meant to tell Cat. Elizabeth was gone. Gone as in forever. Her elopement with some rich Basque rancher had hit the society pages from Denver to Reno. He'd never expected anything else from her first and only visit. *I'm free,* Alex had thought in relief when

Papoo read him the society column of the *Post*. The loss of Liz was no loss at all. The loss of Cat would kill him.

"No. She's nothing like Elizabeth."

"Vanessa has dreams beyond you, and the capacity of her heart to realize them all."

"I have dreams, Pop."

"It takes more of a man to live with a woman's other dreams, Alexander."

Unexpectedly Alex felt his chest tighten. Or maybe his masculine ego swelling, protesting. "Are you asking if I'm man enough for her?"

"Perhaps," Constantine acknowledged, "but not for any reasons of the heart."

"I love her." Between them there had been no embarrassment for Alex's naked state, only the easy, back-to-the-ancients camaraderie of men in public baths. But now Alex felt his sex thickening because loving Cat—even giving voice to loving her—did that to him, and he raised his knee to shield himself from his father's knowing.

The protective movement wasn't lost on Constantine, nor its meaning, for his eyes gave Alex's no quarter. "That is no answer, my son."

"It's the only one I have."

"You love a figment of your dreams—"

"A flesh and blood woman—"

"A woman who would defy everything that's reasonable or holy—"

"Who told me once I am everything she was raised to love or expect—"

"—to bring you back." Constantine held up a hand to forestall Alex's easy answers. "Waking, in the real world, you know nothing of her but her body. She is a defiant soul. She'll fight as hard for a thousand others long after you're well."

It was true. He knew nothing of Cat's life or ambitions beyond the four walls of his own room in his father's compound. But he knew her intrepid spirit. She'd braved the contempt of her family, her fiancé, even her cultural heritage to leave home before marrying, to become a doctor, to stay so unwisely unattached. Maybe she had even cashed in on her virginity, made a deal with God. "Here Lord take it and give Alex back his life." But he didn't believe she'd done it without loving him.

He didn't believe she'd have made such a bargain for anyone else.

Alex's voice was the shadow of a whisper. "I won't give up, Pop. I'll do or become whatever it takes—"

"Then, my son, you must give back more to her than you have taken."

For the first time doubt crowded Alex. Cat had given him back his life, when even his father and Papoo had dared only hope for a miracle. And she'd handed him a second chance. Before Vanessa he'd reconciled himself to a relationship anchored in desperate, barren sex to overcome his aloneness. Sharing Vanessa's body would never be quite enough.

Between his father and himself it was understood; he'd already been given far more than a man had a right to expect.

SHE HAD ALREADY GIVEN more than a man had a right to expect.

The realization paralyzed Alex emotionally for days. He found himself less in control of his life now than before, and all his power over Cat's time and intentions evaporated into the thin mist of memory.

The morning after he came back to life, his hospital bed had been replaced with a real one, and Cat's not replaced at all. She moved into the room across the hall, and there was nothing, absolutely nothing Alex could say or do about it.

She had already given him more than a man has a right to expect.

Three mornings later, she met with Alex's cousin Mike, who flew in from Palm Springs to consult with her on the plans for her rehab center. While Alex wasn't excluded from the talks, he was unable to sit for long stretches of time at the planning table in his father's study, and still less able to contribute ideas of any substance. Cat's other passions quickened, but it wasn't any of his doing, and Alex resented the hell out of it all.

But she'd already given more than a man had a right to expect.

He thought the light in her eyes dimmed in spite of her eager plans. He might have chalked that up to his imagination, but every once in a while he got an overwhelming reminder of what had been between them.

She'd glance up from the sketches Mike drew to visualize some particular piece of her dream. And then their eyes would meet, and Alex could just about hear her heart pumping as wildly as his.

Or she'd touch his thigh in exercise therapy to demonstrate some particular muscle response she wanted. And something powerful would arc between them—a flash of sheer sexual energy.

Or he'd watch her lips while she told him in painful detail why his muscles weren't responding exactly as he wished, and he'd keep watching those sweet, sexy lips until she stopped her doctor-babble. Then he'd touch his fingers to her lips or let them graze her breast.

All that remained of what had been was his wanting her, and her wanting him, and no matter how she busied herself, the need between them was a tactile melody, flowing through every encounter.

His frustration fed on itself because he couldn't pick up where he'd left off. His body had to relearn its balancing strategies, coping with gravity in an upright position and a jillion other functions Cat was only too willing to explain in complete, scientific detail.

He learned far more than he cared to about minimal and maximal nerve stimulation, about action potentials, about myelin sheaths and the excitation of muscle fiber. He couldn't have cared less about *minimal* stimulation, and the only potential he cared about was regaining access to her heart. The only sheathing he was truly interested in was of himself sheathed in her. . . .

Then came the day the baby was baptized—John's new daughter whom John and Andrea named Alexis after her uncle. The family celebrated Alex's recovery as much as the babe's christening, and Alex had one hell of a time singing, toasting *yiassou* and drinking *ouzo*. When he held the infant, the image of Cat's body pregnant with his baby blossomed again.

He was just drunk enough to tell Cat about it.

She was just stunned enough to throw on her coat and take off running into the night before Alex knew what was going on.

By the time he found her in the freezing January night, he was shaking and chilled to the bone. And stone cold sober. She stood in the dark heated garage with her arms on top of her locked VW. And even then, not knowing where the chauffeur had put her keys and angry with Alex for spilling his dreams in front of his father and Papoo and the whole damn family, even then she came to him. She put her arms around him and drew close to his body to stop his uncontrollable shivering.

He clung to her and her warmth, and thought of Richard thwarting Catherine's escape from hell a dozen times over. If he didn't have the guts to do better by Vanessa than that, he deserved to lose her. His lips were numb with the cold, but he managed to ask if she'd leave him if he told her where she could find her keys.

Her head resting against his chest, she told him no, she wouldn't go that night. "I can't, Alex. God help me, not yet."

Relief swam through his veins. "About the babies, Cat." He worked his hand between them and beneath her coat and touched his fingers to a place just below her breasts and stroked down, down.

He swallowed. His throat ached.

She'd already given him more than a man had a right to ask. He'd just meant to tell her that the only thing he had to give her were his babies if giving himself wasn't enough. Now he saw that even babies were only his own selfish need.

"Cat." His voice was scratchy with emotion. "*Harato mou*, you may already carry my—"

She drew back from him. "No, *andras*. There is no baby."

Disappointment made him shiver again. He couldn't have said whether he was more disappointed because there was no baby, or in himself because he hadn't even noticed the pain and moodiness she was prone to, when she must have known for sure there was no baby. He stuffed his empty hands into his pant pockets.

Cat stuffed hers into her coat sleeves. "You will have babies, *andras*," she'd said, her voice ringing with emptiness. "They just won't be mine."

The only thing he had left to give her was himself, and she wasn't taking. Instead, every time he got close, she picked up her emotional baggage and moved back.

He'd had it. Right up to what Cat had once jokingly referred to as the "palpebral part of his orbicularis oculi"—his eyelids. He no longer cared if he ever had children of his own. With or without children, he wanted only Vanessa Koures.

HE DIDN'T KNOW where the next challenge would come flying from, or at what point she'd pick up her baggage and move back home again, but he was ready. It came the eighth morning, smack in the middle of his shaving, which he wished Cat was still doing for him.

She knocked. Knocked on the lousy bathroom door. As if she hadn't ever shaved him, as if she hadn't ever seen his naked chest, as if she hadn't walked into that shower fully clothed and then granted him every right to her body.

She stood at the door in a plaid wool skirt and a white, virginal, prim little blouse, her hair held up by a comb and her reason for leaving on the tip of her sexy little tongue. Alex's temper flared. He wanted nothing so much as to ride roughshod over every last vestige of her corked-up restraint.

He stood there with shaving cream on his face, with his razor held at half-mast somewhere between the sink and his beard, with his low-slung, hip-riding jeans bulging. His eyes fired warnings at Vanessa.

"Don't say it."

She tried to concentrate on his eyes, to counter their don't-cross-me-baby emotion, but her own eyes focused perversely on his tight, beaded nipples, buried in masses of excruciatingly male hair. Her own nipples answered in kind. Her eyes darted to his, held and then darted away again.

"I have to . . . go."

He turned more fully toward her and away from the sink, deliberately, so that his arousal was still more obvious. "Why?"

She swallowed. "Alex, don't."

His eyes glittered.

Hers retreated.

"Don't what?"

Make me want you . . .

"Make you want me?" he echoed her thought. "Make you want more to stay than to go?" He tossed the razor aside. It clattered and plopped into the stopped-up sink while he advanced on her. "I can't do that, Cat."

She trembled, but found her tongue at last. "I have an appointment with a little girl and her parents. Please . . . I have to . . . have to go. I have to."

"Then I'll go with you." He braced himself against the sink vanity, and tipped her head upward with his forefinger. And kissed her in spite of the shaving cream softening his beard. A slow, lazy kiss, tonguing her traitorous little mouth.

No breath left, she said, "Alex, you can't."

Heart beating too hard, he said, "Cat, I can."

Come then, she thought, the ache in her heart mounting right along with every sensation his eyes and his tongue and his lips brought her to. *Come see my world for yourself. Come see how our worlds can never mate no matter how well our bodies do.* Unable to look at the too-rapid pulsing of his heart beneath his ribs, she turned her head away.

Alex reached out to her and stroked her hair. "Cat," he murmured. "My sweet Cat. I have to know what I'm up against.'' Then the comb in her hair was gone, dropped to the floor, and his fingers weaved through her hair.

Vanessa couldn't help wanting to turn her face into his gentle, somehow desperate, somehow demanding hand. She couldn't help wanting to touch her lips to his palm or run her tongue the length of his fingers.

Alex wanted so badly to unravel her, to have her know the flames licking at him everywhere. It had been so long since her body had answered his in kind.... *Why won't you hear what's in my heart now, little one?*

She swallowed, and he knew how exquisitely reminded she was of his first swallow, his laughter, his need of her touch, his invasion of her dreams and finally her body. She thought of *Demon Alone*, thought that she had yet to finish it, and wondered what the point. Richard hadn't needed Catherine. Alex hadn't needed her, either. He'd known his way back.

''Finish shaving, Alex. We have to go in five minutes.''

He'd won. The elation lasted while she picked up her comb from the floor and while she replaced it in her hair. It lasted right up until Cat disappeared through his bedroom door, and then it didn't feel good or right—not like a victory after all.

Sarah Gilles. Alex learned her name, her condition and the gravity of it all on the way into town. He knew by the time Vanessa parked in the staff lot off Colorado and Seventh that Sarah was into cribbage and string games because the exertion level was just right for her, that she'd read *The Little Prince* a dozen times over, and that Vanessa wasn't giving up hope for the little girl anytime soon.

He warned her against slamming the door of his BMW the way she did her own car while he thought, *Vanessa, not my Cat.* The reality of her life apart from him hit Alex like a sledgehammer even before he saw Sarah. Reclining in the rehab labs, a spark leaping in her huge brown eyes, Sarah Gilles broke into tears the moment she saw Vanessa.

The two of them just looked at each other, hearts and minds communicating. Eyes telling all. And the fact that Vanessa, not his Cat, could share like that with anyone but him delivered another blow to his heart.

Those eyes, Alex thought, belonged to a ninety-year-old woman, not a child. Her gaze passed between Vanessa and himself and the first words out of Sarah's mouth followed on the shadow of a smile.

"He woke up!"

"Yes," Vanessa murmured, glancing his way with eyes sparkling, "he did, didn't he? Sarah, I'd like you to meet Alex."

What he heard was, *Alex, I'd like you to meet Sarah, the little girl who did without while I sold my soul to bring you back...*

Sarah Gilles had known about him and given up Vanessa's boundless support—for him. Alex understood in the still-rational part of his mind that the child's therapy had surely continued without Vanessa. In his own soul he doubted very much that in Sarah's place he'd have been half so generous as this sickly, needful little girl.

"Hi, Alex."

"Hi, Sarah." All he could think to do was turn tail and run. Instead he stuck out a sweaty palm to shake Sarah's fragile hand.

He watched while Vanessa shrugged into a lab coat, performed her bag of tricks and then slipped her own fingers in and out of a Cat's cradle with the little girl.

In the end Alex was left to Sarah and her ever-present telemetry box with the wire leads that disappeared into the neck of her child-sized hospital gown. Vanessa took the chance to speak alone with Sarah's parents.

Sarah looked at him for a long, searching moment. "You want to tame her, don't you?"

"Tame her?" Alex croaked.

Sarah nodded solemnly. "You know." Like in *The Little Prince*.

Alex reeled. Had he *heard* her, heard her thinking *The Little Prince*, or had his brain made the connection because Cat had told him the book was Sarah's favorite? "Wasn't it the fox who wanted the Little Prince to tame him?"

"Yeah! Remember? A flower tamed the Little Prince," Sarah explained, "and the fox said if you tame something then it will be unique in all the world to you, and you will be unique in all the world to—"

"—her." Yes, that's what he wanted. To be unique in all the world to Cat, and she to him. His throat tightened unbearably. Falling into the little girl's fantasy, he said, "Yes, Sarah. I would like that very much. What must I do to tame her?"

Again her wide-eyed look reminded Alex of an ancient soul, and her expression told him that she considered him a lot worse off than herself. "You must be very patient, and sit a little closer every day."

Sarah recited the part of the story in which the fox was tamed by the Little Prince, and Alex listened to every precious word. After a while, from the corner of his eye he saw Vanessa appear in the doorway. Somehow he knew that Cat was excited; somehow he knew that she'd been watching Sarah's heart monitor for a while, and something she saw there pleased her very much.

Cat's smile lit a small fire in his gut.

"What's going on here, Sarah? You haven't thrown a PVC in twenty minutes!"

Alex looked questioningly at Sarah, who winked at him conspiratorially. "Premature ven-TRICK-ular contractions," she interpreted. "Don't foxes say the funniest things!"

Foxes certainly did. Alex smiled. He had an ally in little Sarah Gilles. The problem was, patience had never been his strong suit, and he could only sit a little closer every day if Vanessa stopped backing up.

He borrowed Sarah's copy of the Little Prince and sat reading it for an hour while therapists, interns and residents came at Vanessa from fifty directions with greetings, inevitably followed by questions. Did Dr. Koures think Mr. Hayes might safely go on to a seventy-five percent HR max reserve? Mrs. Fenoglio was having inappropriate bradycardia on the prescribed protocol. Did Vanessa think they ought to back off to early Phase I?

He'd just finished reading Sarah's book when a wheelchair-bound man, one of the computer technicians, came looking for Cat. "Dr. Koures, we've got to get the biomed guys up here. The computer imaging is glitching again and I can't figure out what's wrong with it."

Vanessa tossed her clipboard onto a countertop. "Don't tell me. You called and they'll get to it in a couple of hours."

The tech nodded. "Roughly translated, two hours from now—next Tuesday."

"Are you sure you can't patch together something? If we have to wait—"

"Cat." Alex slapped Sarah's book shut and tucked his shirt more firmly into his jeans as he stood. "Maybe I can help." *There are ways,* harato mou, *and then there are ways....*

The tech looked questioningly at Vanessa. *Don't start insinuating yourself into this,* her eyes warned Alex, but she made the introductions anyway. "Tom Sheffley, Alex Petrakis."

"Tom." Alex reached out and the two men shook hands. "I've done a fair amount of work on computer imaging. What's the problem?"

Tom shrugged in Vanessa's direction. "We may not get a better offer for days, Doc."

What's the harm, Cat?

"It won't work, Alex," she protested softly.

He knew she wasn't talking about the computer. She was talking about his ability to fit into her world. "That's the problem, Vanessa. It won't work." He meant to remind her of the forever she'd promised him.

She knew he meant the computer. And that he wasn't going to play fair or give up on them if he had to sit fixing every damn imaging computer in the whole Med Center.

He found the problem, helped Sheffley hack it out and sat through a dismal, tasteless lunch in the hospital cafeteria with Vanessa and Nick. His cousin spent the entire twenty-two minutes directing you-lucky-son-of-a-bitch vibes at Alex.

And then he sat through the silent ride out of Denver and back into the foothills before he hit upon the solution to keeping Vanessa still while he followed Sarah's plan to sit a little closer each day.

"I want to move back into my house. Tonight." Watching her closely, he didn't miss the whitening of her knuckles on the steering wheel of his BMW.

"Why?"

What the hell, Petrakis? he thought. Lay it out for her. "I want you there. I don't want you to leave. I need you to stay with me."

Vanessa glanced quickly toward him and then back to the winding mountain road. "I haven't left you, Alex."

"The hell you haven't!"

"I'm right across the hall—"

"In another room and another bed in my father's house."

"You make it sound like another universe!"

"It might as well be, Cat. We deserve a chance—"

"We don't—"

"What happens between us deserves a chance," he persisted, "and if moving out of my father's house is what it takes, then that's what I want."

She missed the turn into the compound, kept going up into the hills, driving unconsciously. "Moving out isn't what—"

"Isn't it?"

"Don't you get it, Alex? Didn't you get a bellyful of reality back there? I have Sarah and a whole rehab lab filled with patients counting on me!"

"Do you think I'm not man enough to deal with others counting on you?"

"You don't know what it is to deal with, Alex!"

"No. I only know what it's like to be the one counting on you." Alex sank lower into the bucket seat, stretching his legs as he'd have been unable to do in Cat's VW. He pinched the bridge of his nose and reached mentally for strength to make his admission. "Counting on you— counting on anyone makes me feel . . . impotent. Bloody impotent."

Vanessa flinched against his choice of words. *Impotent*. More common than the common cold, more destructive to her patients' self-esteem than...anything. Clearly it hadn't affected him physically. Her heart faltered with sweet, visceral memories of the ways he'd made love to her.

Just as clearly she knew that rejection of any garden variety now could still devastate him.

"And yeah," he continued pensively, "it scares the hell out of me. And yeah, I...maybe I feel a little threatened. But when I think of the alternative, Cat, of not counting on you—"

Threatened. Funny, she'd have labeled *herself* "threatened." "You weren't raised to depend on a wife— I mean a...woman who—"

"*Gyneka*. Woman or wife," he interrupted quietly. "My father called my mother *gyneka*, always. Even a Greek can rise above his upbringing, Cat."

Unable to accept either his reassurances or the parallel between them and his parents, Vanessa pursed her lips against the trembling. "I must—"

"All I want is for you to come home to me. Spend ten hours a day fixing up Sarah, and Mr. Hayes with the 75 per cent HR, and Mrs. Fenoglio with the inappropriate cardia—"

"Bradycardia." Funny, how touched she was that he'd remembered those names, those *people*. Nothing angered her quite so quickly as the pervasive habit of medical types to reduce patients to cases. Nothing could have pleased her more than Alex remembering. She shut the quietly powerful engine of the BMW off and only then realized she'd driven to the plateau where she'd seen the buck and the doe. "It's an undesirable slowing of the heart rate, unlike tachycardia which..."

Alex's fingers reached to caress her cheek. "Which is a very desirable...acceleration of the heart?"

Her voice was a whisper, "Yes."

His was husky. "Please."

"*Andras*! You can't be alone that long each day. You're not up to it."

"I'm not up to being alone at all, *harato mou*."

His eyes reflected primitive need, and her heartbeat crescendoed in her throat.

"Come here, Cat." He offered her a hand.

"Now?"

"Now."

Slowly, her eyes floundering in the golden depths of his, she undid her seat belt. Slowly she wriggled out of her seat to straddle him in his.

Alex pulled the comb from her hair and plunged his hand into russet tresses. His kiss was everlasting and tender, his fevered touch desperate. Up, up her thigh to the garter, under it, into her panties, sinking into deeper sable-dark red curls.

A groan tore through his lips, consort to the cry on hers. She reached for his pant fly, her hands helpmate to his swollen sex. Beyond thought or hesitation or waiting she lifted herself to take him, all of him, into herself.

Her panties tore away in his hand. Driving, thrusting upward, Alex arched into her, lost in the tight, slick, undulating sensations of her small body coaxing him rhythmically, farther and farther into her until it wasn't her body anymore, but the very soul of her that he entered.

"Vanessa . . . Come with me, *gyneka mou*, come with me."

"Alex," she cried. "*Andras*. Yes, I'll come with you."

He thought, if he thought at all, that he'd die of intense, abiding pleasure. The very muscles that thwarted him time and time again in his therapy acceded to the ageless, time-unending thrusts of male into female, man unto woman.

Vanessa clung to him, rocked with him, and thought, if she thought at all, that she'd wither and die without him.

At last his body relaxed and she sank with him, her hands bunching into the fabric of his coat. His arms encircled her, holding her to him. He buried his face in her hair and struggled for a normal breath.

"Vanessa. I can't be alone again. Not ever again. Come with me."

She swallowed hard. He hadn't called her Cat, or used her promise of forever to beat her into submission. He'd called her Vanessa, and somehow opened himself up against the very real possibility that she'd refuse him. This man, this Greek man to whom power was a birthright and feminine submission a given, had left himself wide open, as vulnerable as a man can get.

Nor had she, in her whole life, been so thoroughly defenseless.

Chapter Ten

"WAIT! STOP the car."

"Here?"

"Here," Alex nodded, eyeing the expanse of snow-covered lawn in front of the Petrakis mansion. "Run with me."

"Run with you? Alex, have you lost your—"

"No, I haven't lost anything." Throwing his door open, Alex hefted himself out, only to poke his head back in. Grit mingled endearingly with anticipation in his eyes. "I'm going to take a dash through the snow. You can either be a chicken outfit and drive on around up to the house, or you can *try* to beat me there on foot. Which is it going to be?"

He might never run out of ways to overwhelm her. Still flushed and wanton from his loving, she licked her lips in a blatant siren fashion. "Why? Are you so sure you can take me?"

"I already have, *gyneka mou*," he teased, his grin as evil as grins come, his inflection randy. "But you smell like me, you look like you've had sex, and if you don't run with me, even Nanny will guess what we've been up to."

Her tongue tied in a knot, Vanessa was flooded with fiery embarrassment.

"Crimson becomes you, wench."

"That does it!" she cried. "No mercy for the gimp!"

Her door flew open, and she was out of the car before Alex could respond. And maybe because he gave no thought to the possibility that he'd stumble and fall, Alex maneuvered around the car and ran.

She ran like the wind, but in spite of herself Vanessa had to stop and look back to check on him. But when she did, he caught up with her. Came flying at her. She laughed and screamed and cried for joy at his rediscovered agility. "Alex!"

Too late. He crashed into her and they fell into an enormous, cushioning snowdrift, Vanessa on her back, Alex on top of her, pinning her hands in the snow high above her head. "Gimp? Gimp? Take it back!"

"Never!" she shrieked playfully, with what little breath was left in her.

"Okay," he said, but the devil in his eyes said otherwise. Quite the otherwise.

"Alex, what are you up to?"

"Nothing, Cat, I swear it. Have it your way. Really. I insist." Slowly, taunting her with tongue kisses at her throat, he brought one of her hands to the threshold of his coat pocket. "Are we having fun, Cat?"

"No!"

"Sweet liar," he murmured between otherwise-occupied lips. "Where are your panties, Cat?"

"Oh, no!" Jerking uselessly up against him, she felt her hand being drawn into his pocket. There he let her fingers brush against her own torn silk undies. She felt like a child playing "hot potato." "Alex! How can I go in there with snow in my hair and my panties in your pocket?"

The teasing in his eyes softened to cherishing. "The same way you endured Papoo's interruption?"

"Alex." His name on her lips was almost as endearing and special to her as his kiss. "Give them back to me."

The look in his eyes became possessive. "They're mine, *gyneka*. Mine. Got that?"

More, more by far than her panties were his. "Yeah, *andras*. I got that."

"That's good, Dr. Missy, very good. Because there is much, much more that's mine, as well."

PAPOO CLUNG TO THEM, each in turn, heaping Greek blessings. Nanny snuffled over the enormous picnic basket she had filled to overflowing. Constantine caught Alex fingering something in his pocket, and connected it to the flush on Vanessa's face. Alex smiled. His father cried. Vanessa glowed.

Alex and his father and Papoo poured *ouzo* in the study and smoked rare cigars while Nanny drew Vanessa aside for her own kind of blessing. Pouring hot tea for them both, she sat down at the kitchen table with Vanessa with tears in her eyes.

"These are some consequences Alex is payin'. You were supposed to give him just enough of your heart to bring him back!"

Vanessa drew an unsteady breath. "I did, Nanny. He took the rest."

"All of it, Dr. Missy?"

"All of it that counts."

"And the part that belongs to the others y' care for?"

Vanessa nodded. "Alex met a few of my patients this morning. He says . . . he told me he knows what it is for them to be counting on me. He says he only wants me to come home to him at night."

Nanny clutched at Vanessa's hands. "And y' believe him, lass, truly believe him?"

Vanessa remembered Alex saying how unutterable the alternative to counting on her was. How he loved her. How he couldn't be alone anymore.

"I *have* to help those people," she explained. "He may never really understand, but he spent two hours this morning helping my computer tech fix a problem. And mostly..." Mostly he'd never lied to her, or spoon-fed her platitudes, or gilded the truth. Mostly she had to believe that he meant to accept who she was and what it was she had to do. "I have to think he believes we'll make it together."

Nanny sat back and breathed tremulously. "Y' will, darlin' lass. I've never seen Alex believin' in what he couldn't make happen."

"No, Nanny. I haven't, either."

Nanny clung to Vanessa's arm while they walked out to the entry hall. "May all the angels in heaven be lookin' after y' both.... I guess everthin' is turning out at last. Young Chris will be taking His Greekness back to Crete in a couple of days."

"I'm glad for him, Nanny, but what are you going to do when we're all gone?"

"Pshaw." Nanny sniffed as she rapped at the door to Constantine's study. "I've plenty to keep me busy."

The men wandered out of Constantine's study. Papoo to his greenhouse in search of an airy, flourishing fern to brighten their home. Nanny snuffled some more. Constantine went after the BMW, muttering something about it being a lucky thing the battery still worked what with the lights left on and the doors wide open. He carried one load of belongings out to the car, and then another, and finally the mother plant to Sarah Gilles's staghorn fern.

Vanessa put on her coat again while Alex hugged his father and grandfather.

"Never forget your extraordinary good fortune," Papoo said. "And live forever in your joy."

We will, Papoo. We will.

I know.

Constantine looked on with tears in his eyes. *I see,* yie mou, *my son, that you have indeed contrived to give back to her some of what she has given you.* And although those words were not spoken aloud, either, Alex heard his father's sentiment.

He put on his coat while Vanessa hugged the father of her heart, and his father. There were no words left, not even silent ones, to express the joy in any of their hearts.

IT WAS ALL Vanessa could do to drive Alex's car to Alex's house. Smiling broadly, he fingered the lace in his pocket. Nor could she smother her not-so-secret smile. She insisted he rest while she lugged in the boxes, suitcases and picnic basket. Alex's idea of resting was to build a roaring fire in the Franklin stove in his bedroom. Then they opened Nanny's picnic meal and settled onto Alex's enormous water bed, his legs spread-eagled, hers crossed Indian-style between them.

"Artichokes!" Vanessa exulted.

"And Sparkling Zin."

"Hearts of palm! What's a heart of palm?"

"Open the can and find out."

"With what? My teeth?"

Alex handed her a can opener Nanny had provided, and smiled. Lecherlike. "Save your teeth, *harato mou.*"

"For what, *koukla,*" she asked, all innocence.

"With what, for what," he mimicked. "Must I show you *everything*?" Calmly, deliberately, he peeled away the foil wrapping, shook the bottle and then just as deliberately pointed the neck of the Sparkling Zin at Vanessa. "I almost tore that prim and proper little white blouse off you this morning. I'm glad I didn't, because now—"

"Alex, don't you dare—"

Too late. With expert aim he let the cork fly wide of her, but the spray of wine plastered her blouse to her breasts. Vanessa gasped. The heated look in his eyes countered with sweet intensity the cold shock, and both combined to draw her nipples out like stars in the dark of night. The fire flickered, casting sensual shadows over her.

"There," he murmured. "That's . . . better."

"Give me the bottle, *koukla*," she commanded softly. "Fair is fair."

He held the bottle above his head. "Come and get it, Cat."

Knowing what would happen, knowing that to go after it meant putting her wine-sodden breasts in range of his lips, she braced her knees against the gentle motion of the water bed and reached. Knowing what would happen only heightened the icy-hot frisson shooting through her.

His arms went around her waist, his legs managed to lock around hers.

"I'm thirsty, Cat. So . . . thirsty."

"I . . . please."

Knowing and feeling were poles apart. His tongue stroked at the underside of her breast, and Vanessa shivered.

"Alex!" Vanessa's breath caught in her throat in long ecstatic moments.

Tremors rocked through Alex as he finally lay back. "Ahh, *harato mou*, my joy. We're getting ahead of ourselves."

The weariness in his voice brought Vanessa back to cold, hard realities. "Alex. You're tired."

"I'm hungry."

She moved to sit up by his side. He let her go. "You're exhausted! We should never have tried to do this tonight."

"We had to. I'm hungry. More than hungry, I want—"

"What, Alex? What do you want?"

"I want you to stop thinking of me as an invalid, Cat. As somebody who needs taking care of."

Her heart swelled with tenderness. "Shhh, *andras*. If it were me, if I were sick, wouldn't you take care of me?"

"I'm not sick. I'm not tired, either—"

"Tired is okay, Alex. Answer me! Would you? Would you take care of me?"

"Of course—"

"Can you be so sure?"

"Yes."

"Then let me, Alex. Let me. Please." And then, because he could only look wordlessly at her, she took the bottle of wine from his hand and hurried on. "What would you like? Artichoke?"

"Yeah. Artichoke."

"We'll make a picnic of it, and then we'll go to sleep. Okay?"

Clearing his throat, he said, "Yeah. Then we'll go to sleep." He turned onto his side and supported his head with one bent arm.

In just a few seconds Vanessa spread a checkered tablecloth beside Alex, set out the whole, cold artichokes and placed the mayo-lemon sauce close to his chest. "There."

She pulled a leaf from hers, and Alex, from his. She dipped its fleshy base, and he dipped his. But when she would have brought the treat to her mouth, he stalled her wrist with his.

"A toast, *gyneka.*"

"We didn't pour any wine—"

"No need." He touched his leaf to hers. "Forever."

Echoing him, a silent prayer in her soul, she promised again. "Forever.... Did you know that artichokes are an aphrodisiac?"

"Leave it to Nanny," Alex groused. "Do you suppose she thought I needed it?"

"You're being too sensitive, *andras.*"

"Maybe. Or impatient."

"You have to be patient with yourself. And with me. I don't usually begin affairs of the heart with my—"

"Patients. See what I mean? Aw, hell, Cat. I wanted to make love to you again, not lie here moaning. I . . . come here. Lie with me."

She gathered together the remains of their small feast and set it down on the floor near the bed, then slipped back into his waiting arms.

For long moments she lay there, her head on Alex's shoulder, watching the firelight flickering on the ceiling. His breathing was so even she began to think he'd fallen asleep. The purposeful stroking of his hand on her hip changed her mind.

"I never found out what hearts of palm are."

"Just like the heart of a 'choke, Cat, that's all."

"Have you been the world over?"

Alex kissed the top of her head. She could feel his smile, and hear it in his voice. "Does that have something to do with hearts of palm?"

"In a way." Her hand began unbuttoning his shirt. She wanted closer, to feel the springy masculine texture of his chest hair against her cheek. "When I saw your art I felt, I don't know, provincial, maybe? I've never seen a heart of palm, either."

"Yeah, I've been a lot of places, but...there's nothing provincial about you, Cat. The things you know—"

"Tell me about them. Take me to all those places, Alex. Now. Tell me which is your most favorite."

His nipple rose to the idle stroke of her fingers. "Here, *harato mou*. Of all the places I've been, here in my bed with you is my favorite."

"Mmm." The touch of his fingers along her spine made her shiver. "Where would we be if we were in bed together somewhere else?"

"New Zealand. Maybe we'd be making love in a Christchurch bed and breakfast. Or maybe a Maori hut. Or a bed of moss under a waterfall. I've never seen a more compelling country. They call it a land born of fire and ice."

"Volcanoes?"

"Yeah. And glaciers. Fjords and thermal geysers. The one called the Prince of Wales Feathers is the geyser in one of my photographs. Other places you'd swear there isn't a single square inch that isn't green."

"They're beautiful, Alex."

"What?"

"Your photographs. All of them...but my favorite is *The Man Woman* holograph."

"Mine, too." Now more than ever, because in his heart it was tied forever and closely to Cat.... "There's a place in Stamford, Connecticut, where they display holographic projections. They've even got one of the guy who came up with the technology. It's so perfect people actually wave at him."

Vanessa swelled into Alex's chest, and her tongue nuzzled the nipple buried in his firelit hair. "Did you . . . wave?"

"No, but I'd read about it long before I saw it. The technology, the art—it's seductive." His fingers reached for the buttons on her blouse and began easing them open. "Do you even own a bra, *gyneka*?"

"No." Rampant crazy sensations bedazzled her. "What would be the use?"

"The size of your breasts is unimportant, Cat," he scolded softly. "That they respond to me like this—" His fingers did to her small exquisite breasts what his scattered thoughts could not find words to say.

"What's so seductive about holographs, Alex?" It seemed a provocative challenge to see if they could keep talking while their bodies cried out for more.

"You see something from one angle, but that isn't even a fraction of the whole. Stand somewhere else, and you see something new. You're continually drawn to look for more."

"Have you missed that all these months?" Her fingers worked at his zipper, then closed around him.

"No." His arm tightened around her and he rolled to his side, facing her. "I was drawn into you instead." He thrust into her hand, his eyes locked on hers. "Day after day I lay in that bed, thinking I should get the hell out of it. But then you'd be there, and no matter where I came from in my head, I'd discover something new. You made me laugh. You made me cry. You made me so horny I thought I'd die."

She lifted her leg over his hip and guided him to her.

"You poked and prodded and coaxed—ah, *harato mou*." Each word was accompanied by a deeper shallow stroke until she thought she'd die if he didn't come fully into her—and then he did. "And then you promised me forever."

He held her to him, his eyes courting hers, plunging them both into a daring rhythm, and still he whispered, "You talked to Papoo as if his faded old dreams were the only dreams in the world, and then you made mine come true." He drove into her, more deeply still.

"You were always, always new and special, and I thought, I can't wake up, not now. How was I supposed to give you up? I still don't know, Cat, but I was so scared when you left. So damn scared."

And then he was without words. He rolled to his back, taking her with him, and their bodies soared. But in her heart, and in his, his fears and hers were replaced by an infinite, abiding peace.

INFINITE, ABIDING PEACE. Vanessa and Alex. Alex and Vanessa. His name and hers, linked together forever. She envisioned herself in his arms, safe from an ever-after of loneliness. She imagined the peace of a Christchurch bed and breakfast, the primitive joy of a Maori hut, the timelessness of making love with Alex on a bed of moss beneath the curtain of a New Zealand waterfall.

Then in the waxing light of dawn the beeper in her purse shattered the images of South Pacific bliss. The summons could mean only one thing—that Sarah Gilles had gone from serious to critical.

Fear slashing through her, Vanessa eased out of Alex's arms. She grabbed for the beeper, listened intently for the phone number and recognized it for the cardiac intensive care unit at University Hospital. She stabbed out the numbers on the touchtone in Alex's study and only then realized his line had been disconnected.

"Dammit! Sarah..." she cried. "I'm coming, sweetheart."

Her body battled the lethargy of a night's loving and her heart the anguish of leaving Alex alone. But Alex would wake up, and Sarah could be on the operating table, fighting for her life. Nothing mattered so much at this moment as getting there for Sarah.

Vanessa dumped her purse onto Alex's antique carpet, snatched her toothbrush and paste and headed for the bathroom. In something short of five minutes she'd showered, dressed in jeans and a sweater and found the keys to Alex's BMW.

She'd call him later. No, she couldn't. The phone line was dead. Hurriedly, she reached into one of the boxes she had carried in the night before for something to write on. Her fingers encountered *Demon Alone*. She slid it along the floor toward her purse, and then dashed off a message on the back of some research papers.

"Alex," it read, "Sarah's very bad—in cardiac ICU—took the BMW—would call but can't—Back ASAP—Yours—V."

The drive from the southwest Denver suburb was a nightmare. Who'd have thought there would be so much infuriating traffic at dawn? But there was. She sped up Broadway, turned east on Sixth, and proceeded to shatter the speed limit.

When she got there she found a very frightened but heavily sedated little girl connected to a respirator, three separate IV lines, and a heart monitor recording tachycardia and irrationally frequent PVCs. Passing in and out of consciousness, Sarah clung to her hand.

Vanessa didn't recognize the smooth-faced intern on the cardiac service. Haggard and gangly, he looked grimly up at the monitor through thick glasses.

"Is she scheduled for the O.R. yet?"

The intern shook his head. "Can't till she settles down. At least that's what I'm told."

Can't wait, either, Vanessa thought, but a surgeon had to make that decision, and she was no cardiac surgeon. "Where are Bonnie and Sean?"

"The parents? Markson's office."

Vanessa knew Todd Markson. If he thought he could take Sarah to surgery, he'd have done it in a flash. "He's got about two minutes," the intern warned, "before he's due to crack open somebody else's chest. Who are you?"

No matter how many times she heard it, the coldly dispassionate lingo didn't get any easier to take. Her stomach rolled over into knots at the very suggestion of Sarah's body being so ravaged in the name of healing. "Vanessa Koures. I've been—" *off falling in love* "—on a sabbatical of sorts. Sarah was under my care after her first operation back in October."

He nodded. "Koures. Markson speaks highly of your rehab lab. I take it she didn't do very well."

"For a while, she did." *Until I left.* But Vanessa turned away from the guilt setting up house in her conscience. The stop-gap surgery Sarah had undergone was just that—stop-gap. No one involved had any illusions to the contrary; only Vanessa had held out any hope that the precious little girl's respite would last longer than it had.

"I was here yesterday morning. Sarah went through an extended time without throwing any PVCs." *Alex.* Alex had been with Sarah then. Coincidence? Probably. "Look, I know this is kind of unorthodox, but I'd like to turn off these lights. I'll stay with her."

The intern shrugged. "Whatever you say. I'll kill the lights and okay it with the charge nurse."

"Thanks."

The weary young doctor ambled out, and Vanessa left Sarah long enough to search around for the worn copy of *The Little Prince*. Sarah whimpered softly.

"Shh, sweetheart. I'm still here. Shall I read to you about the Little Prince?"

"It's dark . . ." Sarah whispered.

"Only so you can sleep, *koukla*. But I can sit here by the window, hold your hand and read, too. Where shall I start?"

The ghost of a smile played at Sarah's still-bluish lips. "Chapter twenty-five."

Vanessa read. The chapter was about the anniversary of the Little Prince's descent to earth. A peculiar sadness lingered, for the main character was filled with a fear of losing his friend, this magical little prince. It ended, "I was not reassured, I remembered the fox. One runs the risk of weeping a little, if one lets himself be tamed . . ."

"Don't foxes say the funniest things?" Sarah had said to Alex.

THE DAY WORE ON. Nick came. Nurses bustled around endlessly while Bonnie and Sean Gilles paced anxiously in the ICU waiting room. Sarah rested more easily as Vanessa read on and on from the storybook. The surgery was set for seven o'clock that night.

Nick came by again. "Hi, sweet stuff. You want to go get a cup of tea?"

Vanessa shook her head. "I need to be here, I think."

"What you need is to get out for a while, Van. Besides, I learn my lessons well. I just asked. You can't let that go unrewarded."

"Nicholas..."

"Okay, okay. I get the picture." He disappeared into the ICU lounge and returned with a stale donut and two cups of tea. He handed her the donut and one Styrofoam cup, then pulled up another chair. "Now talk."

Vanessa took a bite of chocolate off the top of the donut and glanced at Sarah's monitor. "What do you want to hear, Nick?"

"How's Alex. How's Vanessa and Alex?"

A slow, satisfied smile crept onto her lips.

Nick rolled his eyes. "Say no more, 'he begged'."

Her smile gave way to laughter. "Really? 'He *begged*'?"

"Begged? Who me? A Petrakis never begged, Van. Never. So tell me more."

She was only too willing to tell him more. "I'm happy, Nicholas. Truly, truly happily-ever-after happy. We went home to Alex's house last night. We drank some Sparkling Zin and toasted forever with some artichoke leaves and—" Nick's expression stopped her. "What? What did I say?"

"If you're talking happily-ever-after, Van, why were you so upset when Alex started spouting off, the night John's daughter was baptized, about filling your belly with his babies?"

Shock went through her like a blizzard. And then anger. "Dammit, Nick, will you ever get off his case?" she cried. "What do you want me to say, that he's a selfish bastard with no thought of anyone's happiness but his own? Dammit!"

She hurled the crusty donut remains into the trash, and then, realizing Sarah still lay sleeping uneasily in her intensive care bed, forced her voice lower before he had a chance to answer. "If that's what you think, Nicholas, you're wrong! Alex was desperate enough to think loving me wasn't enough, that he could *give* me his babies, and maybe somehow that could make up for the rest!''

Nick bounded out of his chair to slide the door to Sarah's unit closed. "Take it easy, will you please?"

"No, Nick, I won't take it easy! Every time we talk about Alex I wind up defending what I've done—"

"That's not true, Van." He interrupted angrily, his voice a harsh whisper. "Last time we talked about Alex, *I* was defending the things you've done. Remember? I just want you to think about why you ran away when Alex started talking babies. What is it his babies should make up for, Van? Your father's life? Sarah's? What?"

The anger seeped out of Vanessa by degrees, leaving her defenseless. She'd spent her whole life trying to make up for those things, for her father's wreck of a life, for other people like him, for other people's babies like Sarah Gilles. And if she had a dozen babies of her own, none of that would change. She'd still go on fighting for them all, defying their deadly aches and their truly broken hearts. But how very special to have her own babies. Alex's babies.

How very unique....

At last Vanessa discovered Sarah's meaning. It was she, Vanessa Georgina Demetra Koures, who, like the Little Prince's fox, had been tamed. First by a little girl named Sarah Gilles, and then by a man named Alex Petrakis.

Alex. He was the prince of her dreams, the one man on earth able to ease her heart's longings. To Vanessa, unique in all the world.

She smiled at Nick through tears that put prisms and rainbows on everything she saw. She had only now discovered for herself why she'd fled from the specter of her body in bloom with Alex's seed.

"I ran, Nicholas, because in my heart of hearts I was sorry there was no baby already."

Chapter Eleven

ALEX DISCOVERED HER MISSING from his bed, discovered a trail of her clothes, and then discovered her hastily scribbled note atop a box of her things. None of his discoveries made him happy.

He considered flying into a jealous rage, then he felt like a heel. After all, he'd met Sarah. How could he even half-heartedly begrudge the ailing child the comfort of Cat's presence?

He considered throwing on some fresh clothes, calling a taxi and going after her, then remembered the phone was dead.

He considered tearing up the earth to find someone who could fix up Sarah's heart once and for all, so he wouldn't have to feel so contemptibly guilty for wanting Vanessa back. Was it so wrong to want her back, *now*?

He decided, finally, to just sit back and try to figure out if there was a limit to Vanessa's caring and compassion. Or if he could deal with being so vulnerable to her.

For a while he paced. He knew the word *vulnerable*, could cite its etymology, meanings and implications. He had even put it to devastating use in his screenplays. But Alex Petrakis was not—repeat not—vulnerable. Or defenseless or powerless or thin-skinned or naive.

"Yours—V," her note had said. The cynic in his head said otherwise—Yours and Sarah's and Hayes's and Fenoglio's and a parade of other, future walking heart attacks..." Renewed guilt shut the cynic's voice up.

He slept for a while, then woke up and consumed an entire loaf of Nanny's homemade bread with crabapple jelly. He slept again and then showered. He poked steadily at the fire. All day long he stoked it with Ponderosa pine until the flames leaped high and crackled some poor semblance of conversation back at him. At last he pulled a box of Vanessa's papers to the foot of the water bed and leaned against it with his bare feet stretched out toward the fire.

Then he read and reread Vanessa's note.

To stifle the cynic's voice, he hurled the sheaves into the fire. And snatched them out again, beating the small flames out on his jeans. The papers were Vanessa's. Maybe important.

Idly, he turned them over. A yellow Post-It sticker, covered corner to corner in cramped handwriting, read, "VK: Final draft to JAMA eds,—assured publication July, in time to cite as a ref. your publication? Many thanks your time and revision suggestions. WR."

His meandering attention finally snagged, Alex lifted the sticker. He got so far as the title and cross-references. "Sexual Rehabilitation in the Cardiac-compromised Adult Male," by Walt Richards. "See also Rehabilitation, Sexual; Sexuality, Male; Surgical Implications, Sexual, Male Ego."

Inexplicably Alex's mouth went dry. He threw the papers aside and reached for the still-open bottle of Zin. It was flat, but it quenched his sudden thirst, and he felt its warming effects almost immediately. He glared at the faintly accusing papers, swore and picked them up again.

He read three pages into the body of the paper. His hands began shaking but . . . this had nothing to do with him. The writer in him began critiquing—verbose style, overblown, self important... Surely it had nothing to do with him. He hadn't suffered a heart attack. Still he brought the wine bottle to his lips three separate times and drank.

How about an aperitif of Hemlock, Petrakis?

He began to feel no pain. Wine was supposed to be the nectar of the Gods, but it was less ambrosial than Cat's lips. He'd never before taken so much as a sip of wine from a bottle. Chalices, yes. Glasses of every description. Even leather wineskins. But the bottle? Never.

Then he turned the page and found his name penciled in the margin next to an underlined paragraph. Cold shot through him like an Arctic wind through the Rockies. Numbly as if his fingers were frostbitten, he turned the papers over to compare the *A* in the Alex of Cat's note to the *A* in his name by the underlined words.

He began again to feel pain.

"The shame, Your Honor," he testified to an imaginary magistrate. Even he could hear the wine-induced slurring of his own words. "*Same*, I mean, but it is a bloody shame. Can't of course be absolutely certain without a positive graphoanalysis, but, Your Honor, consider the circumstances. Consider," he said, warming now to the prosecution, "the likelihood."

Alex began to read aloud.

"There can hardly be any single factor more crippling, indeed disabling, to the self-esteem and subsequent recovery of the physically compromised patient than a rejection of his sexual expression. Lest the patient suffer irrevocable damage and setback, physician, therapist, nurse and family must equally convey not only acceptance at the critical juncture, but approval of any and all appropriate sexual behavior, appropriate defined to include—"

He stopped reading, and the ache in his chest increased.

Now he knew. There were no limits to Cat's compassion. By her uncanny empathy she'd sensed his need, and responded. What else could she do? It was exactly as she had told Papoo. He could hear her giving the old man her steadfast assurances. But now he found that Alex Petrakis had been nothing more to her than the most recent and demanding object of her compassion—the physically compromised patient in desperate need of her sexual acceptance. She would do anything, whatever it took to redeem herself and take away the guilt she harbored for failing her father.

Or was it all—her touch, her touching confession, her lovemaking, her moving him home—all for the rehab center of her dreams?

A woman with dreams, his father had said. *It takes more of a man to deal with a woman's dreams...*

Numb, he wondered how much more wine it would take to blunt the throbbing ache. How much more to render himself senseless. How much more to forget pewter-blue eyes and lips more intoxicating than—

"Alex? Alex, where are you?"

Cat? Where are you?

He said nothing, couldn't have squeezed an answer past the throbbing pain in his throat if he tried. He dragged the wine bottle to his mouth one more time and drained it dry.

"Alex? Hi..." She tossed her purse onto the tangled bed clothes where just the night before... Peeled off her gloves... Stood there in her sexy-assed little jeans looking at him as if he were the only man on earth... What a laugh. What a goddamn belly laugh.

"Alex, you're... you're drunk!"

"Nope," he rasped. "Not even close, *harato mou*. Matter o'fact, I'm pleasantly tuned, and only just beginning to read the han'writing on wall—which is clever of me, don't y' think?" He tipped the empty bottle backward in his hand and examined its bottom, then hurled it at the Franklin stove. The clang was suitably loud but the bottle didn't shatter.

She sank to her knees beside him. Pleasantly tuned or tuned in, he felt the compassion rolling out of her in tidal waves. What else had he expected from the inestimable Dr. Koures?

"Alex, what's happened? What's wrong?"

"You left," he accused.

"Sarah is very sick—"

"I'm sick! Here," he said, thumping at his chest.

Her chin rose defensively. "Is this feel-sorry-for-Alex time?"

"Gee, I don't know." He brought his bare foot to the box containing her papers and shoved, hard. The box fell over behind her; manila files by the dozens slid out. "Got a paper on the proper handling of the belligerent, self-pitying, emotionally compromised male?"

"No! I—Alex, please! What are you—"

"You used me, Cat."

"I never—"

"No? Well, tell me this," he demanded roughly, and threw the scorched article into her lap. "Have you had one, even one genuine emotion since you came to me, or do you just soak up everyone else's and dole out the right responses like pain pills?"

Vanessa paled. His honey-shaded beard was unshaven, and his hair curled wildly. Naked but for his Levis, he fulfilled her every dream. Her lashes lowered, her wavering vision fixed on the damning papers. She knew without looking what they were.

Before her silence condemned her further, she answered him the only way she knew how. "This had nothing to do with why I . . . touched you, Alex."

I wanted you, Cat, not your charity.

Andras! I only wrote your name there when . . . afterward . . . later. Later, at my mother's house, when I was trying to justify to myself what I'd done.

But the time for hearing what the other only thought was past.

Her fingers tingled, ached with the tactile, sensual memory of his swollen sex in her hand, and his male flesh hardened, ached with the memory of that same, exquisitely poignant touch.

His eyes followed hers to the blatant evidence of his burgeoning response. His voice was gritty and thick with the hurt, "Gonna give a gimp another thrill, Cat?"

"You bastard!" Her hand shot out at him, but in spite of the wine there was nothing wrong with his reflexes. He caught her hand wide of his anger-flushed cheek.

Enraged, she jerked back, but he held tight. Their gazes crossed like fencing foils.

Monstrous disappointment overtook her. This was the prince of her dreams? Damned if she'd shed her tears for him.

The muscles in his jaw grew taut. Damned if he'd apologize for the truth.

The pain in her breast increased, but she hadn't lived for endless weeks with Papoo's rapier wit or Alex's devastating humor for nothing. Having learned her lessons well, she lashed out, aiming to wound as badly as she'd been wounded.

"Lighten up, Petrakis. My motives were far more selfish than that. It isn't ev—every gimp who has his way with a virgin, and anyway, I just needed a w—willing stud to do the honors."

Her black humor cut him to the quick. His Cat might use "gimp" in play, but never, never in such an ugly context. It shocked him, and for one stunned, inadvisable second his fingers relaxed. Vanessa jerked free of him. She was on her feet and out the door with her coat flying behind her before he could react.

"What the hell—"

The oak door in the foyer slammed shut against his imprecations. Stiffly he rose and went after her, opened the door and stepped bare-footed out into the snow. Vanessa was about to climb into his BMW.

"What the hell is that supposed to mean?" It was snowing hard, and the only sound in the darkness was that of his bellowing.

Fury riding high in her own heart, she turned on him. "Just exactly what it sounded like!"

Snow flakes piled on his shoulders and clung to the hairs on his chest, but he was beyond noticing. "Wait a minute, that's my car!"

Frustration built on her anger. "So it is!"

"Dammit, Cat, get your ass back in here, *now*!"

She reached for the car door and gave it a walloping good slam, then threw the keys at him and took off through snow, eight inches deep, in her five-year-old Reeboks.

Alex hopped back into the house and slammed *that* door, jammed his frozen bare feet into a pair of cowboy boots and jerked a sheepskin coat on over his naked shoulders.

Muttering every Greek, English and Portuguese profanity he knew, he went after her again. He followed in her tracks because seeing her through the thick snowfall was impossible. He stumbled once, and another time his feet almost went out from underneath him, but he ran until he caught sight of her dogged, narrow shoulders, and her small feet kicking through the drifts.

Finally he drew abreast of her. "Dammit, Cat, stop. Where do you think you're going?"

"To call a cab. Go home, Alex. Leave me alone."

For all the weeks that she'd manhandled him, his manhandling her was no problem. He stepped in front of her and grabbed her by the shoulders. His eyes in the light of a streetlamp promised her trouble. "No, you're not. Not until you tell me what you meant by that stupid remark back there!"

Oh, Alex you stupid, stupid man. Twice, *twice* she'd left a very special little girl to her own fragile devices for him. She crammed her gloveless hands into the opposite sleeve of her coat and stonily met his gaze. Snowflakes had the temerity to gather on his lashes instead of succumbing to the fire in his eyes.

How could she brazen this out? Fear coalesced into an icy certainty that she'd done him no favors. Loving him first had stripped away his masculine prerogative and he resented her, just as she'd always known he would.

"Get this straight, Alex. I saw my opportunity and I took it. Nothing more, nothing less. I used you."

A lie. He'd grown used to her chronic, endearing little lies, and this was one of them. He could hear it in her voice and see it in her daring, gut-this-one-out eyes. She was no more capable of using him than of turning her back on Sarah Gilles. Could she possibly have played sex surrogate to his needs without loving *him*?

He scraped a hand through his hair and shivered. "I can't live with your mercy, Cat." He could forgive her anything but her acts of humanitarian compassion.

"And I can't bear you thinking that, Alex." For what was love, if not an abiding mercy?

Desperate to erase the sense of losing her, Alex crooked an elbow around her neck and set a half-mad palm to her bottom, hauled her against him, and then crushed her lips to his. He had to know. Angry and upset, she wouldn't cooperate now if her compassion was all that had ever been between them.

Fury and love and every nameless fascination she'd ever known with him spilled into her blood. Her hands pulled free of her sleeves and met the warmth and furriness of his chest. Her breasts beneath her parka flattened against him, and her lips fell prey to the punishing, nipping, suckling pressure of his. Her fingers slid up the warm wall of his chest, and her left hand encountered the small scar left by the IV line. A renewed rage at what had happened to him played into her emotions.

Not fifty yards from a stranger's house, she began returning his bruising kisses. His tongue plunged into her mouth and hers fought back. His hand at her bottom lifted her closer, and her legs went around his, clinging. His hand sank into her snow-dampened hair and pulled, and she offered no resistance, only her throat with a daring sort of vengeance. *Here, take me.*

Against her frantically pulsing neck he commanded, "Say you love me, Cat."

"No!"

He relaxed his hold on her, and she slid to her feet. His hands cradled her cheeks, wet from the snow and his kisses, and his eyes drew hers. "Say it, Cat."

"No..."

He released her altogether, stood back and jammed his hands into his pockets. "Say it, Vanessa. I won't ask again."

"You haven't asked yet," she answered defiantly. "You've only *told* me—" But her heart was clamoring, and she knew if ever there was a time to shut up, this was it. Her eyes glanced heavenward and she swallowed her tears. "All right. I love you."

The breath he'd been holding gushed out, and he reached for her.

She skipped out of his reach. "I love you. But right now I'm going to walk up this hill and over it and into that Seven-Eleven and call a cab, and you'd better not try to stop me." *Yes. I love you—you stupid man!* "Loving someone and living with it are not the same thing, Alex. Or being so vulnerable to each other—and living with that. You figure it out." And for all her resolve, all her promises to herself, tears leaked onto her cold-blistered cheeks. "I guess we've discovered we're neither one will— willing to be that vulnerable, are we?"

Wind and bits of snow whipped through his open coat, and he shivered violently, but the cold outside was nothing like the cold inside him. He watched her turn away, watched her slow progress up the hill, watched until, she disappeared.

BY THE TIME Vanessa reached the Seven-Eleven and called a cab it was 2:00 a.m. Sarah Gilles was three hours postop, and in a second phone call Vanessa learned from the intern she'd met earlier that Markson had put Sarah's chances of surviving at one in five—better than expected, less than Vanessa hoped for. A half hour later she climbed into the Yellow cab and directed the driver to University Hospital.

She thought she'd known what a broken heart felt like. She'd endured her father's heart attack in a Chicago hospital bed across the hall from him; a defenseless child with no notion of what was happening to her.

The pain in her heart now was far, far worse. There was no physical basis for this pain, nor the slightest hope for a cure. Vanessa's instincts had told her, before she'd ever shared a thought with Alex, that he'd resent her. That coaxing him back to life was tantamount to usurping his power; that he'd only let her love him when, asleep, he had nothing to lose. Now every time he looked at her he'd be reminded that it was due to her that he lived. Still worse, he'd never believe after reading that paper that she loved *him*, to distraction, beyond decorum.

She watched out the back windows of the cab as the driver headed north on Sante Fe, but the mesmerizing snowfall blurred through her tears. The prisms of light she saw now were just stabbing pains in her eyes, and rainbows were just God's covenant with the world. No more floods.

No more tears.

AT TWO IN THE MORNING Alex bashed his fist through his kitchen window. He'd locked himself out and couldn't find the keys Cat had hurled at him, for all the snow. His contrary heart found all sorts of perverse amusement in his dilemma.

Locked out, bud? it taunted, making the wholly unnecessary and cruel connection for him between being locked out of his house and Cat's heart. *Fancy that. Estranged? Alienated? Exiled? Banished, bereft, forlorn, forsaken? Take your choice, Petrakis. Or take them all.*

Glass crunched under his boots as he stepped into the kitchen. He'd never wanted anyone or anything like he wanted Cat to be his, uniquely his. He wished to God he'd never woken up.

At least in his sleep he'd found a way to connect with her like no man and woman had ever connected before. Or ever would again. In his sleep he could suffer his ignorant bliss and believe Cat hadn't touched him first out of some misguided sense of charity.

There was nothing even vaguely civilized about his need for her, or the need to transform himself back into someone vulnerable. Nothing civilized at all. If he had doubted that he was a man who could live with sharing her with her dreams, he'd just learned differently.

He couldn't stay away. She'd be with Sarah, he knew that, but there were other ways to be with her. He'd simply wait at her place until she went home. First he had to find his keys.

He forced himself to clean up the broken glass, to put on a pot of coffee, and then to sober up with it like the civilized man he was supposed to be. The better part of an hour passed before he found the keys Vanessa had hurled into the snow, and another quarter hour to drive the BMW up to the pay phone Cat must surely have used. There, he called Nick. It was by then nearly three-thirty in the morning, and his cousin didn't take pleasantly to the call.

"What on earth can possibly be so important?"

Alex swallowed his very uncivilized curse and made up a story as he went along. "Vanessa's been up at the hospital all night with the Gilles girl, and she'll probably be there all day. She'll need some fresh clothes only I forgot to get her key. I'm at a pay phone and I need to know how to get into her place.'' The address he'd already found in the directory.

The silence from Nick's end of the line grew suspicious.

''C'mon, Nick. It's late and it's colder than a witch's tit—''

''Nice try, Alex. Really nice, except that Van showered and changed into fresh surgical scrubs an hour ago. I've only been home that long.''

His grip on the receiver tightening in frustration, Alex rammed three fingers into the front pocket of his Levi's and started backpedaling. ''Look—''

''If you want to wait at her place, just say so.''

Breaking into her place seemed reasonable about now. ''I want into her place, okay?''

''Yeah. Okay.''

''How do I get in?''

''Is this a riddle?'' Nick jibed.

His civilized veneer was rapidly growing thin. ''For Pete's sake, Nick! What the hell—''

''Pardon me,'' Nick grated, ''if I don't have a lot of sympathy for a world-class jerk—''

''She told you—''

''She didn't say one word about you, but it doesn't take a real genius to interpret the symptoms of pain.'' Nick paused thoughtfully, then continued. ''Forget waiting at her place. Van's got a small sofa in her office and she'll go there if she goes anywhere. So help me, Alex, family or not I'll personally take you apart if—''

But Alex was gone, and the receiver swung from its metallic cord in the booth.

Getting into Cat's office proved amazingly simple. Staying was another matter, for the first thing he discovered was a final draft of her postdoc paper with a covering letter, and the second was a photo of her parents.

Paging through her draft, he discovered only one minor reference to the paper he'd read and accused her with. The more blatant truth came from the fifties-vintage picture. Alex sat in Cat's uncomfortable chair, mesmerized by the eyes of Georgiou Koures. Eyes so full of exuberance, so vital, so like Cat's. This barrel-chested, virile-looking man had lived the life of an invalid?

The more he sat in that chair and looked at the picture, the more starkly clear it became to Alex why Vanessa would go to any length to preserve another life against such a fate. His life.

It took him an uncivilized amount of time to get around to accepting the truth. Cat had come to him first with her guilt and her empathy and her good intentions, and only afterward had she loved him. Loved him when he was as powerless as a babe in arms. Dared to love him in spite of every moral and ethical argument against it. And he'd thrown it all back in her face, because Alex Petrakis was not vulnerable to loving.

Just as he'd discovered the charms of Papoo's bird milk good fortune, he discovered now the hidden allure of *vulnerable*.

His mind strayed backward in time to images of Cat. Reacting to the intense sensuality of *The Man Woman*. Shaving him for the first time. Touching him, angering him, goading him, watching him. Watching him as he took her that first time. There could never have been a more poignant, more needy first time.

And again, there was nothing civilized about the myriad ways he wanted her.

HE FOUND HER crying over his *Demon Alone* script at the side of Sarah Gilles's bed. One hand planted high on the doorjamb, his other hand helplessly crammed into a Levi's pocket, he watched her. Willed her to look up. Begged her silently to hear him now as she'd heard him for so many weeks, because whenever he opened his mouth, something truly stupid came out.

Do you see at last, Cat, that even when Richard knew his way out, he knew nothing?... You promised, *harato mou*. Promised me forever....

Sarah whimpered. Vanessa read on, and the only way Alex could see she was aware of the little girl's stirring was the tightening of her fingers on Sarah's.

Dawn broke. The long, endless night was over, along with the punishing blizzard. Piercing rays of sunlight sliced through the slats of the blinds at the windows of Sarah's ICU cubicle, but Vanessa read on, oblivious to the sunlight and to him.

I was wrong, little Caterpillar. I love you. If I don't say it, only think it, will you hear me? Will you believe me?

Sarah moaned again, and Alex had the incredible notion that it was the child who heard him. The pattern of bleeps from her monitor increased, in tandem with his own.

Vanessa lost her place as more tears welled up from nowhere. All her tears should have been long since spent. She should have read the final act of *Alone*. She should have known Alex had more to say to her than that he'd known his way back all along.

She should have known better. Should have asked. Should have told Alex long before he woke that she loved him.

She should have known. Richard would have chosen the frozen caverns of hell all over again—over any Paradise—to have Catherine, just as Alex had prolonged his sleep to elude giving up what he had found with Vanessa, and she with him.

Whether it was the denouement of Alex's heart-rending script or the subtle change in Sarah's heart rhythm or Vanessa's sudden instinctive awareness of Alex's presence, she didn't know. She simply couldn't trust herself to look up into his penetrating hazel eyes.

His heart seemed to climb high into his throat and lodge there. *Sweet, chronic liar. You know I'm here. Pretending I'm not won't make it so.*

The tilt of Cat's head acknowledged she knew.

Sarah tugged weakly at Vanessa's hand. Alex tugged at her heart and mind. *I won't let you welsh on your promise, Cat. You said you'd be mine forever if I woke up. I did and you are. You're mine, Caterpillar. Mine...* "Just the way you are, Cat. Dreams and all," he finished raggedly, and aloud.

'Nessa? It was Sarah.

Vanessa's eyes darted to Alex and held. The script slid from her lap as she rose. To Sarah she asked, "What is it, *koukla*," but her eyes never left Alex's.

His words are invisible, aren't they?

Vanessa swallowed and bit her lip to stop its trembling. Alex's eyes held hers in thrall. "I'm sorry, *koukla*. I don't know what that means..."

Sarah faded back into her sedated sleep, and still Alex looked at Vanessa with pain in his eyes and uncertainty in his words. "The fox, Cat, in *The Little Prince*..." His voice seemed unnaturally quiet, an echo perhaps, of the thoughts he sent her. *"What is essential is invisible to the eye."* *I've only just learned the Fox's secret myself, sweet Cat.*

"Alex—"

Sarah's respirator huffed and whooshed rhythmically. The cardiac unit buzzed with activity as the morning shift arrived and the graveyard crew departed. Alex still blocked the doorway into Sarah's room, and no one, not even Markson deigned to intrude.

Alex stood stock-still in that ethereal, enchanted moment, captivated by Vanessa and the surprising rose-colored surgical garb that dwarfed her and suggested she had no shape. He knew better, and it took no particular flights of fancy to imagine her otherwise.

"I want to make love to you, *gyneka mou*, in the meadow where the buck and the doe bring their young. And then I want to sink the first shovel into the ground and lay the first brick of your rehab center. And then I want you to come away with me to New Zealand—a month—two if you can." *A honeymoon, Cat. Will you come away with me?*

He went to her, then, and cupped her face in his shaking hands. Silver-pewter depths had returned to her wide, luminous eyes, and he'd gladly spend a lifetime ensuring they stayed there.

"The first shovelful is yours, *andras mou*. And the first brick. But then you must promise me you'll bring *Demon Alone* to life." *I will come away with you, for I am yours, just as I promised.*

Cat . . . She still held Sarah's hand, and Alex knew he couldn't love her more than in this moment as she clung so fiercely to life and love and a child not of her body.

"And then, Alexander *mou*," she warned, meeting his own hazel shade of passion, "I want a brood of excuses to sit in the Petrakis rocker."

The breath went out of him, and out of her, and Sarah Gilles smiled in her sleep. His arms went around Cat, doubling desperately across the narrow breadth of her back.

It took no particular flights of fancy for either to imagine her small, delicate breasts laden with the milk of their own good fortune.

And they lived happily ever after, but we are even better.

From *New York Times* Bestselling author
Penny Jordan, a compelling novel of ruthless passion
that will mesmerize readers everywhere!

Penny Jordan

Silver
Real power, true power came from
Rothwell. And Charles vowed to have it,
the earldom and all that went with it.

Silver vowed to destroy Charles, just as surely and
uncaringly as he had destroyed her father; just as he had
intended to destroy her. She needed him to want her . . .
to desire her . . . until he'd do anything to have her.

But first she needed a tutor: a man who wanted no one.
He would help her bait the trap.

Played out on a glittering international stage,
Silver's story leads her from the luxurious comfort of
British aristocracy into the depths of adventure,
passion and danger.

AVAILABLE IN OCTOBER!

 HARLEQUIN

SILVER

Six exciting series for you every month... from Harlequin

HARLEQUIN

The series that started it all

Tender, captivating and heartwarming...
love stories that sweep you off to faraway places
and delight you with the magic of love.

◆

Harlequin Presents®

Powerful contemporary love stories...as individual as the women who read them

The No. 1 romance series...
exciting love stories for you, the woman of today...
a rare blend of passion and dramatic realism.

◆

Harlequin Superromance®
It's more than romance... it's Harlequin Superromance

A sophisticated, contemporary romance-fiction
series, providing you with a longer,
more involving read...a richer mix of complex plots,
realism and adventure.

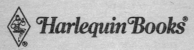

**From America's favorite author
coming in September**

JANET DAILEY

For Bitter Or Worse

Out of print since 1979!

Reaching Cord seemed impossible. Bitter, still confined to a wheel-chair a year after the crash, he lashed out at everyone. Especially his wife.

"It would have been better if I hadn't been pulled from the plane wreck," he told her, and nothing Stacey did seemed to help.

Then Paula Hanson, a confident physiotherapist, arrived. She taunted Cord into helping himself, restoring his interest in living. Could she also make him and Stacey rediscover their early love?

Don't miss this collector's edition—last in a special three-book collection from Janet Dailey.